Merlin did not hesitate again.

He shouted, weaving a spell out of hand and voice together.

The long-dormant waterfall burst from the cliff above. The water sparkled in the sun as it sprayed down, dousing the dragon and turning the earth beneath its feet to mud. As the beast wallowed through the mire, trying to reach firmer ground, Merlin gestured again, and a thousand green tendrils burst up out of the ground beneath the dragon's feet. The shoots swarmed over its haunches, dragging it back toward the ground . . .

ALSO BY JAMES MALLORY

Merlin: The Old Magic

HALLMARK ENTERTAINMENT PRESENTS
SAM NEILL   HELENA BONHAM CARTER
JOHN GIELGUD   RUTGER HAUER
JAMES EARL JONES   MIRANDA RICHARDSON
ISABELLA ROSSELLINI   MARTIN SHORT
"MERLIN"
LEGEND ADVISOR LOREN BOOTHBY
MUSIC BY TREVOR JONES
CREATURE EFFECTS BY JIM HENSON'S CREATURE SHOP
EXECUTIVE PRODUCER ROBERT HALMI, SR.
PRODUCED BY DYSON LOVELL
TELEPLAY BY DAVID STEVENS AND PETER BARNES
STORY BY EDWARD KHMARA
DIRECTED BY STEVE BARRON

ORIGINAL SOUNDTRACK AVAILABLE ON VARÈSE SARABANDE COMPACT DISCS

Merlin

The King's Wizard

James Mallory

HarperCollins*Publishers*

Voyager
An Imprint of HarperCollins*Publishers*
77–85 Fulham Palace Road,
Hammersmith, London W6 8JB

www.voyager-books.com

A Paperback Original 1999
1   3   5   7   9   8   6   4   2

A catalogue record for this book
is available from the British Library

ISBN 0 00 651290 9

Set in Times

Printed and bound in Great Britain by
Caledonian International Book Manufacturing Ltd, Glasgow

For Betsy, Jane, Jaime, Fiona, and Russ,
for all their help and support,
and for MJ, for the usual.

C ⊕ N ✝ E N ✝ S

Merlin
The King's Wizard

Previously, in
Merlin:
The Old Magic

Mab, Queen of the Old Ways, desperately seeks a champion to preserve her people from destruction and destroy the New Religion: Christianity. At first she chooses Vortigern the Saxon, but when Vortigern takes the throne, Mab discovers that he cares for nothing but himself, and the devastation becomes even worse.

Enraged, Mab vows that she will create a champion for Britain who cannot betray her, one who will be both wizard and king: Merlin. But Mab's powers have grown too weak for her to do all she wishes, and she is forced to implant the spark of Merlin's life in the young novice Elissa, one of the Guardians of the Grail at Avalon Abbey.

Elissa's pregnancy causes her to be cast out of Avalon, and Merlin is born in Barnstable Forest, under the watchful eye of Ambrosia, who was once a priestess of the Old Ways. When Mab comes to claim the child for her own, Ambrosia demands that Mab leave young Merlin for her to raise, hoping to teach him human love to balance Mab's thoughtless cruelty.

Mab agrees, but says that on the day Merlin first uses his magic he must come to her to be tutored in the Ancient Arts.

Merlin grows to manhood among the forest creatures unaware of his true heritage, but when he rescues the Princess Nimue using magic, Mab sends for him. Still unaware of Mab's plans for him, Merlin journeys to the Land of Magic, where he is instructed in the Old Ways by Queen Mab and her gnomish servant Frik.

But the destiny Mab sees for him is one that Merlin is increasingly reluctant to accept, and when Mab's sister, the Lady of the Lake, tells him that Ambrosia has fallen ill, Merlin hurries home to her.

Mab, fearing Merlin's untimely departure will deprive her of the champion she needs to restore the Old Ways, reaches Ambrosia before Merlin does, demanding that Ambrosia send Merlin back to her. When Ambrosia refuses to tell Merlin to do anything but follow his own heart, Mab lashes out in anger, leaving Ambrosia dying. Merlin, stumbling over the body of his foster mother, realizes Mab is evil. He tries to fight Mab, but fails to defeat her because he has not yet mastered the highest levels of magic to become a Thought-Wizard. Merlin swears he will never be what Mab wants him to be, and vows he will never again use his magic except to defeat her.

Mab, feeling that Merlin's capitulation is only a matter of time, abandons him to his solitary life in the forest, waiting for the day she can use Vortigern to make Merlin break his rash oath. . . .

CHAPTER ONE

The Throne of the Greenwood

his name was Merlin, and he was the child of the Queen of Air and Darkness and a mortal maiden. His human mother Elissa had died when he was born, and he had grown up happy and free in the deep forest under the care of his foster mother Ambrosia . . . until the day that the Queen of the Old Ways, Queen Mab, had taken him to learn the arts of magic in her land under the hill.

To become a wizard.

At the time it had seemed like such a simple thing to become a wizard, passing through the three stages of magic to become a Wizard of Pure Thought, but Merlin had quickly realized that things weren't simple at all. He'd come to perceive that Mab saw him as nothing more than a pawn in her plan to restore the Old Ways to a Britain increasingly falling beneath the spell of Christianity—and that Mab saw no difference between Good and Evil, so long as she got her own way.

Perhaps it came from being half-human, but Merlin *did* see a difference between Good and Evil. Under his foster mother's guidance, Merlin had chosen the ways of the Good, and that simple choice had set him and Mab upon opposing paths. He would do anything to keep from becoming her tool for changing the world from what it was to something it could no longer be.

Inevitably the day had come when Merlin had fought against his magical mentor.

"I'll never forgive you—never!" Merlin shouted. He held his foster mother's body in his arms.

"I'm sorry about your mother and Ambrosia, but they were casualties of war," Mab said insincerely. "I'm fighting to save my people from extinction."

But to fight this war, Mab had sacrificed everything that made life worth living.

"I don't care if you die and disappear," Merlin said furiously. Mab had killed Ambrosia out of spite— and to reclaim Merlin's loyalty. He knew that in her total heartlessness, the Queen of the Old Ways would try any trick, take any hostage. . . .

"I will, unless I fight and win!" Mab assured him seriously. "That was why you were created." To be Mab's tool against the New Religion, to bring pain and suffering to thousands just like Ambrosia.

"I will never help you," Merlin vowed.

"You will," Mab purred, her green eyes gleaming with wolf-light. "I'll make you help me."

But he had sworn a bitter oath on the forest graves

of his mother and his foster mother—both now dead through Mab's treachery—that he would never use his wizard's powers except to defeat Queen Mab.

But Merlin now knew how infinitely clever and treacherous Mab was, and that was why no action was safe. His only safety from Mab lay in being more cunning than she was, more clever. So Merlin would follow the way that Mab's sister, the Lady of the Lake, had unfolded to him in the Land of Magic. Merlin would study wisdom, not magic, and all of Mab's plots to make him her tool would fail.

But as the years passed, Merlin realized that though he had not lost his fight against Mab, he hadn't won it either. Though Merlin had escaped the twisting paths of the Land of Magic to live safe and unmolested in the forest that had been his childhood home, he knew that in the world beyond the forest, Queen Mab was still scheming and planning to make her dreams for him come true.

His visions told him so.

The ability to dream true was not a talent that Merlin had learned in the Land of Magic or a gift granted by the Lady of the Lake. It was a skill that he had been born with, something in his blood from earliest childhood. Now that he had turned away from wizardry, Merlin's prophetic dreams were much stronger, and through the years, he had come to rely on them. Though his dreams always came true, sometimes they were so confusing that he didn't realize the truth they contained until it was too late. But they were the only weapon he had. As a boy, Merlin had cherished dreams of being a valiant knight, but his wizardhood had forced him to set aside his boyhood dreams long ago.

Through his dreams Merlin watched all of Britain as it writhed in the terrible grip of its tyrant king, Vortigern.

Vortigern the Saxon ruled as he had for Merlin's entire lifetime. He crushed all rebellion with an iron hand. He was neither Christian nor Pagan, and there were only two things he could not control.

One was the Great Dragon, Draco Magnus Maleficarum. The fire-breathing monster ravaged the West Country with his insatiable appetite for flesh. Only magic could defeat the Great Dragon, and King Vortigern was no wizard: instead, the King preferred to slake the beast's appetite with flocks of sheep and the occasional virgin sacrifice, rather than fight it and lose. Vortigern wished to save his army for other things, like his other great nemesis, Prince Uther.

Prince Uther was hungry for more than roast mutton. He was the rightful heir to old King Constant, from whom Vortigern had stolen his blood-soaked throne. As a child, Uther had been smuggled out of Britain, and grown to manhood exiled in France. All his life he'd been waiting for his chance to take back what was his by right of inheritance, gathering ships and men across the channel in Normandy. Now that he was grown, Prince Uther wanted two things: his father's throne and Vortigern dead. And he would wait no longer to attain either of his desires.

Merlin's visions told him that Uther would soon meet the king on the battlefield, but his visions did not tell him whether the Old King or the Young Prince would win the war to come, nor what the cost to Britain would be of the winner's victory.

A high one, no matter who wins, Merlin thought with a sigh. There had never been a year of his life when Britain had been free from the shadow of war. Even if Uther gave up his hopes of the crown and settled peacefully in France, there would still be war in Britain, for Vortigern had no heir to set upon the throne when he died, and Vortigern's nobles watched the aging king hungrily, each one certain that he would be king hereafter.

Wolves have better manners than that lot, Merlin thought sourly as he opened his eyes, shaking off the last of sleep. His night had been restless, filled with dreams of dragons and swords.

He stretched and sat up, looking around the snug forest cottage that had been his home from earliest childhood. He had been born in this very room, to a mother who had died only moments later, the first victim of Mab's meddling in his life. Since he had returned from the Land of Magic years before, the little hut in which his foster mother Ambrosia had raised him had been his home and his whole world.

It was late autumn, a few weeks past Samhain. Unconsciously, Merlin always expected trouble to come at the beginning of the dark half of the year, and when the festival time had passed, he assumed the rest of the year would be quiet. But the morning wind had brought him the news that strangers trespassed in his beloved forest. There was danger afoot.

Merlin rolled to his feet, shivering in the cold of

the small forest hut. He'd slept in his clothes: a rough tunic of brown homespun and leggings over which he wore a long vest of deerskin to protect him from the worst of the winter cold.

Wind whistled through chinks in the thatch of the cottage, and Merlin moved quickly to poke up the fire on the hearth, holding his hands out to the warmth he raised. Without the use of his wizard's powers, he was as helpless as any mortal man before the forces of Nature. Fire was the earliest magic, and a touch of wizardry would warm him, but he would not use his magic for his own comfort. It was reserved for only one purpose: Mab's destruction.

As he prepared his simple breakfast of herbal tea and acorn bread, Merlin's mind was far from the simple homely tasks. What did the coming of the strangers mean to the peace and quiet of the life he had made for himself here in the greenwood? While a part of him hoped he would be let to live out his life within the confines of Barnstable Forest, he had always known that this was an unattainable dream. He had always known that his fate would find him someday.

And suddenly, someday was today.

As he had learned to do over the years, Merlin calmly awaited what was to come. He finished his morning meal and then went out into the clearing in the forest to meditate. He sank down gracefully into a seat amid a drift of autumn leaves. All around him the circle of young trees stood like the pillars of a cathedral—a cathedral of the Old Ways that grew from the living earth, and was not made of dead stone as were the churches the New Religion built.

As soon as the thought came to him, Merlin pushed it away. To think in terms of the Old Ways versus the New Religion was to fall into the same trap that Queen Mab had, a trap made of hatred and distrust. Merlin chose to walk a third path, neither of Black Magic nor White Light, a path grey as mist, where everything must be judged upon its own merits. He would not hate the New Religion or follow the Old Ways. He would simply be as he had always been: Merlin the Wizard.

As he closed his eyes and settled into a meditative trance, the forest seemed to unfurl below him as though he were a bird soaring far above its leafy canopy. In the eye of his imagination, he could see glints of metal far below, the helmets and lances of his uninvited guests. They were warriors wearing the sign of the white dragon: soldiers of the king.

Why had Vortigern sent them? Even as he wondered, Merlin knew he would have to wait for that part of his answer. He was only a thread in a pattern that forces greater than himself had begun to weave long ago, and over the years Merlin had learned to save his strength for the most important battles.

At midday he finally heard them approach—a troop of mounted soldiers crashing through the winter-killed underbrush. There were half a dozen of them, and riding at their head was an old man dressed as a Druid, though the reigns of two draconian kings had managed to nearly wipe that ancient priesthood from the face of Britain.

So Vortigern has discovered he now has some use

for magic? Merlin thought to himself. *This should be interesting.*

He got to his feet and turned to face the soldiers just as they entered the clearing.

Their captain was a man of a type Merlin knew all too well: a brute, but a clever one, who served a ruthless master with efficiency and without conscience. The old Druid riding with him simply looked terrified, but despite that he was obviously the real leader of the little party. "Seize that man!" the Druid blustered, pointing an accusing finger at Merlin.

Merlin tried his most disarming smile. "Welcome to my home, sir," he said mildly. "How can I help you?"

To live in perfect trust was the first lesson that magic taught. As the years had passed here in his forest home, Merlin had learned to live and act as if he expected goodness from all men, and such was the power of expectation that he had rarely been disappointed. Even now such humble sorcery worked its subtle magic. The old Druid dismounted from his horse, and when he spoke again, his tone was very different.

"Well, *er,* the king wants to see you," he said in apologetic tones, taking a step toward Merlin—or more precisely, *away* from his armored companions.

Now that he was close enough, Merlin could see how the old man's face was marked by lines of care and worry—though that was hardly unusual with Vortigern on the throne.

"You have only to ask," Merlin said gently. Because of his forest seclusion, Merlin had been spared most of the fear that the ordinary people of Britain faced in their daily lives. But if Vortigern was asking for him, Merlin knew that Queen Mab must somehow be behind it.

"You'll come voluntarily?" The old Druid did his best to conceal his surprise. "Ah, that's good. Most people are reluctant to meet King Vortigern. In fact, they're usually dragged in screaming. Not that I blame them," he added hastily. The last of the pretense of command seemed to leave him now; as he sighed, his shoulders drooped and he suddenly looked like what he was: a frail, frightened old man in the grip of forces larger than himself.

"I'm the king's Soothsayer," he explained dolefully.

Even Merlin in his isolation had heard of Lailoken, Vortigern's Soothsayer. No wonder the old man looked so weary. The poor creature was hated by the Christians for his pretense of Pagan wizardry and despised by the Pagans for serving Vortigern. It was a hard life when you fit in nowhere, and no one knew that better than Merlin, who was himself half-fairy, half-mortal.

"An important position?" Merlin asked Lailoken politely. Vortigern was notorious for ignoring advice, no matter what its source. He wasn't likely to pay any more attention to his soothsayer than he did to his generals.

"And a fragile one," Lailoken agreed. "I'm the third Royal Soothsayer this year."

"He must get through them at an alarming speed," Merlin commented. He did not need to ask why the previous soothsayers had retired. There was only one way to retire when you worked for Vortigern.

By now the rest of the soldiers had spread out around the clearing, surrounding him and incidentally cutting off his path of escape. Merlin saw that Vortigern's men had come well prepared: all of them were armed to the teeth. More to the point, they'd brought a spare horse for him to ride.

"He gets through *everything* at an alarming speed," Lailoken said gloomily, as if agreeing with Merlin's thoughts. The soothsayer shuddered, glancing at the ring of soldiers surrounding them both, and then, as if only now remembering his duty, said: "You *are* Merlin, the man without a mortal father?"

"Yes," Merlin answered, wondering why Lailoken was asking. There was no point in denying who—or what—he was: a wizard, created by the Queen of the Old Ways to be her champion and born of a mortal mother—but a champion who would not fight, and a wizard who rejected magic.

"I'm afraid the king wants you urgently," Lailoken sighed. He seemed to sincerely regret his part in the proceedings, whatever it was.

Without being asked, one of the soldiers led the riderless horse into the clearing. The man's expression said clearly—though silently—that Merlin would mount the animal one way or the other. Bowing to the inevitable, Merlin vaulted gracefully into the saddle, and from that vantage point took a last look around his forest home.

Something within him told him that it would be a very long time before he saw it again.

In moments, Merlin and Lailoken were surrounded by mounted soldiers whose horses were moving at a brisk trot along the road that led out of the forest, the road that led west . . . toward Pendragon Castle, and the king.

In the month since the last architect had been executed, little had changed here on the Welsh border. The building blocks of what was intended to be Vortigern's most formidable castle still lay scattered across the landscape as if they had been dropped by an angry giant. The tents that sheltered the members of the court obliged to attend the king here still decorated the grassy plain near the ridge like bright mushrooms. Beyond them, the tents housing the workers and soldiers spread in somber and orderly rows. All day long, masons and laborers toiled to repair the destruction of the tower's last collapse. All of them hoped there would not be another—none more fervently than the man who huddled over a table of curled velum drawings, cringing beneath the king's bright gaze. He was not the best builder in all of Britain, but he was certainly the most unlucky, for no architect in the last ten years had been able to make Vortigern's fortress stand.

"It'll hold this time, Your Majesty, never fear," Paschent said nervously.

"I never have," Vortigern said simply.

It was no more than the truth. For more than two decades, the Saxon king had ruled Britain as king by right of conquest, and he had done it without help from either magic or religion. But Time had taken its toll, and now the aging ruler, his kingdom beset by threats from within and without, was willing at last to seek out new alliances. It was why he had demanded that his soothsayer discover why the tower would not stand, even though Vortigern had never found that magic could accomplish anything muscle could not.

As he regarded Paschent, there was a sudden rumble from behind him.

He heard the screams of desperate men, the scraping sound made by granite blocks as they ground together like monstrous teeth chewing workmen to pulp. The ground shook as the walls bulged and buckled, spitting out building stones that struck the earth like the footsteps of giants. Suddenly the air was thick with rock dust and the powdered mortar that rose from the destruction like morning mist before beginning to drift down the hill. The screams of the dying dwindled to whimpers and sobs, and the frightened murmurs of the survivors were punctuated with urgent cries for help.

Through all of the upheaval, Vortigern didn't turn around. He didn't need to. He could see all he needed to see in the architect's face.

"You were saying?" Vortigern's voice was soft with menace. His hand dropped to the dagger at his belt and he watched Paschent's face go grey with the realization of the magnitude of his failure.

"Your Majesty!" a voice called from behind him.

Vortigern turned away from the trembling architect. A troop of his soldiers had just ridden into camp with the soothsayer at their head. Lailoken actually looked pleased to see Vortigern. This was an event so unusual that it took the king's mind completely off the latest collapse of his stronghold.

There was a young man with Lailoken, an unpre-possessing lad dressed in threadbare rags and animal skins. Vortigern was surprised: Lailoken had actually found the fabulous creature he'd gone in search of.

The old Druid dismounted hurriedly and shuffled toward the king. The young man stayed by the horses, regarding the camp with watchful eyes.

"Your Majesty, I've found him—the man without a mortal father!" Lailoken announced excitedly.

Merlin contemplated the king with interest. This was his first actual sight of the man who had haunted his entire life with his bloodstained deeds, the man who had persecuted Christians and Pagans with a monstrous evenhandedness. Perhaps unconsciously Merlin had expected to see a misshapen creature as fearsome as any he had encountered in the Land of Magic, but Vortigern was only a mortal warlord.

In a way, Vortigern reminded Merlin of Idath, Lord of the Wild Hunt and the Kingdom of Winter. And Idath, like the winter cold, could be a fearsome enemy.

"If this is another of your moth-eaten tricks—!" the king snarled, and Merlin saw Lailoken cringe back. The wind on this hilltop cut through Merlin's tat-tered clothing like a knife, and Merlin could see the more-warmly-dressed Lailoken shiver with more than cold. He took a few steps forward, knowing that there was nothing he could do to save the old man from Vor-tigern's capricious wrath.

"No—no!" the old man protested. "It's all true."

Vortigern turned his attention to Merlin, and the

impact of the king's arctic gaze caused Merlin to take an unconscious step toward him.

"There's only one way to find out," the king growled. With a swift stride forward, Vortigern punched Merlin in the stomach. "Get a knife and a bowl and cut his throat."

Merlin fell to the ground, gasping for breath. The winter-dry grass crackled beneath his weight. He could dimly hear Vortigern calling for someone to cut his throat, and Lailoken's feeble protests. Merlin shook his head sharply, hoping to clear it, and struggled painfully to his feet, still panting from the pain.

"He doesn't look much like a wizard," Vortigern commented.

"You caught me by surprise," Merlin answered honestly. What did Vortigern see when he looked at Merlin? A sacrifice for some ritual the Saxon didn't even believe in? "Why do you want to cut my throat?"

"It's not personal," Vortigern said. There was a dagger in his hand. "I have to mix your blood with the mortar in the castle. This toothless old fool says it's the only way to make the building stand. You'll die easier knowing you die for your country." Vortigern smiled mirthlessly.

It wasn't hard for Merlin to suppose who had put such an outlandish idea into the king's head. Queen Mab must think that if Merlin was faced with death, he would have to draw on the power of the Old Ways to save himself, breaking the oath he had sworn over Ambrosia's grave.

But Mab was wrong. Merlin had other resources

than magic to draw upon. He had his heart, his will, and his mind.

"I'm afraid Your Majesty is giving the impression of being invincibly stupid," Merlin said kindly.

Vortigern's head snapped around. "What was that last word?" the king asked dangerously.

"Stupid," Merlin repeated clearly.

There was an electric moment of absolute silence, as everyone who had been close enough to hear what Merlin had just said held their breaths and pretended they hadn't.

Vortigern's face revealed nothing. Then, suddenly, the king roared with laughter. Relieved, the others joined in.

"This man thinks he's me!" Vortigern said, and then, barely pausing for breath, "Why did you call me stupid?"

Merlin took a deep breath and marshaled everything he knew of human nature. "Because it's obvious why you can't build a castle there. Look—"

He gestured, pointing confidently toward a narrow fissure in the cliff just below the castle. When he had been a young man growing up in the Barnstable Forest, Merlin had been taught natural history by an old hermit named Blaise. From the furrows in the rock, he could tell that a stream had flowed there a long time ago. He also knew that by now Vortigern must be looking for a face-saving excuse to abandon this building project without having to admit failure. Perhaps this could be it.

"I'm looking," Vortigern growled.

"I don't see anything," Paschent said, clutching his architect's tools nervously against his chest.

"Can't you see the stream?" Merlin asked persuasively. He visualized the stream in his mind as it must once have run, a sparkling rill leaping from rock to rock, and willed the others to imagine it as well.

"It runs into a great cavern below." And that meant that if Vortigern ever managed to get the tower to stand, its weight would cause it to collapse and break through the roof of the cavern below anyway.

"There's no water there—I swear," Paschent said frantically.

"I can see it," Vortigern snarled menacingly, turning on his architect. "We can all see it. You wanted to build a castle on *water*?"

"But—but—but—" Paschent stammered.

Now was the moment when Merlin should have taken control of the situation, persuaded Vortigern that he'd discovered the underground stream through his own common sense, and found some way to slip invisibly away from the king's notice. But even as he formed the thought it floated away, just as his consciousness was. *No! Not here!* Merlin cried silently, but the force of the vision was too strong. Merlin became only a fragment of awareness, a leaf in the gale that was swirling him up to heaven. The mantle of prophecy descended upon him, blotting out everything else.

"That's not all that's wrong," he heard himself say distantly. "You've woken the dragons. . . ."

The outside world vanished. With his inner sight, Merlin saw the vast grey landscape of dreams, and on that infinite plain two mighty armies clashed. The winter chill no longer troubled him; though the wind was enough to loft the armies' banners into the sky, Merlin did not feel it. He was a disembodied observer, nothing more.

Above the two hosts flew their battle standards: one a white dragon on a black field, the other a red dragon against a background as white as snow.

"I see two dragons, a red and a white. . . ."

"My crest has a white dragon," Vortigern said excitedly.

As the armies ran toward each other, the bright flicker of light on their sword blades became the dazzle of sunlight on the scales of two enormous dragons flying above them, one white as frost, one red as flame. As Merlin watched, the two beasts and the armies they embodied met in a clash of swords and scales. Their roaring deafened him, the screams of fury and pain chilled his blood.

In moments it was over. The dragons faded away to become pieces of cloth once more. The black banner hung limp and tattered, while the red dragon waved triumphantly against a sapphire sky.

Merlin blinked, refocusing on his surroundings with difficulty as the images of his vision slowly faded. Everyone was staring at him, some frightened, some hopeful.

"What did you see?" Vortigern demanded.

"The red dragon conquered the white," Merlin answered simply. He didn't believe in lying, and even if he did, he suspected it would be very unhealthy to lie to Vortigern, no matter what the truth was.

"It's an omen!" Lailoken said, before he remembered who his audience was. Vortigern's banner was the white dragon. "Er . . . wouldn't you say, Sire? I mean, it *could* be an omen . . ." the old man's voice trailed off uncertainly.

Vortigern looked from Lailoken to Merlin, his eyes narrow with suspicion. Merlin could tell that Vortigern had not quite decided what to do, but the king was legendary for swift and ruthless decision-making. He was obviously waiting for more information.

Just then, there was a clattering sound as a large party of knights rode into Vortigern's camp in a great hurry. Before the horses had stopped moving, the knight in the lead had vaulted from his horse and rushed to the king's side.

"Your Majesty—Prince Uther has landed from Normandy with a great army!"

"He's marching on Winchester," said a second knight, coming up behind the first.

Vortigern's response was an elemental howl of rage. He glared at his men, about to leap into action against this new threat, when suddenly he remembered Merlin.

"You foresaw all this," Vortigern said, his voice a deadly adder's hiss.

"I am Merlin. I see things unknown," Merlin said, with more confidence than he felt at the moment. It was as much truth as boast, but saying it aloud made him uncomfortable. It seemed too much like tempting Mab to attack him.

"What are your orders, Sire?" Vortigern's commander asked urgently.

"Gather my armies. We march on Winchester," Vortigern said, turning away from Merlin.

The wind caught the king's black cloak and filled it like a sail, whipping it away from his body so that his scaled golden armor gleamed in the sun. The king took no notice. His knights hurried to obey him, and all around them the camp began to seethe like a boiling cauldron as the news of Prince Uther's landing spread through it.

The construction of the tower that had obsessed Vortigern for the last seven years was forgotten as if it had never been. The king had a new and more urgent threat to face.

"Why doesn't it ever stop?" Vortigern asked, as if only to himself. Suddenly he drew his sword with one fluid motion and laid it against the side of Merlin's neck. "I've been fighting my enemies for twenty years. I crush one and another takes his place."

More knowledge than that of the white dragon's defeat had come to Merlin in his vision. He had a part to play in Vortigern's destruction, though he did not know precisely what it was yet. But perhaps through destroying Vortigern, he could strike at Mab as well.

"Perhaps you need me to foretell the future," Merlin said smoothly, trying to ignore the cold weight of the sword at his throat. "Then you could crush them all before they had a chance to cause trouble,"

The words were spoken lightly, but Vortigern took them at face value. "Yes, that would be helpful, Merlin," he said seriously.

"Of course, then you couldn't cut my throat," Merlin added.

"No. . . . You're obviously an extraordinary man." Vortigern lifted the sword away from Merlin's neck. "Bu I can't have extraordinary men running around loose."

Before Merlin could react, Vortigern leaped forward and struck Merlin a hammerblow to the side of the head with his mailed fist. The young man dropped senseless to the ground.

"You're just not quick enough," Vortigern said smugly to the unconscious wizard. "It's a mistake my enemies make, too. They always think before they act. I act before I think, so I act first! That's why I always have the advantage. . . ." He prodded Merlin with the toe of his boot, and then, satisfied that the young prophet wasn't shamming unconsciousness, motioned to his guard to take him away.

"Mount up! We ride for Pendragon Castle—not you, you're out of a job," he added, pointing a minatory finger at Lailoken.

"But Sire . . ." the old soothsayer quavered. He wasn't quite sure what Vortigern meant, but he knew that leaving the king's service was usually fatal.

Captain Rhys led Vortigern's black stallion forward. Vortigern vaulted into the saddle. He shouted with laughter, looking down at the expression on Lailoken's face. "Why so surprised? You must have known this would happen. You're an expert on the future!"

Vortigern rode away, still laughing. Lailoken stared after him for a moment, then began to shuffle in the opposite direction as fast as his old legs would carry him, lest the king change his mind. A moment later, Paschent joined him.

Pendragon Castle stood as it always had, a brooding presence looking down upon the River Thames from the ancient Roman city of Caer Londinium.

Once this city had been sacred to Lughd of the Long Hand and Bran of the Ravens, and ravens still flocked around the tallest tower of Castle Pendragon. But Bran and Lughd had been supplanted by Mars and Apollo and the eagles of Rome, and Lughd's Dene had become the City of Legions. In the end, even Rome had left, and for a time the New Religion had reigned here, until Vortigern had taken the throne by treachery and betrayal. Vortigern worshiped no power but his own dark ascending star, and in his name crimes were done that shocked the ancient stones of Pendragon Castle.

Princess Nimue sat in her inner chamber, her back resolutely turned to the narrow window-slit. Her embroidery sat forgotten on her lap. It was too dark to sew by now, and in any event she'd dismissed her waiting women—most of whom were Vortigern's spies—in order to savor a little precious solitude. Any time that she did not have to play-act for the king's benefit was priceless . . . the Princess Nimue had been given years in which to lose all taste for duplicity.

Her childhood dreams of freedom had all been for nothing—she had simply exchanged her little lodging at Avalon Abbey for an equivalent cell within the walls of Pendragon Castle, and the life of a royal captive.

Her world was still limited by blocks of stone and rules made by others.

Nimue did not like to think of how many years had passed since she had become King Vortigern's prisoner, one of the many men and women held by Vortigern as security for their fathers' good behavior. "Hostage" was a kinder word, but the reality was the same: if she displeased the king, if her father Lord Ardent displeased him, Nimue would die.

Her life was not hard. Just as it had been at Avalon, her life at Pendragon Castle was circumscribed with prayer and study. Though here at Pendragon the omnipresent threat of death hung over her, Nimue found she did not fear death as much as she feared never having lived. Would she grow old here in her stifling stone cocoon, a caterpillar who never had the chance to become a butterfly?

If Uther took the throne, things would be different. Uther would unite the land and bring it under Christian rule once more. Nimue longed for his coming the way the nuns at the Abbey longed for the return of the Grail. When Uther came, there would be peace and justice at last.

Suddenly her thoughts were interrupted by the clatter of the gates being dragged open, and the shouting of many voices. Someone was coming to the castle—from the sounds of it, a large party, and Nimue knew that the king was not expected to return to Pendragon for some months yet. She sprang to her feet and ran to the window, leaning as far out as she could in order to see. She blinked as her eyes adjusted to the dark.

The first thing she saw was the glitter of torches stretching in two lines up the road as far as she could see. It was an army! For a moment her heart leapt—had Uther come?—before she realized that the castellan would never have opened Pendragon's gates so easily to Vortigern's enemy. If there was an army outside Pendragon's gates, it was the king's. But why was Vortigern bringing his army here?

The outriders clattered through the open gates holding their torches high. The light glittered on the gold crown Vortigern wore upon his armored helm. She could see him plainly as the horsemen milled in the castleyard beneath her window, and Nimue drew back a little in fear the king might see her as well.

Vortigern had a new prisoner with him. Nimue watched as soldiers pulled the unconscious man from the back of the horse over which he had been tied like a sack of meal, and held him between them. Nimue could see that he was moving feebly—Vortigern could see it too, and took a torch from one of his men, thrusting it toward the prisoner's face as he examined him closely.

Her fear forgotten, Nimue leaned out her window again, peering into the frigid dark. The prisoner bore an elusive familiarity, though he must be a peasant, dressed as he was in rags and animal skins. Who was he? How did she know him?

Satisfied with what he saw, Vortigern turned away and strode into the castle. The soldiers followed with their prisoner.

"My lady! My lady!"

Nimue barely had enough time to move away

from the window and sit down again before Mistress
Olwen burst into the room. The lady in waiting was
agitated, her cheeks flushed and her wimple askew.

"My lady—it is war! Uther has landed and attacked Winchester—and they say a Pagan wizard saw
it all and predicted it at the moment it happened!"

A wizard! Suddenly Nimue remembered where
she'd seen Vortigern's prisoner before. They had met
in a forest, many years before. . . .

"Merlin. . . ."

It was amazing, Merlin reflected gloomily, how
much difference being able to leave a place made to
one's feelings about it. While it was true that his tiny
cell was dark, wet, and freezing, he'd happily poked
around in caves that were just as inhospitable. The
only difference between the two was that he could
have left the cave at any moment, and here an iron
door barred his escape.

Merlin glanced toward the tiny window set high
into one of the cell's slanting walls. It provided the
only light and air the chamber got, though at the moment all it admitted was moonlight and frost. It, too,
was barricaded with a grille of cold iron, but, like the
door, it could provide no real obstacle to magic.

Magic.

The power of the Old Ways could free Merlin in
an instant, whisk him back to his woodland home and
protect him from the king's anger. Merlin could feel its
power pulsing at his fingertips, just waiting to be used.
A word, a gesture, and he would be free . . . and lost.
The moment he used his magic, Merlin placed himself

more firmly in Mab's power, there to become her tool for every sort of evil.

A flicker of darkness appeared at the edge of his vision. Merlin turned, unsurprised, to see that Frik, Mab's gnomish servant, had appeared in his cell.

Mab always likes to keep a close eye on her triumphs.

On this occasion, Frik was not wearing any of the disguises he so loved, and his plain, close-fitting black cowl and garment made his pale face and long curving ears seem to float like disembodied shapes in the dimness. He smiled grotesquely at Merlin.

"Hello, Frik. How are you?" Merlin said easily. Frik was his only pleasant memory from his time in the Land of Magic. Frik had genuinely seemed to care for him. The gnome was Mab's servant, but he'd never tried to trick Merlin as Mab had. And he'd never killed anyone Merlin loved.

"Overworked and underpaid—how terribly sweet of you to inquire," the gnome answered with a toothy smile. He turned away, examining Merlin's cell fastidiously. "How did they ever make a vulgarian like Vortigern king?" he mused, with a moué of distaste for Merlin's surroundings. "You mortals have no sense of the fitness of things; how appalling."

Merlin shrugged. Frik drew himself up, seeming to recollect his purpose. "Anyway. I'm here with a message from Queen Mab."

"Naturally," Merlin said with a faint bitter smile.

"She's going to punish you," Frik announced portentously.

"She hates me," Merlin explained kindly. Perhaps

the explanation was even necessary—human emotions were largely a mystery to the Fair Folk.

"No," Frik corrected him with schoolmasterish fussiness, "but she's rather disappointed that you've refused to use your magic powers. *Why* won't you use them, Master Merlin?" Frik asked mournfully.

"Because Mab wants me to!" Merlin snapped. The hot force of his anger surprised even him—after so many years, he'd thought his feelings for Mab had hardened into a cold hatred. He turned away from Frik, staring up and out through the grille, yearning for the open air. The night was clear and bitterly cold.

"You will in the end, you know," Frik said, with what almost sounded like compassion in his voice. He touched Merlin's shoulder gently. "She's a terrible enemy, Master Merlin, and a very poor employer. Well, I mean, I could tell you *stories . . . !* But enough of my problems—" There was a ripple in the darkness, and Frik was gone in midsentence.

Merlin stretched his cramped arms, then blew on his fingers to try to warm them. Mab thought that confinement in this dismal prison cell would do what Merlin's self-imposed forest exile had not . . . but she was wrong.

If Mab is a terrible enemy, Frik, then so am I. She'll see that before this is over. I will not rest until my dead are avenged—the dead, and the living as well. . . .

Princess Nimue slipped along the castle wall. Pendragon Castle seethed with activity, and the news that Winchester had fallen to Uther had seemed to madden

Vortigern. Nimue's father was one of Vortigern's captains, loyal to him since before he became king. But after Vortigern executed Hawdes and Aerlius on the mere suspicion of treason, not even those who had been loyal longest dared to do anything that might anger him.

It had been a relief to everyone when Vortigern had finally ridden out to inspect the army massing a few miles away on the Downs, and Nimue had seized her chance. Vortigern's special prisoner was sure to be somewhere in the dungeons, and with winter coming on, the worst of the cells were the ones that were open to the outside air.

The first few cells Nimue checked were empty, but at last she came to one that was occupied. At the bottom of the narrow slanted shaft she could see a man dressed in deerskin and rude homespun lying on a crude cot.

"Merlin?" Nimue whispered softly.

He roused at the sound of his name and saw her. As he climbed from his bed and made his way stiffly to the window, Nimue could see how pale and haggard he looked. Ill as he was, though, his face lit up at the sight of her.

"Nimue!" he said.

If he climbed the rough wall as far as he could and stretched toward the sky, and she knelt and thrust her arm down between the bars of the grate, their fingers could just touch.

"Merlin—it *is* you!" Nimue said, holding his fingers through the harsh iron bars. The years had turned him from a boy into a man, and there were new lines of care and worry in his face. "You said we'd meet again," she said, remembering that long-ago day. "I thought I recognized you last night when they brought you in . . . they said you were a wizard."

"I am," Merlin said, before he remembered Nimue was a member of the New Religion. Christians hated wizards with a special intensity because of the power of the Old Ways that flowed through them. But no shadow of that prejudice touched Nimue's face.

"Not much of one, if you can't even escape," she said, teasing him gently.

"I can, but I won't," Merlin said. "I'm Vortigern's prisoner, and so I'll stay. But why are *you* here, Nimue?"

"I'm a hostage," Nimue told him. She smiled wryly. "Vortigern wants to make sure my father doesn't join Prince Uther. The cage is bigger, but other than that there's not much difference between us."

"What difference there is, I'm grateful for," Merlin told her softly. She was more beautiful than he'd remembered, the lovely young girl having ripened into a desirable woman. He could almost be grateful to Vortigern for having brought them together again. "It seems I said the wrong thing when I told him Uther would defeat him."

"Oh, I hope you're right!" Nimue said, lowering her voice even further. "If he comes soon, I think there is hope for both of us."

Merlin wanted to ask what she meant, but a sudden sound behind her made Nimue rise to her feet. "I must go," she told him hurriedly. "I'll come again."

*   *   *

Merlin lost count of the passing days, but Nimue visited frequently, growing bolder as her visits went unnoticed.

Without Nimue Merlin would have died. She brought him food in secret, but though the winter nights were icy, and frost had begun to form upon the walls of his cell, she dared not bring him blankets, or anything his jailers would find. Merlin shivered without cloak or covers to warm him, but a worse torture than the cold was the imprisonment. Merlin was a creature of the wild open spaces. The man-made walls seemed to loom inward, crushing the life from his body, until he began to wonder if Vortigern had simply forgotten him, leaving him to die here alone.

Other than Nimue, Merlin's only companion came from his visions; as he grew weaker, he drifted in and out of dreams, seeing jumbled meaningless images of events yet to be.

"Merlin!" Nimue's urgent whisper roused him.

He blinked, gazing upward toward the light. His body felt heavy, as though it were turning to stone in sympathy with the walls.

"Merlin!" she called again.

He wanted to tell her he heard her, but when he tried to speak, no words would come. He raised a hand weakly, and realized he could move no more than that. His visions always told him he would not die here, but lately he was coming to doubt them. And if he died here, had Mab won? Or had he?

"Merlin, what's wrong?" Nimue's voice was filled with unshed tears. "What has he done to you?"

"Nothing." Speech was an enormous effort, but somehow he managed it. "I just need . . . space to breathe. These four walls are suffocating me, Nimue." He looked up toward the window he could no longer reach.

"I won't allow that." Nimue's voice held a hardness he'd never heard before. "The king is back. I'm going to demand that he release you."

"Nimue!" Fear for her did what fear for himself could not—but by the time Merlin had gotten to his feet, Nimue was gone.

It felt good to be at war again, the king decided. Vortigern was far more cheerful than he meant to let his captains know as he called them together in Pendragon's Great Hall for a council of war. When the two armies clashed next spring, the slaughter would be glorious. Uther had taken Winchester, and the Celts and Picts of the North were rising for him, but Vortigern held the South and the West. The Anglos, the Saxons, and the Cornish would fight for the crown like demons, and the Welsh archers could put an arrow through the heart of a sparrow on the wing. Vortigern had nothing to fear. He had a trained army and years of experience. It would not be that hard to defeat a callow youth in his first battle, and in the process Vortigern thought he'd be able to get rid of a number of troublesome political enemies on his own side as well.

But in order to win his war, he first had to inspire his captains.

"Now . . ." Vortigern said, leaning forward on his throne.

At that moment there was a commotion outside the Great Hall. Suddenly the doors flew open and a young woman in a coronet and dark velvet mantle marched in. After a moment Vortigern recognized her: Nimue, Lord Ardent's daughter and one of the royal hostages.

"I didn't send for you," he observed.

"That's why I'm here," Nimue said calmly. His words didn't seem to faze her.

"I've killed men for such insolence," Vortigern said. All around him, the chamber was filled with the stifled sound of battle-hardened warriors trying not to be noticed.

"And women?" Nimue asked. She really wasn't afraid of him. Vortigern found this astonishing.

"Yes. And children," he said, smiling his predator's smile as he stalked toward her.

Astonishingly, Princess Nimue laughed. "See? I'm trembling," she said, holding out a steady hand.

"What makes you so brave?" Vortigern asked in wonder. He circled her menacingly.

"Knowing that if you hurt me, my father and his men will go over to Uther," Nimue said calmly.

Vortigern grimaced. Kill the girl and he lost his hold over Ardent, and his hold over the fathers of the other hostages was weakened. He could not afford that, least of all now, when Uther waited ready to welcome any disaffected band of warriors to swell his army's ranks.

"Yes," he said consideringly, "that would make you brave enough to face me. So what do you want?"

"Merlin—the wizard—is sick."

"Then get him a physician," Vortigern growled, once he remembered who she was talking about. The moment was sliding from drama into farce, and if any of the fools gathered in this room laughed he'd have to kill the girl just to save face. Maybe he could feed her to the Great Dragon and kill two birds with one sacrifice.

"There's no cure but his freedom," Nimue announced.

"I can't give him that," Vortigern said. For a moment he wondered if somehow Nimue was in communication with Uther. Christian or not, Uther must know that a wizard as powerful as Merlin would be a great ally in the war to come.

"Then he'll die," Nimue said.

As if I care, Vortigern thought. A dead wizard could be of no use to his enemy, and that was more important than the aid Merlin could be to him. "We all die eventually," Vortigern said, sweeping his captains with a menacing glance. "Even wizards."

Nimue turned to go, as if she had given up. As she reached the doors she stopped and looked back, as if a thought had suddenly struck her.

"If he does, you'll never know about the battle. He's had another vision. Don't you want to know how to win?"

CHAPTER TWO

THE THRONE OF TRUCE

T rapped in his cell beneath the castle founda-
tions, Merlin drifted in a dream of banners and
clashing swords. Victory for the red dragon . . . or the
white. But which—and when? The sounds of the battle
merged with the sound of the key turning in the lock of
his cell door, so that Merlin did not truly wake until
Nimue knelt beside his cot.

"Merlin—you're free. The king wants to see you,"
she said, shaking him gently awake.

"Why?" Merlin asked quietly. Over her shoulder
he could see his guards standing in the doorway, regarding him uneasily.

"I told him you'd had a vision of Uther," Nimue
said, her voice low. "I lied—but you can make something up, can't you?"

Merlin smiled painfully. "As it happens, that
won't be necessary. Help me up."

*   *   *

The soldiers almost had to carry Merlin up the steps that led out of the dungeon, but once he emerged into the clear winter sunlight of the castle courtyard, strength seemed to seep into him with the sun's warmth. Though still very weak, he was walking under his own power by the time he entered the corridor that led to the king's Great Hall.

The news that Uther had taken Winchester without a battle frightened Vortigern's men more than Vortigern had expected—and terrified men, the king knew, were difficult to panic further.

"I have the biggest army Britain has ever seen," Vortigern said impatiently. If he couldn't frighten them, then he wanted to refocus their thoughts on his inevitable victory.

"It may not be enough," Sir Egbert said nervously.

Sir Egbert had led the scouting party that assessed Winchester's defenses, and ever since he had tried to avoid reporting his findings.

"Uther and his men follow the Christian way."

Christians, Vortigern knew, would fight on behalf of other Christians as Pagans would not. Hawdes and Aerlius had been Christians—it was one of the reasons Vortigern had been forced to execute them. "I thought they didn't believe in killing," he muttered.

"They'll kill in a holy cause, Sire. And destroying you is a holy cause." Sir Egbert, hearing his own words, looked stricken, but Vortigern couldn't work up any interest in tormenting him just now.

"How convenient. They kill when it suits them," he muttered.

"As do we all, Sire," Yvain the Fox said. He bowed slightly when Vortigern's glance fell on him.

"What I want to know is: when will Uther attack?" Vortigern asked.

"Not before Spring," Sir Gilbert said decisively, and the other lords nodded. It was one of the rules of war: fight in summer, rest in winter. None of them would do otherwise, no matter the cause.

"Good. Then I'll use Winter as my ally and take him by surprise."

The stir of astonishment at the king's words almost masked the sound of the doors to the Great Hall opening once more. Vortigern glanced toward the doorway, and saw Merlin and Nimue entering, followed by several guards. He bounded to his feet and crossed the room, smiling a crocodile smile.

"Ah, Merlin," he said, reaching out to clasp the wizard's shoulder. "I need your help. I know I've been a little hot-tempered," he added without contrition, "but patience was never one of my virtues."

"You have so few, I wouldn't trouble myself about that one, Sire," Merlin answered. He longed to return to the sunny courtyard, but he refused to allow the king to see what his captivity had done to him. "What do you want?"

Vortigern shrugged off the veiled insult. "I have to know: can Uther be defeated?"

His words woke a piercing memory of the teasing fragments of dreams that had tormented Merlin during his imprisonment. Red dragon or white? "I dreamed a battle near Winchester," Merlin said, smiling faintly at the king's frustration. "But I couldn't see how it ended. I was too weak."

"Dream it again!" Vortigern snapped. "I want to know who wins!"

The tension in the room was palpable, and Merlin could feel the hatred and distrust of magic that radiated from the British lords. Once they would have welcomed magic as their natural ally, but it had been too long since a king of the Old Ways had ruled Britain. Though he wished them no harm, even Pagans thought of Merlin as their enemy.

"And *I* want fresh air and sunlight!" Merlin responded in frustration. "Without them I can't dream dreams—see visions. I need the sun!"

He'd exposed the depth of his infirmity, but Vortigern, like many bullies, was mollified by a display of his victim's weakness.

"Is that all?" the king said expansively. "Why didn't you say so? There's plenty of sun up on the battlements." He nodded toward the guards, who stepped forward meaningfully. "Go bask in it. And come back soon with what I need to know."

Merlin and Nimue walked along the stone and wood battlements of Pendragon Castle, able finally to touch, to be together. Here in the south, the cold weather was not yet as established as it was in the north, and the air was soft. Merlin drank in the sunlight and clean air as if they were life itself, and the disturbing clamor of events not yet to be faded from his mind.

But the need to make a decision remained. Should he place his prophetic gifts in the service of Mab's ally? Merlin hesitated at the thought. The last time he had prophesied to Vortigern, it was almost by accident, but this time it would be a deliberate decision. There were two kings upon the chessboard of Britain—Uther and Vortigern. Which should he help to victory? Whose victory would hurt Mab most? The choice seemed obvious, but Uther was far away—and Vortigern held Nimue as his hostage.

How can I let anything happen to her? Merlin wondered despairingly. For the first time in many years, there was something that mattered to him as much as his vow to destroy Mab—Nimue—and for the first time Merlin was unsure of what course to take. How could he save his love and keep his oath?

Nimue took his arm. What lay beyond the castle walls was apparently as new to her as it was to him, and she pointed and exclaimed at the hurry and bustle going on below them and in the surrounding countryside.

"Oh, Merlin, look! It is as if there is another city surrounding this one," Nimue exclaimed.

"A city of legions," Merlin said, smiling faintly at his own jest. Scattered across the rolling fields outside the walls of the city, Merlin and Nimue could see the tents of Vortigern's army as it massed for war. The host was enormous: through the years, Vortigern had drained all Britain's resources to keep his forces armed and supplied, and now, inevitably, they would be used

. . . but the young lovers found it hard to care. Fate had tossed them together once more, and for the moment, that was all that mattered.

They continued their circuit of the castle walls, and Merlin felt himself growing stronger by the moment. The thought that Vortigern might once more lock him in that foul cell beneath the earth was a terrifying thought. What would he do to escape that?

Merlin shook his head, willing the dilemma far from him. He had made his decision long ago, and he did not want to be faced with any new choices. He only wanted Nimue . . . and freedom.

"What do you hope for most, Nimue?" Merlin asked. "When Uther and Vortigern fight, one must triumph and the other die."

Now Nimue stopped, pointing toward the distant horizon.

"Way over there, beyond those hills, is an island called Avalon," Nimue said wistfully. "Joseph of Arimathea came there from Jerusalem with the Holy Grail. It has the power to feed the hungry and heal the sick. It is lost to us now, but one day a man with a pure heart will find it and peace and happiness will return to us."

"It's a lovely story, and so are you," Merlin said.

Nimue smiled at him and took his hand, ignoring the guards that loitered several yards away. Her hand was soft and warm against his work-hardened ones, and in that instant it seemed as if they could take up where they had left off on that long-ago summer's day, as if the intervening years of trouble and danger they had both endured simply had not existed.

Perhaps those years had been the dream and not this shining moment. Perhaps Merlin could simply step aside from his half-glimpsed destiny into a world where he could love and be loved as an ordinary man.

He did not then realize that his wish was so fervent because it was for something he could never have. All around him Britain was tearing itself to pieces, and in this moment Merlin didn't care. All that mattered was Nimue.

Far away, that golden afternoon was reflected in a giant crystal sphere that seemed to hang weightlessly in darkness. The great scrying ball was at the center of the midnight rainbow chamber that was the heart of Mab's power. Within this spherical sanctuary all went on as if the New Religion had never come to Britain. Here the power of the Old Ways reigned unchallenged.

Mab stepped through the concentric rows of glittering crystals that stretched as far as the eye could see. As she crossed the mirrored floor her reflection seemed to follow her, a silvery ghost. Approaching the ball, she tapped its surface with one long lacquered talon. A large oval ring with a blood-red stone flashed on her forefinger, secret fires churning at its heart. The tiny images of the lovers embraced, oblivious.

Mab smiled, baring sharp white teeth. Merlin thought he'd seen her trap and escaped it by refusing to use his magic to escape Vortigern—but the blade now laid at his throat was far sharper and more inescapable. He'd chosen to be ruled by his human heart and humans were subject to falling in love.

Mab didn't understand love, but she knew its

symptoms and its effects from long observation. Lovers would do anything to keep one another from harm.

Even break an oath sworn on their life's blood.

"Frik!" Mab rasped. "Come here. There is a journey I need to make. . . ."

Merlin and Nimue had dined privately in her rooms. The sun had set, and the full moon was visible in the night sky outside her window. Her disapproving ladies in waiting hovered around them until Nimue shooed them out.

"Vortigern will expect you to prophesy for him soon," Nimue said when they were alone. "He isn't a patient man."

"I know," Merlin said, rubbing his still-bruised jaw reflectively. "But when the time comes, he'll have his prophecy. I don't think he'll like what I'm going to tell him, though." Merlin smiled.

"Are you really a wizard?" Nimue asked wonderingly, studying his face.

"A Hand-Wizard," Merlin said apologetically. For the first time in years, his failure to master Frik's teachings bothered him. Now at last Merlin wanted to be great, in order to be worthy of Nimue's love.

"You mean there's magic in hands?" Nimue asked, enchanted. She didn't understand. Merlin realized that to her, magic and wizardry were only a wonderful game. Nimue followed the New Religion; the Old Ways were less than a legend to her, and she had no idea what his words implied.

"They can say so much more than words," Merlin

answered. "They can welcome, beg, pray—" His hands made graceful gestures in the air. "They can even pluck down the moon for you."

He reached up toward the night sky, his thumb and forefinger framing the edges of the radiant moon. "If only we could keep everything simple, like the roundness of the moon. Look at its simplicity, Nimue. Everything equal, no part more important than the rest."

He gestured, and Nimue's eyes grew round. She was seeing what Merlin meant her to see; the moon, like a round silver penny, running over his fingers like a magician's coin-trick. He closed his fingers over its light and offered the hand to Nimue.

Her hands cupped his own. Her face was flushed with awe.

"Ah, but the moon's not so easy to catch and hold. . . ." Merlin grinned, opening his fist to reveal emptiness.

Nimue glanced up toward the sky to where the moon rode serenely, and laughed with delight. "I thought you weren't going to do any magic," she said, her face clouding with worry.

"That wasn't magic," Merlin told her gently. "Magic's real. That was a trick."

"How did you do it?" she demanded eagerly.

"Ah," said Merlin wisely. "It's a secret . . . and if I told you it wouldn't be a secret anymore."

Nimue shook her head, smiling at his foolery. "Can you tell me something plain . . . without tricks, Merlin?"

"Yes. Just ask." In that moment he would have given her anything.

"What do you want?" Nimue asked seriously.

"I want you," Merlin said. And in that moment it was all the truth in the world. If he could have Nimue he would want nothing more.

But Nimue was shaking her head. "That's not what I meant. What do you want from life?"

And to that question, the young wizard had no answer.

Plans for the coming spring's battle went forward in the autumn days that followed. Vortigern was confident that his plan to attack Uther in winter would succeed, but he also had to convince his officers to follow it. The weight of custom was a heavy yoke: to wage a winter war, supplies must be gathered, horses shod, arrows fletched out of season. Without the force of the king's will, everyone would settle back into the traditional ways, doing nothing. But by spring Uther might be strong enough to cause real trouble. Vortigern's days were full.

Messengers rode back and forth between Pendragon Castle and the sprawling army camp that grew beside it. Scouts rode north to spy out the extent of Uther's defenses at Winchester, and to tally the number of soldiers loyal to him. Vortigern was mindful that the young prince should gain no information about his forces in return, and stationed sentries everywhere.

And one morning, when the sun was only a few hours high, Vortigern's outriders rode for Pendragon with an incredible tale. It was amazing enough to bring

the king from a conference with his generals to stand
upon the wooden stairway that led down into the castle
courtyard. Vortigern stood and watched as the wooden
gates of Pendragon swung inward to admit a woman
like no woman he had ever seen.

She wore strange silver armor and shining black
robes, and she rode a magnificent white horse whose
silken tail brushed the ground. Her hair was braided
with jewels, and her lips were a glistening inhuman violet. Nine maidens in hooded black gowns, crowned
with golden diadems, rode behind her, each horse as
spotlessly white as their queen's. No one moved to
stop her; soldiers and peasants alike were struck spell-
bound by this strange apparition. At a majestic walk,
she rode forward until she was directly beneath the
stairway.

"Hail, Vortigern, King of Britain. I am Mab,
Queen of the Old Ways," she said, raising her hand in
salute.

Vortigern stared at her with narrowed eyes. As if
he had always remembered it, a moment more than
half his life ago came vividly into his mind. A landless
Saxon raider had dreamed of seizing the throne of
Britain. Though she had clouded his mind afterward,
Mab had been with him that night, urging him forward
for her own purposes.

*"Who are you?" asked the Saxon warlord he had
been on a night long ago.*

*"One who can give you what you desire," Queen
Mab had answered. "Land. Power. A kingdom. A name
that will live forever. You will have power and rich*

lands beyond imagining. You are Pagan, and I do not care who rules there so long as the people return to the Old Ways," Mab had said.

She had been the most beautiful creature he had ever seen—ravishing and terrifying at once. But still Vortigern had broken their pact—if pact it had been. He'd cared not what gods or spirits existed or didn't so long as he ruled. Britain had become Vortigern's kingdom, not Mab's. He'd slaughtered her priestesses and looted her shrines, and she had done nothing.

But then, Uther didn't have the power to stop him, either, and Uther was beginning to be actively annoying.

"What brings you here, Madame?" he said slowly. Vortigern was determined not to be impressed. If Mab had truly possessed the power to stop him, he told himself, she would have done it years before.

The woman below him raised her head proudly and stared into his face with inhumanly-bright eyes. "I can tell you how to defeat Uther," she said.

The morning sunlight slanted through the high windows of the Great Hall. It stood empty, its door barred, save for two figures.

Vortigern sat upon the throne he had taken from Constant, crowned and armored as the king he had become. Across the room, Queen Mab stood facing him across the straw-strewn floor, veiled in the power of the Old Ways.

"What will this alliance cost me, Madame?" Vortigern asked, breaking the silence. "There's a price for everything."

Mab regarded Vortigern with grudging respect. He had betrayed her years before when she had chosen him as her champion to wrest Britain away from the Christian King Constant. Mab had set Merlin in his place, and she did not intend to give Vortigern the opportunity to foil her plans again. Let him think she had come to aid him in fear of Uther and his Christian priests, or to take simple vengeance upon her renegade wizard. Once Merlin had returned to her side she could dispense with Vortigern. She would need no other allies!

"The wizard, Merlin. I want him," Mab said.

Vortigern settled back on his throne, smiling faintly. This was a game he knew well.

"He's too valuable to me. He sees things—he has visions."

She had not known that—it was nothing she had taught him—but Mab dismissed it easily. "Anyone can have visions. Don't you see visions? Don't you see yourself winning?" she asked persuasively.

"Always. But I don't see why you would want to help me," Vortigern said cynically.

He was more clever than she'd thought; a scornful realist in a world of frightened, superstitious fools.

Just as she was.

"I'd rather see you on the throne than Uther," Mab told him truthfully, walking toward the throne. The fact that she would rather see Merlin on the throne than either one of them was something that need not be mentioned.

"Why?" Vortigern demanded again. "I don't believe in your Old Ways."

"You don't believe in anything!" Mab said indignantly, stopping in front of his throne.

Vortigern leaned forward until their faces were very close.

"I believe in me," he said fiercely.

"It's not enough to make us win!" Mab answered with equal fierceness. If only Merlin had been as true to her vision as Vortigern was to his own, she would have accomplished wonders by now. The New Religion would have been swept away, Avalon destroyed, and the Old Ways would reign supreme once more.

But Vortigern discerned something she hadn't intended him to discover. He smiled.

"I understand," he said, sitting back and smirking. "Uther will bring Christianity to the people and that will be the end of you."

He was too stubborn! Mab raged. Vortigern was blind to his own advantage while he sought the hidden motives of others. She could not persuade him to aid her, and it was far too late to try any of her old tricks. She would have to find another way. Perhaps Uther would be more sensible. Mab turned away.

"All right," Vortigern said unexpectedly. "You can have your wizard. But how do I defeat Uther?"

You never will, Mab vowed. It would be Merlin who defeated the Christian king. But Vortigern did not need to know that. Not yet.

"Sacrifice Nimue to the Great Dragon," she said.

Let Vortigern think that this was what would bring him victory, and Merlin's life was merely a price for the knowledge. But Nimue's death was the linchpin of Mab's plan. Even if Merlin would not use magic to save his own life, he would use it to save his beloved's.

And then Merlin would belong to her.

But once more the king balked. "That's not so easy," he said slowly.

"Ethics?" Mab mocked, cocking her head with a birdlike gesture.

"Politics," the king answered. "I'm holding Nimue hostage so her father won't join Uther."

Mab nodded, understanding her ally's misgivings completely. Vortigern would sacrifice anything to victory, but he would not sacrifice victory itself.

Frik! she demanded silently.

In the empty hall outside the royal chamber, the air flickered and the black-clad form of Mab's gnomish servant appeared. In a moment he had transformed himself from an obsequious gnome into the image of the timid Sir Egbert. Vortigern trusted Sir Egbert as much as he trusted any of his captains, knowing that if Sir Egbert could manage to nerve himself up to mention something, it was something worth hearing. In this disguise, Frik flung open the doors of the throne room and assumed a look of frantic agitation.

"Urgent news, Sire! Lord Ardent has defected! He's joined Prince Uther!" He dropped to one knee and gazed up gogglingly at Vortigern, and at Mab standing behind him.

"How convenient, Madame," Vortigern said. He doubted the spontaneity of Ardent's defection, but if

Mab had the power to arrange that, then she certainly still had the power to make Vortigern's battle with Uther end in his victory as well.

"For both of us," Mab pointed out. She gestured, and Frik scampered away. It wouldn't do for the *real* Sir Egbert to appear while her gnomish servant was impersonating him.

"The girl dies," Vortigern agreed.

"Let Merlin watch . . ." Mab hissed.

Merlin slept, in a sleep too profound for even dreams to reach him. Dimly he could hear the shouts of fleeing soldiers, and the clatter of horses' hooves on the stone as their riders made their escape. But a closer sound penetrated the veils of sleep, a rhythmic sorrowful sound whose source Merlin thought he should know. Eventually its riddle forced him awake to the sound of weeping.

"Merlin!" Nimue screamed his name as she saw him move.

Slowly Merlin puzzled out his surroundings. It was just before dawn, and he was tied to a tree at the bottom of a deep gorge cut through the bones of the earth. He could not remember when he'd fallen asleep, or imagine how it was that he'd come here. He had passed this place with Lailoken several weeks ago, on his way to meet Vortigern. This place was near the site where Vortigern had sought to construct his ill-omened tower.

The ground around him was littered with bones, some charred to black, some grey-white with the weathering of passing years. A few yards away an iron stake, thick as a man's arm, was bedded deep into the rock—and Nimue was bound to the stake, her fine gown muddy and torn.

Just as the first rays of dawn touched the valley floor, Merlin heard a rasping sound coming from behind him, a sound as if a chain-mail shirt were being dragged over the rock. Suddenly he smelled a faint musky stench, recognizing its source with a flash of horror.

Dragon. Draco Magnus Maleficarum, the Great Dragon of the North—and Vortigern was offering Nimue to it. The creature was used to receiving offerings here, just outside its lair. In moments Nimue would be dead.

No! He could not bear the thought of seeing her die. But to save her would take magic.

Magic he had sworn not to use.

There must be another way! Even as his thoughts tumbled wildly, he struggled like a madman to free himself.

He could not break his oath.

He could not let Nimue die.

The unbearable choice paralyzed his brain as his body struggled instinctively. In moments he was rewarded by a loosening of the soil about the roots of the tree.

He could see the dragon now as it slithered along the ground toward its prey. Its thick leathery hide was green and yellow, almost the color of the lichen-covered boulders here in the valley. It stopped, seeing Nimue, and reared up on the hindmost pair of several sets of legs. Wings like pleated parchment fans snapped out from its sides, giving the dragon the terrifying aspect of a monstrous insect. It whipped back its long narrow head and roared.

Nimue screamed, and at that instant Merlin would have been willing to perform any feat of magic to save her. He would break his oath—dishonor his mother's memory—anything! But the crowning irony was still to come. Merlin was as powerless as any mortal. For all his training on the Land Under Hill, Merlin was only a Hand-Wizard—one whose magic was invoked through gestures of the hands and fingers—and his hands were bound.

Nimue screamed once more, in an agony of helpless terror, and Merlin struggled harder against his bonds. Suddenly the roots of the tree to which Merlin was lashed came loose. Merlin staggered forward, unbalanced by the weight and length of the trunk still bound to him. His magic forgotten, all he could think of was placing himself between Nimue and the dragon. He bent forward, and the crown of the tree lashed the rearing dragon across the face, startling it. Caught off balance, the dragon dropped back to all sixes again, lashing its long serpentine neck back and forth and belching a great gout of flame at its tormentor.

Merlin fell back, his shoulders aching with the strain of holding the tree, and once more the Great Dragon lurched toward Nimue. But the moment's struggle had been enough to allow Merlin to free his hands. Now he could fight.

Tears gathered in his eyes, and in that instant Merlin seemed to hear Mab's mocking laughter ringing faintly in his ears. He had been a fool to think that Mab would confine her attacks to him alone. Once again she had reached out to warp his life, bringing harm to those Merlin loved.

And it was all happening so fast. If there were more time, would he see another way out of the trap? Would he be willing to sacrifice Nimue to his pride?

Never. That was Mab's way.

Merlin did not hesitate again. In this moment he had discovered what the most important thing in his world was.

Nimue.

"Malence llanertal toderis Segninore!" he shouted, weaving a spell out of hand and voice together.

The long-dormant waterfall that had so plagued Vortigern's fortress burst from the cliff above. The water sparkled in the sun as it sprayed down, dousing the dragon and turning the earth beneath its feet to mud. As the beast wallowed through the mire, trying to reach firmer ground, Merlin gestured again, and a thousand green tendrils burst up out of the ground beneath the dragon's feet. The shoots swarmed over its haunches, dragging it back toward the ground.

Draco bugled its fury as it struggled, and the ground beneath its haunches began to open and subside, dragging the creature deeper. The creature could have ripped any single one of the vines free, but not all of them—they covered its body like a living net, tightening as they pulled the dragon into the earth.

Nimue—Nimue! Merlin's mind raced ahead of the

moment. His loss—his self-betrayal—was too new for him to really feel it. All he knew in this moment was that he was sick of the fight, of his own emptiness. He would take Nimue—together they could flee beyond the vengeance of Vortigern or Mab. At least they could salvage their love from the ruins of this day.

But the Great Dragon had lived since before the dawn of man, and it would not go to its defeat quietly. As its body sank beneath the surface of the earth it gathered its power for one last defiant act. It bellowed a great jet of flame directly toward the wizard whose magic had destroyed it—and at Nimue, still chained to the stake just beyond.

Desperately, Merlin raised his shield of magic, his fingers working frantically. But the oath he had broken exacted its vengeance now. Too many years had gone by since Merlin had practiced his wizard's arts, and the power that should have come to him with long years of discipline was not there. His shield buckled under the force of the blast of dragonflame, and Merlin fell to his knees, stunned.

With a last mournful howl, the Great Dragon was gone. Dazed, Merlin staggered to his feet. Something was burning.

Nimue.

Merlin ran toward the iron stake. Nimue sagged in her chains, the left side of her face, of her gown, charred, the exposed skin crisp and bleeding.

At Merlin's touch the iron chains whipped away, and Merlin could cradle her in his arms. The fine silk of her gown turned to ash in his hands.

It had all been for nothing. His sacrifice, the loss

of all he believed in. He had given up everything he was, and had still lost everything. Nimue was dying, and magic could not save her.

And when she died, there would be nothing left in all the world that mattered to him. Mab's plotting would have taken the lives of the three women who had loved him.

There must be someone who would help them— some place where Nimue could be healed!

Avalon. Nimue had been raised there, and it was a place that Vortigern's wars had never invaded. She would be safe there. If he could get her there.

Merlin found Nimue's cloak lying on the ground a few feet away and gently wrapped her in it.

But the Isle of Avalon was many leagues from here, in the uttermost west. The dragon's gorge was miles from any habitation. Merlin had no horse. By the time he could carry Nimue to Avalon Abbey on foot she would be dead.

Merlin clenched his fists in fury. He would not accept that. There must be a way! His magic must find him one.

Half-forgotten scraps of wizardly learning came back to him as if the past were only yesterday. There were still forces he could call upon, and an ally given to him not by Mab, but by her antithesis, Idath, the Winter King.

"Sir Rupert!" Merlin shouted.

There was a moment of stillness, and Merlin feared that his magic had failed him at the moment he needed it most. Then he heard a sound of hooves striking stone, and a sturdy grey horse with a dark mane and tail—fully saddled and bridled—cantered down the valley.

"Sir Rupert, old friend!" Merlin cried. The flood of relief he felt at the sight of Sir Rupert was nearly overpowering. "Help me!" He scrambled to his feet, Nimue in his arms. Even in the anguish of the moment, Merlin felt as if a long-dormant part of himself was wakening into life once more, and he did not know whether to exult or grieve.

I will do all I can, the horse answered, bowing its head.

Avalon Abbey lay far west from the lair of the Great Dragon, but Sir Rupert had been sired by a stallion of the Wild Hunt, and it was only minutes before he brought Merlin and his precious burden to the coast. The Isle of Avalon stood serenely, reflected in the still water of the ocean, for the tide was in and it was completely cut off from the land. But Sir Rupert did not even slow down; Idath's gift to Merlin galloped across the water as surefootedly as he had galloped across the land. In moments Merlin had reached the gates of Avalon Abbey.

Once upon a time long ago, Joseph of Arimathea had brought the Christians' most precious treasure to this place: the Holy Grail. Now, Merlin brought Nimue—his most precious treasure.

A group of the monks and nuns who lived there had gathered to watch his arrival. When they saw Merlin's burden, the Healing Sisters clustered around his horse gently taking Nimue from him, and wrapping her in a thick wool blanket they had brought. Among them was the cowled figure of the Father Abbot, ruler of Avalon.

"Help her, Father!" Merlin implored.

"We help all who come to us," the Father Abbot said kindly. Behind him, the nuns gently carried Nimue away.

The autumn day was dark and cloudy, and rain threatened. *Mab has made me break my vow.* Merlin numbly waited in the Abbey gardens to hear the Healing Sisters' verdict. Someone had brought him a cloak, and he wrapped it closely around him, although he was too tormented by his thoughts to feel the cold. *How could I—could we—have come to this? Oh, Nimue, I have brought you nothing but pain!*

The stones of the cloister gave no reply, and the slow hours passed in silence. There were walls all around him, but the roof of the garden was open to the sky, and so he was not too uncomfortable. Slowly his sorrow gave way to a certain interest in his surroundings. This was the first time in all his life that Merlin had been in a Christian place, and despite himself he was curious about those people whom Mab considered her deadliest enemies. Ambrosia had once told him that his mother had come from here, so in a sense Avalon was as much a part of Merlin's being as the Land of Magic.

He stood in the middle of an herb garden. All around him grew many plants with which he was familiar for their healing properties, and more which he did not know, brought to the Abbey by its fellowship across the sea. He knew that Avalon was famous for its apples as well. Despite their religious devotion, the lives of the monks and nuns here could not be so very different from those of the simple farmers and herders Merlin knew best.

The scrape of a sandal on stone warned him that someone approached. Merlin got to his feet and saw the Father Abbot approaching from the direction of the hospital.

"She's very badly wounded," the cleric said as he faced Merlin. "The sisters are doing all they can, but you must pray with us." He gestured toward the chapel that lay at the heart of Avalon.

"Why should I pray to your god if he's going to take her from me?" Merlin demanded bitterly.

"This isn't God's work," the Father Abbot answered quietly.

"No," Merlin said consideringly. "You're right. It isn't." Nimue's injury was Mab's doing, not God's.

He felt the old man look at him curiously. "Do you know who did it, then?"

"Oh yes, I know . . ." Merlin said quietly.

Ardent was loyal—Vortigern would have had no other reason to sacrifice Nimue to the Great Dragon without Mab's meddling, of that Merlin was sure. And without magic, the king's soldiers would never have been able to deliver Merlin to the dragon's cave while Merlin lay unconscious.

Suddenly he felt as if the stone walls of the Abbey were closing in on him, crushing him just as the walls of Vortigern's dungeon had. He brushed past the old priest and fled, running for the open air.

*   *   *

The sea air did nothing to calm Merlin's anger at what Mab had done. He'd hoped to foil her plans by simply not allowing himself to be used, but she would not let him go. She'd destroyed his life.

As now he would destroy her. He was no longer a child. He was a man, and he would use her own weapons against her.

"Mab!" he shouted, raising his arms to the storm-clouded sky. "Mab—do you hear me?"

"Yes, Merlin."

An unnatural wind rushed toward him from the land, and Merlin could feel the tingling of sorcerous power over his skin. The clouds above the island boiled as if in the grip of an oncoming storm, and suddenly Merlin could see Mab's face in their shapes.

In that moment he truly understood for the first time why the Christians hated the Old Ways. What right did Mab have to meddle in his life? No right but her power. Her power was what gave her the right. In this world, in this time, absolute power was absolute freedom . . . to persecute.

"You destroyed everything I love!" he shouted at her. "My mother, Ambrosia—and now Nimue!"

But if he had expected to see remorse on the face of the Queen of the Old Ways, Merlin was disappointed.

"The end justifies the means," Mab answered, and her voice was as inhuman and elemental as the roaring of the storm. "I did it for you. I want you to use the power in you. Rise up dear, *dear* Merlin, and be great!"

He could not bear the note of gloating pride in her

voice, as if Merlin were merely some possession to be used or discarded at her whim.

"No, Mab!"

The wind tore at his thin clothing, but his fury warmed him like a thick fur cloak. He'd been wrong to hide in his forest and deny his birthright. Mab would not fade away if he ignored her. She must be blotted out like the plague she was.

"I'll destroy you for what you've done to me!" he shouted.

"You can't, Merlin," Mab said, almost sadly. "I'll always be too strong."

He could feel her disappointment in the air around him. Had she truly believed that once he'd broken his vow and used his magic again he would come back to her?

As Mab spoke, the sky flickered above Merlin, and the sea suddenly rushed toward him as though its force could overwhelm him. But Merlin was not afraid. Anger lent him a strength and focus he had never had before, and the desire to hurt Mab as she had hurt him burned in his heart as if it had been transfixed by a sword of ice.

"I'll find a way!" Merlin shouted, shaking his fist at the sea and sky. "I'll find a way!"

"Never . . ." the world around him seemed to whisper. "Not ever. . . ."

It was the need for revenge that sustained Merlin through the harrowing days that followed. He would not join the monks at their endless praying, but he did find a small measure of peace among the Healing Sisters, who used the ancient power of the land in the service of humanity.

Though the nuns also prayed to the One God whom the Romans had brought to Britain, Merlin sensed that they were a true link with the Old Ways that had gone before. He would have honored them for that alone, even if their dauntless fight to save his beloved Nimue had not already gained his deep admiration.

Each day that Nimue survived was a small victory against the despotism of the Old Ways, but in Merlin's heart, these victories were not enough. He wanted to win the war, to utterly defeat Mab . . . and her allies.

For Merlin knew that she must have allies. Mab could not use the power of the Old Ways to kill—that was the ancient law. She could never have harmed Nimue directly. For that she had needed help.

Vortigern.

Without the king's assistance, none of this could have happened. And if Mab had made a pact with Vortigern, she would work with all the power at her command to bring him victory . . . and to destroy his enemies.

In his visions Merlin had seen Uther—the red dragon—triumph over Vortigern, but that had been before the king had gained the help of the Queen of the Old Ways. The future could be changed. One triumph did not guarantee victory. Mab would do her best to see to that.

But for Nimue's sake if not his own, Merlin would thwart her meddling, and see a Christian king set upon the throne of Britain.

*   *   *

Nimue drifted for a long time in a trackless half-world of suffering and fear. Pain blotted out all orderly thought, but over and over again she remembered the moment Vortigern's guards had dragged her from her room, the moment when she realized that her father's name and title could no longer protect her from anything the world might choose to do.

She remembered the terror she had felt at the sight of the dragon—an unnatural creature, created out of the magic that ruled the Old Ways. Its flame had not killed her, but even now, she knew that what it had done to her was even worse.

Nimue's beauty had always served her as a protection from the worst of the danger the world could present, but now her beauty was gone, wiped out in an instant by a burst of sorcerous fire, and the eternity of terror when she had faced the dragon lived on and on, its memory scarring her soul as badly as the dragon-flame had scarred her body.

Try as she might, Nimue could not forget that the Old Ways had done this to her . . . and that Merlin was a part of them.

No! she cried silently. *I love him!*

But the love for Merlin that she had cherished in her secret heart for so many years had been permanently tainted. Nimue had always been fearless, and now her every conscious moment was consumed by fear. Each time she thought of Merlin the memory of the dragon returned—a creature the Christians taught was a symbol of the Devil—and each time it was harder to separate them: dragon and wizard, wizard and dragon. . . .

The sound of the church bells ringing out on the wintery air soothed Nimue, driving away the monsters in her dreams. She realized she was back at Avalon where she had always been safe. Nothing could hurt her here. All the brutality of the outside world stopped at the Abbey gates, unable to enter these holy precincts.

Here she was safe. Only here.

After what seemed like years spent in a timeless healing sleep, Nimue slipped closer to the borderlands of wakefulness until at last, in response to insistent gentle coaxing, she opened her eyes.

The first thing she saw was Merlin. He was sitting on the edge of her bed, gazing down at her with grave pity.

"Hush," he whispered, when he saw she was awake. "Don't say anything. Save your strength."

Nimue could taste the bitterness of healing herbs upon her tongue and feel the thick weight of bandages covering her face and chest. Painfully, she moved the tips of her fingers, and felt the tightness of the burns along her arm. Once again she relived the moment that the dragon's flaming breath had licked over her, searing and scarring her face and body.

Forever.

She moaned and tried to turn away. She did not want to see Merlin now, not when she had the power to hurt him so deeply with her helpless cruelty and revulsion against what he was. She knew that wizards could see things unknown: he would see into her heart and see the fear there.

"No. Don't turn your face to the wall," she heard him plead.

"I'll . . . be . . . scarred," Nimue said painfully.

Forever. I will never again be the girl you loved. How can you still love what I have become? Oh, Merlin. . . .

Merlin's hands were gentle as he turned her face toward him. Even though when Nimue looked into his eyes she saw nothing but love, the sight of him terrified her. She would never be able to be open and honest with him again. The attack had stolen an innocence that she had not known she still possessed.

Her eyes filled with tears and Nimue shut them tightly. Merlin was honor itself. If she lied to him he would learn to hate her, and she could not tell him the truth. Not now.

Perhaps not ever.

Merlin smiled gently at his love, though inside he was howling with rage. Half of Nimue's face was swathed in wide linen bandages covering a mask of herbal ointment. Though the Healing Sisters had saved her life, there was no possibility that she would recover completely unscathed.

It was true that Nimue had been beautiful, in the way that mortals reckoned beauty, but it was not her beauty that Merlin had fallen in love with on that long-ago summer's day. It was her spirit, that joyful dauntless thing that he had glimpsed in the moment their eyes first met.

He'd seen the fear in her eyes when she'd looked at him just now. The smiling young woman who had laughed in Vortigern's face was gone forever as surely as if Mab had cut her throat, and Merlin vowed vengeance. He could not bear the thought of leaving what had been done to her unpunished.

Vengeance is mine. . . .

"Nimue, I have to go away for a little while," he said gently. "When I come back, it'll be forever." *If I come back.* "You'll always be beautiful to me," he pleaded urgently as she closed her eyes once more. *Nimue, don't shut me out. I have given up everything for you.*

He kissed her gently and felt her yearning—not for him, but for the inviolate love they had shared, a love that had been a shining shield against the cruelties of the real world. Now that sanctuary was gone.

Vortigern and Mab would pay. The Queen of the Old Ways had wanted Merlin to use his magic? Very well. Merlin smiled savagely. Let her see what a great enemy that magic could be.

The seasons had turned while Nimue lay injured, and it was now close to the Feast of Midwinter, the time at which Pagan and Christian alike celebrated, though for different reasons. Merlin found nothing to celebrate; the wizard rode through a landscape as cold and wintery as his own heart, toward a destination only he could reach. Sir Rupert's silver-shod hooves covered the frozen ground in a tireless gallop, and Merlin's long dark cloak of pheasant and owl feathers, trimmed in the skulls of ravens, billowed about him as he rode. Beneath it he wore rich clothing donated to the Abbey by some pious pilgrim, but the cold that burned him came from within, and no amount of fur and velvet could shut it out.

The Enchanted Lake glittered under the harsh winter sunlight. Its surface was frozen into a smooth layer of sparkling ice, and the reeds and bushes along its shoreline were stiff and glittering with the frost and snow that enveloped the landscape. This region looked like the mirror image of the Land of Magic: light where that was dark, bright where that was shadowed. But where the Land Under Hill was lifeless and crystalline, beneath the surface of the Enchanted Lake, life still burned.

Merlin dismounted from Sir Rupert's back and walked to the edge of the frozen water. Mist rose from the ground, shining with the light of the winter sun and turning everything ethereal, unreal. In counterpoint to that insubstantiality, Merlin's boots crunched loudly through the brittle surface of the hard-frozen snow.

"My Lady of the Lake!" Merlin cried. His breath made white clouds on the air and there was frost on his hair and eyelashes. He stepped carefully out onto the frozen surface of the lake. It was a darker silver than the land that surrounded it, humming faintly with its own weight.

"It is I, Merlin. I need your help. I need a sword!"

A sword with which to cut out Vortigern's heart.

For a long moment the young wizard did not think the Lady of the Lake would answer his cry—perhaps he had somehow angered her, or perhaps she had dwindled and disappeared into nothing as humankind forgot her, in just the way that Mab feared to do. But at last Merlin saw the glint of movement beneath the surface of the ice, and the figure of a pale shining woman who glowed like the full moon looked up at him through its frozen surface.

"For what purpose, Merlin?" the Lady of the Lake asked. Her voice shimmered, chiming like the ice-covered branches of the winter trees.

"To defeat Vortigern," he said. "He is Mab's ally, and a tyrant." He spoke the words that had formed in his soul through all the desolate nights he had watched by Nimue's bedside.

The Lady of the Lake shook her head slowly, sadly. "Good king . . . bad king . . . you judge too easily, Merlin. You'll learn," she sighed.

Her image faded away beneath the ice, and Merlin was alone.

She would not help him.

He shook his head. He tried not to be disappointed that she had refused him. The Lady of the Lake went her own way, as subtle and mysterious as the deep waters that were her realm. He would find another way to aid Uther and destroy Vortigern.

Merlin turned away, and as he did there was a rumbling explosion behind him. He turned back. Slabs and shards of ice were sprayed across the frozen surface of the lake, and a glowing woman's arm, garbed in shining white, thrust up through the surface of the ice. Rings glittered on her fingers.

In her hand she held a sword.

"I give you—Excalibur!" the Lady of the Lake cried.

Excalibur! Sword of the Ancient Kings, summoned out of the Lands of Magic and now a part of the

World of Men once more. The blade was as long as his arm, and shone brighter than anything Merlin had ever seen, brighter than candle flames reflected in wine. Its hilt and fittings were gold, almost in the Roman style, but decorated with the triple spiral of the Great Goddess.

Slowly, Merlin walked out onto the surface of the frozen lake and took Excalibur from the Lady's glowing white hand. Magic thrilled through him at the touch of the hilt and he swung the sword into the air. It sang a high sweet note, as if he'd struck it against a blacksmith's anvil, and the scent of magic filled the air as the humming grew louder. Excalibur was to the Old Ways what the Grail was to the Christians. So long as the sword remained unbroken, the land it served would endure.

Merlin looked down at the sword he held. In his hands he held the soul of the land, the secret history of Britain.

At the dawn of Time, when the tribes first came to Britain from the uttermost East, they had brought with them the gods who knew the secret of working cold iron. In that unimaginably ancient era, the Queen of the Old Ways had summoned a star down from heaven and from its fiery body had forged . . . Excalibur! From god to king to hero the blade had been handed down, always returning to the Ancient Ones who had forged it when its time on Earth was done. It was the sword of Weyland, of Lughd, of Taliesin—the sword of Maxen Wledig, last emperor of Britain before the Dark Times came. And now Merlin would use it to put a new king, a good king, upon the throne of Britain once more.

Merlin held the sword skyward in triumph. The blade flashed silver in the winter sun, and once more he heard the faint song of the blade's inviolable magic. Excalibur granted victory to any who wielded it and made them unbeatable in war. Merlin swore he would never allow the sword to be used except for a good purpose.

The cold of its blade burned his fingers. Holding the sword in his two hands, Merlin walked back to where Sir Rupert stood patiently. When he reached Sir Rupert, he found a swordbelt and scabbard hanging from his mount's saddle.

So this was meant to be, Merlin thought to himself as he buckled on the swordbelt. It was of soft golden leather, very plain, but worked by a master hand. When Merlin slid Excalibur into its sheath, the new weight at his hip felt right, as if it had always hung there. In a way, he felt that his life began at this moment.

Merlin had always thought that his future would hold great deeds. It had begun when he had slain Draco Magnus Maleficarum, the Great Dragon. Now, armed with the sword of the Just, he was going to face another dragon—a red one.

The red dragon was Uther's crest, and Merlin was about to make it supreme—if Uther would let him.

And he would slay a king.

CHAPTER THREE

THE THRONE
OF BATTLE

The Roman legions had worshiped Mithras as
the Unconquered Sun at this season, and now
the Christians worshiped a different Son in his place.
There was a cathedral at Winchester; its presence was
one of the reasons Uther had chosen to make that city
his stronghold. The Young Prince was holding
Christmas Court in Winchester Castle. His forces had
doubled and doubled again in the weeks since his
landing. All those who resented Vortigern—or had
royal ambitions of their own—had flocked to Prince
Uther's red dragon standard.

The red dragon will fight the white come spring.

Uther was a young man, who wore his dark hair
short and a neat beard in the Roman fashion, as well
as a Roman cloak and armor. The Continental courts
were still run very much in the Roman style, and the
boy who would be king had grown up there, as a

landless beggar suppliant at the foot of a Norman throne, existing in the shadow of his mother, Queen Lionor, King Constant's widow.

He had not enjoyed the experience.

Time and again Uther had fretted beneath the yoke of patience, waiting—always waiting—for the moment of his ascension. A thousand times he would have resigned his claim on Britain to become the Norman king's vassal, but his mother had always dissuaded him. To the day of her death, Lionor had believed that Britain was a rich prize worth fighting for, but that it could only be won when the time was right.

And at last Uther had come to share her vision. He had watched and waited until he was a man grown, until King Vortigern was old, and rotted through with mistrust, and had oppressed his people for so long that they looked back on the reign of King Constant as a golden time. Then Constant's son had sold his mother's jewels, borrowed all the money anyone would lend him, and sailed for Britain with the cross of the New Religion held proudly before him.

Though he still marched beneath the red dragon standard of his Pagan ancestors, Uther was a Christian king, and meant to make Britain a Christian land. The Christian lords of Britain had flocked to him to pledge their support as soon as his ships landed, and the Bishop of Winchester himself had opened the gates of the walled city to Uther's troops.

The fighting that followed had been brief and apathetic, and ended with the lordling who had held the

castle hanged from the highest tower while his men-
at-arms pledged themselves to Uther.

Now secure behind Winchester's walls, Uther
gathered his resources and drilled his army, and
blessed the winter that kept him safe from enemy attack. Vortigern's army was ten times the size of
Uther's. He needed time to prepare.

"Can we count on your people for supplies,
Cornwall?" he asked. Uther's knights were gathered
in the throne room, having come from early Mass to
hear the reports of the army scouts.

Gorlois, Duke of Cornwall, looked up from the
letter he was reading. "They will do what is right,
Your Grace, in the name of Christ our Lord."

Gorlois's wife Igraine held Tintagel Castle
against attack while Gorlois—a loyal and sometimes
overdevout Christian knight—was here. Uther
counted on Cornwall for food as well as men-at-
arms, though he knew Gorlois was ambitious and
hoped for Cornwall's independence once Uther tri-
umphed.

Suddenly the door of the Great Hall opened. A
servant crossed the room to whisper into Uther's ear.
His lords looked on curiously at the figure standing
in the doorway, awaiting permission to enter.

The man who stood there was about Uther's age.
In comparison to Uther's Romanesque armor, he was
dressed like some wild Pict from over the Wall, in a
long cloak trimmed with shining black feathers and
tiny animal skulls.

"You're welcome to Winchester Castle, Merlin,"
Uther said urbanely. A man who wished to challenge

a warlord such as Vortigern must be prepared to take his allies where he found them.

"Oh, are you Merlin the wizard?" Gorlois asked with false surprise. A ripple of tension went through the men in the room. Uther saw Lord Ardent—he had brought his troops over to Uther after Vortigern had sacrificed his daughter Nimue to the Great Dragon—whispering intently to Sir Boris.

"Wizard?" Sir Boris said indignantly, stepping between Merlin and the king's throne. "We're all good Christians here! We don't believe in your blasphemy!"

The young man—or wizard—smiled gently, refusing to be insulted. "That's your choice, sir," he said, bowing in acknowledgment. "But Christian or Pagan, I hope you believe in fresh news."

"Well, is it good or bad?" Uther asked, sitting back and crossing his legs. This wizard looked as if he'd at least be more interesting than another dull day spent reviewing battle plans.

"It depends on how you use it," Merlin said smoothly. He walked toward the king, one hand upon the hilt of the sword at his hip, and the lords who were gathered about Uther fell back.

"Vortigern will attack you within days," he said.

The tension in the room dissolved as the nobles laughed loudly, dismissing Merlin's words as those of a madman or a fool.

"No one fights in the winter," Gorlois said, his pale eyes boring into Merlin's. He fingered the golden cross at his throat as though it could protect him from Merlin's wizard-magic.

"It isn't done, sir!" Sir Boris blustered. He was a round, redheaded man whose small suspicious eyes gave him the look of a pig. "Rules of war. We fight in the summer and rest in the winter. It's *tradition!*" His tone was condescending, as if he thought Merlin could not be expected to understand the ways of civilized men.

"Vortigern isn't interested in rules or tradition," Merlin answered evenly. "He wants to win. If circumstances were different, I'd favor him."

He ignored the jeering nobles and spoke directly to the Young Prince. He was the only one in the room who mattered. Uther understood the necessity of kings. He would listen because he had to. Now that he had returned to Britain, he must win at all costs.

"His army's already on the march. Take it or leave it." He shrugged, turning away from the throne.

Before Merlin had gone more than a few steps, Uther had risen from his throne to follow him. He put a hand on the shoulder of the young wizard, turning him away from the gathered nobles as they walked together.

"Why are you telling me this?" Uther asked in a low voice.

"Vortigern is the friend of my enemy, Mab, so my enemy's enemy is my friend. Besides, I've seen the Red Dragon defeat the White, and I think you might make a fair to decent king," Merlin answered simply. It was no more than the truth.

Uther smiled, taken off guard by Merlin's presumption of treating him as no more than an equal. Raised in a French court, he'd never before seen any of the wizards and wonders that Britain was said to abound in. He found himself liking this Merlin-the-wizard.

"You think so, do you?" Uther jibed.

"King Constant wasn't," Merlin continued in that same confidential tone. "You'll have to do better than your father. But I offer you my services as a wizard."

Uther laughed, and held out his hand. After a moment, Merlin took it.

The bargain was sealed.

The next morning, Merlin, Uther, and his two closest companions, Lord Gorlois and Sir Boris, rode out to scout the territory over which they were soon to fight. When they reached the edge of the river that flowed south of the city, Merlin dismounted and walked out onto the ice. The surface of the river was as flat as a table, covered with snow and frost. It seemed as if Merlin were looking for something.

The other three watched him closely. Sir Boris thought that Merlin's mere presence in Uther's army was heresy; Gorlois worried about that and also feared that Merlin would give Uther more power than was good for him. Uther ignored them both. Scouts had ridden into Winchester at dawn, bringing the same news that Merlin had delivered the previous day: Vortigern's army was marching toward Winchester.

"Merlin, I owe you an apology," Uther called cheerfully. "You were right about Vortigern."

"What a fool," Sir Boris grumbled. "Fighting in winter!"

"Perhaps I was the fool, thinking winter would make me safe," Uther answered slowly. "But we'll be ready for him now."

"We must choose our battleground, Sire," Gorlois said, impatient with Merlin's slowness.

"Here," Merlin called back to them from across the ice. The cold of the north had frozen the water into ice at least a foot thick, strong enough to bear the weight of horses and men.

"You mean by this river?" Uther asked, puzzled. He would have chosen a site farther from his own stronghold, to keep Vortigern from besieging it with a second force during the fighting.

"*On* it!" Merlin answered. "Vortigern has to come down here through the pass and cross on his way to Winchester."

Uther looked at his companions. Neither of them trusted the wizard at all, and, despite the warning about Vortigern's plans he had brought, Uther himself wasn't quite sure about Merlin the wizard.

"Uther, this is where you meet Vortigern—and crush him!"

Merlin's words had the force of a prophecy—or a vow. At last Uther nodded. Here he would meet Vortigern . . . and pray that his new wizard spoke the truth.

It was Christmas Eve. Tomorrow morning, Vortigern's army would meet Uther's. Though many hoped and prayed and conjectured, no one truly knew what the outcome of that battle would be.

King Vortigern—for whom Christmas was just another day—lay resting upon his bed in the royal tent. Though his eyes were closed, he wore full armor, and clasped the hilt of his naked sword against him much as if he were posing for the lid of his own sepulchre. Later he would go and rally the troops for tomorrow's battle. They would fall upon Winchester like wolves upon a fat and unsuspecting lamb, and by nightfall his crown would be secure once more.

Sometimes he wondered why he bothered.

Just as his mind shaped those words, he felt a breath of cold air fill the tent.

"Uther knows you're going to attack," a familiar voice hissed above his head. "He's waiting for you."

Vortigern didn't bother to open his eyes and look; he knew who it was. "I wonder who told him I was coming?" he said mockingly.

"Merlin." Mab spat the name as if it had a bad taste.

"The dragon didn't kill him?" Vortigern was mildly surprised. Draco hadn't eaten a single peasant in the last six weeks, and Vortigern had assumed it was resting up after a big meal. "What about the girl?"

"She's alive," Mab admitted. She turned away from the bed and stalked to the far end of the tent.

"So much for your magic." Vortigern opened his eyes and sat up. "It doesn't matter. I never believed in it anyway."

Mab turned and glared at him. She was dressed

as if for battle, her hair braided up into a Medusa's nest, her eyes painted wide and dark and her body sleek in a tight corselet of gleaming silvery leather. Jeweled bracers were laced onto her forearms, and her boots were long and sleek. A shimmering cape of violet silk hung from her shoulders. She looked as beautiful and as dangerous as a venomous serpent.

"You're a very brave man, Vortigern—but so stupid! You *have* to believe in something now!" she cried in her harsh voice.

"Like what?" Vortigern scoffed. *Why does everyone keep calling me stupid? First the wizard and now Mab. You'd think they weren't afraid of me!* He stabbed his sword at the carpet that covered the floor of the tent. Its sharp blade sliced through the weave, into the earth below, and Vortigern smiled. He liked destroying beautiful things.

He folded his hands over the hilt and looked at Mab for a long moment before he spoke again. "I've been king for twenty years. I've never been defeated, and I didn't use any magic. I did it with my bare hands."

And just as well, in Vortigern's opinion. The one time he'd dabbled in magic, it had cost him a valued ally. After he'd given Nimue to the Great Dragon, Ardent had gone over to Uther's side. Deep down, Vortigern was sure that Mab had tricked him to her own advantage somehow, and his enemy was the stronger for it.

Looking at the Queen of the Old Ways across the length of the tent, Vortigern thought he could see tears well up in her eyes. There was a glitter as something fell, and when Mab approached him, there was a tiny oval jewel in the palm of her hand. It sparkled like sunlit ice, casting bright shadows against her skin.

"What is it?" Vortigern asked. For the first time since he'd known her, the Queen of the Old Ways looked less than confident.

"It will protect you," Mab answered.

"What are you afraid of, Madame?" Vortigern asked. He took the hand that held the jewel, and drew her down to sit upon his knee. Her face was inches from his own.

"The world is passing you by, leaving you behind," Vortigern said, answering his own question. "Old ways—new ways—it will all come together in the end. I've never been afraid, and I never will be."

And if he must die tomorrow, he would not try to elude his fate. He would meet it with eyes open, as he always had. With a quick gesture, he plucked the crystal teardrop from her hand and flung it into the brazier that sat at the foot of his bed. There was a spark, a sizzle, and the talisman was gone.

Mab gazed into his eyes, and now there was sorrow instead of fear in her stare. "Vortigern—" she said, and her voice held a last despairing warning. "Vortigern, it's your pride that condemns you."

"No," the king said quietly. "You've shaped my whole life, but you never trusted me enough to give me victory. If I die tomorrow, Madame, it is you who have been my executioner."

*　　*　　*

It was still dark when Uther's army took its place on the bank of the frozen river. There'd been some grumbling from the men at taking orders from a wizard, but in the end they had all done what they were told. Merlin placed them carefully: pikemen in the first rank of the center wing, archers behind them. What little cavalry Uther had was evenly divided between the left and the right. He held back no reserves. If they were to win this day, it would not be through a contest of endurance.

The Bishop of Winchester had come out to say a Mass and bless the troops. His elaborate jeweled robes sparkled as if they, too, were made of ice, and the censer trailed clouds of fragrant incense that hung upon the air like fog.

Merlin had withdrawn from the others, not wishing to give offense to the Christian priest. He stood now on a high hill overlooking the river valley. Though he could not see them, his magic told him that Vortigern's forces were just beyond the ridge.

His magic. It was such an easy thing after all these years to fall back into using the powers Mab had given him. All that his renunciation of his abilities had done was doom the woman he loved to a travesty of life and validate his path. Mab had been so certain that using his magic would make him return to her, but he was using those powers to fight her. Because Mab wanted Britain to return to the Old Ways, Merlin would set a Christian king upon its throne. Everything Mab wanted, Merlin would work to destroy.

It had become as simple as that.

* * *

"What if they don't come?" Godwin, a young archer in Uther's army, stared out into the dark nervously. This was his first battle. His friends said that was lucky for him, because this was Uther's first real battle as well and he would share the Prince's luck.

"They'll come," the man beside him said. "And all too soon."

But as the sky lightened and the sun rose, it began to seem as if Vortigern's army would not come, and Uther's soldiers had lost their Christmas feast for nothing.

"Look!" someone shouted, pointing toward the ridge across the river.

Vortigern's army lined the horizon, its numbers stretching as far as the eye could see.

King Vortigern sat easily in the saddle of his warstallion, indifferent to the tension of the knights around him. His battle-standards—a white pennon embroidered with red runes and a ram skull mounted on a long pole—were displayed prominently in the front ranks of his troops. They were Pagan symbols, but those members of Vortigern's army who followed the New Religion did not think it wise to object to their presence.

Sir Gilbert and Sir Egbert were at his side, awaiting the command to charge. The sky lightened, and still Vortigern did not give the signal to attack. It was as if the king was waiting for something.

"Look!" Sir Gilbert said, pointing toward the enemy host. "Lord Ardent! The traitor—he has changed sides!"

The king shot Gilbert a look of disgust and raised his arm. The sword he held flashed in the rising sun.

Uther waited, resplendent in his red-crested Roman armor, every muscle tense. If he attacked too soon, the battle would be fought on the far bank of the river and in the dark, and Merlin had assured him that victory would come only if he fought Vortigern *on* the surface of the river itself. He must trust the wizard's advice. It was the only advantage he had against an army three times the size of his own. Compared to Vortigern, Uther had no cavalry worth the name, and a mounted knight could cut a foot-soldier to pieces within minutes.

At last the first moment came when there was light enough. "Loose!" Uther shouted, and the air was filled with arrows.

The volley of arrows rattled through Vortigern's line like a shower of pointed hail, claiming few casualties. Though one of the victims was Sir Egbert, Vortigern did not flinch as the man beside him fell from his saddle.

"Charge!" Vortigern bellowed, bringing down his sword. The shout was taken up along the line, and within moments the army was in motion, charging down the hill.

Uther's pikemen ran forward to meet the foe. He'd had to give the order—he could not have held them back in the face of the oncoming cavalry. Quickly, the young prince gestured his troops forward, and heard a whooping cheer run up and down the line. He drew his own sword and ran toward the frozen river, shouting his battle cry.

Vortigern hung back only long enough to select his targets. Ardent first, just to warm up with, and then that upstart boy who wanted his throne. And then Merlin, just to spite the lynx-eyed serpent, Mab. All his enemies would be dead before nightfall. Vortigern spurred his warhorse forward.

From his vantage point upon the hill, Merlin saw the king's white stallion charge forward. He began to walk slowly down the hill, Excalibur flashing in his hand.

In the moment that the two armies met, Uther saw the wisdom of the wizard's plan. When the horses reached the ice they went down. Vortigern's cavalry was useless. In moments the battlefield became a tumult of screaming horses and shouting men. The momentum of Vortigern's charge was broken, and the fallen horses were doing more damage to their own side than to Uther's.

In the distance, the Young Prince saw Vortigern galloping toward him. Hacking around him with his sword to clear his way, Uther began to forge through the tumult of fighting men to meet him.

The stallion fell the moment its hooves touched the ice, trapping the king beneath its flailing body. Three of Uther's soldiers turned toward what they saw as easy prey, and in a moment Vortigern was buried beneath a pile of soldiers stabbing and hacking at him.

But if he had been that easy to kill, the king would have been dead long ago. Groping around with his free hand, Vortigern seized a spear that had been dropped by its former owner. He used it as a bludgeon, and in moments he had fought his way free, killing all three of his opponents, and was able to retrieve his sword from its sheath on his horse's saddle. Standing alone over the bodies of his foes, Vortigern saw Ardent a few yards away, fighting gallantly against zealous foes. Eager for prey, Vortigern waded back into the battle that raged all around him.

Ardent saw the king and rushed toward him, his sword at the ready. For half his life he had groveled and toadied to Vortigern, serving him faithfully, guessing at his moods, and the king had repaid him for his care by feeding Ardent's only daughter to the Great Dragon. Now he would do what he should have done years ago, and kill the Saxon usurper.

"Vortigern!" he shouted.

Vortigern closed with Lord Ardent, who quickly found that righteous rage was no substitute for regular sword practice. In moments Vortigern had beaten through his guard and bludgeoned the older man to the ground. Setting the point of his sword carefully into the center of Ardent's armored chest, Vortigern hammered its point home with heavy blows of his mailed fist. In moments Ardent lay dead, his blood spreading through the snow beneath him.

"Ardent," Vortigern said softly.

Merlin strode through the middle of the battle, paying no attention to the carnage around him. He wore no armor, only a close helmet of leather and bronze upon his head and his usual long feathered cloak. His lack of armor did not distress him. He had eyes only for Vortigern, and as if Fate itself had decreed that nothing should prevent their meeting, none of the other soldiers' combats touched him. It was as if Merlin moved through a world that held him alone.

At last he reached the king.

Vortigern stepped over Ardent's body and sneered mockingly when he saw Merlin. "Are you going to use some of your magic on me, Merlin?" he asked tauntingly.

"I'll kill you any way I can, Vortigern—but I will kill you," Merlin answered evenly.

In that moment Vortigern swung at him. Instinctively, Merlin raised Excalibur to block the blow. The sword hummed sweetly, and there was a ringing sound as the swords met. But Excalibur only shuddered in Merlin's grip. Vortigern's blade was sheared off at the hilt.

King and wizard both stared at the enchanted blade. When Merlin looked up, he could see the knowledge of defeat written plainly on Vortigern's face. As Vortigern began to step backward, Merlin raised the sword high above his head and brought it down again, but this time Vortigern was not his target.

The tip of the sword touched the ice gently, and the ice exploded away from the blade. In moments a deep fissure appeared in the frozen surface running directly toward Vortigern, and widening as it ran. The surface that had been so solid a moment before gave way beneath the king's feet, and Vortigern fell through the ice into the icy black water beneath.

For a moment it seemed as if he would drag himself onto the ice again. His mailed hands scrabbled at the edges of the ice as he strained to save himself, but the cold leeched the strength from his limbs as the weight of his armor pulled him inexorably down into the chill lightless dark. He screamed as he sank from sight, and his last despairing scream echoed through the icy air, unnaturally loud, startling the men who fought around him. The ice closed over him as Vortigern struggled desperately to reach the air once more, entombing him like a dragonfly in amber.

As the men around Merlin realized what had happened, the fighting stopped. Men lowered their weapons, turning to stare at the spot where the king had vanished. Slowly the clash of weapon against weapon died away, until the entire battlefield was silent, waiting.

Merlin stared down at the shining blade of Excalibur, and at Vortigern's dead face gazing up at him from beneath the ice.

"Surrender!" The cry was taken up by others; it rippled through the soldiers like wind over summer wheat, and men began to throw down their weapons.

"That's a mighty sword," said Uther—King Uther, now.

Merlin had not seen him approach. The force of the rage that had sustained him ever since the moment he'd seen the Great Dragon attack Nimue had ebbed at last, leaving him hollow and sickened by what he had done. He had used his magic, or the sword's, to kill—and in this moment, standing in the cold bloodstained snow, Merlin could not remember why killing had seemed so important to him.

"It's Excalibur . . ." Merlin said. He offered the sword—still unstained by blood—to Uther, who took it reverently. Swords like Excalibur were for executioners and kings, and Merlin did not wish to be either.

"It can only be used by a good man in a good cause," Merlin said, though even as he spoke he knew that was not true. Excalibur would grant victory to any who held it, but they must look elsewhere for wisdom.

"I understand," Uther said. He flourished the shining sword in the air, and his men closed around him, cheering his great victory over Vortigern as if Uther had won the day by force of arms alone.

No one in Uther's Christian army wanted to congratulate Merlin, and he was able to slip away, unnoticed, from the king's side. He walked steadily, empty-handed now, through the men and the horses, the reddened snow, and the vast landscape of the dead.

Vortigern was dead. Only one tear had ever been

shed for him, and his pride had cast it away. In the end, he had paid for that pride with his life.

Now Uther was king, and his Christian rule would heal the scars of the land and so defeat Mab. Merlin could return to Avalon Abbey, and Nimue.

Merlin looked back toward the frozen river, and saw that the men were carrying Uther on their shoulders, cheering as lustily as if so many of their fellows did not lay dead at their feet. Now they would crown their new king. The Red Dragon had defeated the White, and the prophecy that had called Merlin from his forest home was fulfilled.

But a strange sense of uneasiness filled his thoughts, as though—somehow—he was wrong.

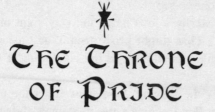

The Throne
of Pride

eep under the Hill, in the Land of Magic, Mab gazed into a scrying crystal that showed her only ice, and a battlefield long cleared of bodies. She felt a curious pain in the place that had once been her heart at the knowledge that Vortigern was dead. The two of them had fought from the moment they had met. Mab had tangled the threads of his life and denied him the chance to found a dynasty, but now that he was dead, she would miss him. Of all her cat's-paws down through the centuries, Vortigern had been the only one to go to his death clear-eyed and accepting.

She waved her hand over the surface of the glass, and the scene changed. Now the crystal showed a nun's cell in Avalon, where a Healing Sister helped Nimue to take her first unsteady steps. The heavy bandages were gone, and the girl's face was veiled in a hopeless attempt to conceal her scars, even when there was no one to see.

So Merlin's love hated the very sight of herself, did she? That might prove useful, as time went on. Mab smiled as she waved her hand to clear the glass once more.

Now the scrying glass showed her the makeshift chapel at Pendragon Castle. Its stained-glass windows cast rainbows of light over the nobles standing to watch their new king being crowned. Mab's gaze wandered over the crowd until it settled on the Duke of Cornwall. His lovely dark-haired wife Igraine stood beside him, holding the hand of their only child, a girl who'd had the misfortune to be born with a cast over her left eye. Her pious father naturally assumed that such misfortune was due to divine—or infernal—punishment, and reproached both his wife and his daughter frequently for their imagined sins.

Yes, here was something she could use to pull down Merlin's puppet king and show him he must take the power for himself. Mab smiled as she raised her hands above her head.

Igraine would do what Vortigern had not. And Merlin would not suspect his doom until it was too late for the knowledge to matter. . . .

The coronation took place at Pendragon Castle on New Year's Day.

Word of Uther's victory had spread across the land with the speed of summer lightning, and the nobles of Britain hurried to do him honor—or to fortify their castles—according to their natures.

The Bishop of Winchester was to have his early loyalty rewarded by being the one to crown the new king in the name of Holy Mother Church. Old King Constant's crown had been lost with Vortigern's body beneath the winter's ice, and so Uther had ordered a new one fashioned, its band carved with symbols drawn from the Christians' Holy Book—loaves and fishes, stalks of wheat and spring lambs. Upon the brow was the image of a rising sun. A Christian crown for a Christian king, and Merlin thought that if Uther had the perspicacity to rule with a light hand, the people of Britain would do for love what they never would have done for fear, and Britain would become wholly a Christian land at last.

And that would be Mab's destruction.

The Great Hall at Pendragon had been decked for feasting. It was filled with tables laden with delicacies to the point of collapse, and with nobles arrayed in their best clothes and largest jewels. They had been at the church earlier, with their wives and their brothers and their families, to see Uther crowned, and in every heart, Pagan and Christian, was the same prayer: *Please let him be a better ruler than the old king.*

At the top of the room, Uther seated himself upon his throne as his nobles cheered him. His rich vermilion robes gleamed, but not as brightly as the wide band of carved Welsh gold that sat upon his brow. Excalibur was by his side, and his hands lingered upon its golden hilt.

Merlin stood beside the throne, as Uther had asked him to. He had stayed for the coronation and the feast that was to follow, though he yearned to be with

Nimue. But this was Uther's moment, the day he had worked toward, and the king naturally wanted all the world to know that he had the aid of a powerful wizard.

Sir Boris glared distrustfully at Merlin as he pledged his fealty to the new king, but said nothing aloud, for Boris was an old campaigner and a practical man, despite his religion. Merlin stepped farther back into the shadows as Gorlois came toward the throne with his wife and daughter.

"Cornwall," Uther greeted him affably. Gorlois's presence at the feast was a welcome surprise, if it meant that the young Duke would support the new king and not demand sovereignty for his Cornish lands.

"Your Majesty," Cornwall said, giving Uther his new title, "May I present the Lady Igraine . . . and my daughter?"

There was a long hesitation before that last phrase, as if Gorlois would rather have not mentioned his daughter at all. But Igraine was holding so tightly to her hand that there was no way of overlooking the girl.

Igraine and her daughter both made deep curtseys, and as they rose, Mab appeared behind them like a flicker of black flame.

No one in Uther's Great Hall could see her—not even Merlin, for all his power. She took Igraine by the shoulders, and that touch was all that was needed to invest Cornwall's wife with fairy glamour. Over Igraine's shoulder Mab saw Uther's expression soften and his eyes fill with a foolish, demanding lust as his eyes rested on the face of Cornwall's wife. Mab stepped back as Uther spoke.

"You are welcome to Pendragon, my lady, and you, miss—"

"Morgan le Fay, Your Majesty," the girl said promptly, curtseying again. She was quick and alert, and if not for her deformity, would have been a child to make any father proud.

"Cornwall, will you permit me to dance with your lady after the feast?" Uther asked. His eyes never left Igraine's face.

Gorlois looked from his king to his wife, and his mouth set in a hard line. "If Your Majesty pleases," he said reluctantly.

"Oh yes . . . yes," Uther said, nearly gloating. "It will please My Majesty very much. Merlin?" he said as Gorlois shepherded his wife and daughter away.

"Uther?" Merlin answered. Something terribly important had just happened here, and he wasn't quite sure of what it was.

"Igraine," the new king said. "She's beautiful, isn't she?"

Please, let this be a joke! Merlin thought in sudden incredulous horror. For an instant he almost longed for Vortigern, alive and king, once more. Vortigern had been a paranoid tyrant, but he had never lusted after other men's wives.

"Beautiful—and someone else's wife," he said lightly, trying to make a jest of the matter.

"But still beautiful," Uther said. "What does the rest matter?" He stared after Igraine fixedly.

Merlin followed the direction of Uther's gaze and

his heart sank. He'd thought Uther could be a good king, but he was beginning to wonder whether he'd expected more of Uther than a young man raised as a pensioner at foreign courts could deliver. Now that Uther was king, he was also greedy for everything he had been denied in his previous life. Merlin sighed, seeing the future troubles of Uther's reign clearly now. He'd been far too optimistic. It was his own fault for seeing the good in men instead of their weakness; it was the weakness that destroyed them in the end.

Another noble came forward and Gorlois and Igraine vanished into the crowd. Uther's attention returned reluctantly to the business at hand. Merlin took the opportunity to make his escape and mingle with the crowd of revelers. If the king had another request to make of him, Merlin didn't think he could bear to hear it just now.

He was standing in the doorway, watching Uther on his throne, when he felt a tug at his cloak. He turned to see Gorlois's little daughter watching him. Merlin was no judge of children's ages, but he thought she could be little more than eight. Morgan le Fay was her name—Morgan of the Fairies. An odd name for so devout a Christian as Gorlois to give his daughter. Merlin thought that Gorlois must be regretting the decision to court the new king's favor just now. But who could have foreseen that Uther would be so willful—and so stupid?

"Are you weally a wizard?" the girl demanded seriously. In addition to her marred face, little Morgan had a pronounced lisp. But though she must be used to being badly teased for it, she spoke up boldly.

"So they say," Merlin told her gravely, trying to hide a smile. He respected courage, whatever form it came in.

"Do some magic for me," she ordered with all the imperiousness of a duke's heiress.

"Do you wash behind your ears?" Merlin asked her. He reached down and plucked a gold coin from Morgan's ear and showed it to her.

But she did not laugh, as he had when his old friend Herne had first demonstrated this bit of sleight-of-hand to him. Instead, Morgan regarded him as though he'd done something particularly pointless.

"That's not weal magic," Morgan said scornfully. "It's a *twick*. Anyone can do it."

"Anyone?" Merlin asked her, still smiling. "You do it, then." He bent down so that she could reach his ear. As he did, he made a small gesture with his right hand.

Right hand to summon, left hand to banish. I still remember your lessons, Master Frik, even after all these years. . . .

Unhesitatingly, Morgan reached out and plucked three gold coins from behind his ear.

"Theww, you see?" she said triumphantly. "I did it!"

"You're right," Merlin said, smiling. "Anyone can do it."

"Morgan!" Gorlois called for her, and Morgan scurried away, still clutching the coins. She didn't look back.

But Merlin watched as Igraine put her arm around her daughter and hurried her toward the door, Gorlois following closely behind them. Merlin watched them leave, certain he knew where the young duke was going. To the stables, and then home to Tintagel Castle as quickly as the horses could carry them. The meaning of the look Uther had given Igraine was unmistakable, and Gorlois was a proud and jealous man.

Well, at least that's settled, Merlin thought. Igraine would be out of Uther's reach by morning, and surely Uther would not be so rash as to pursue her, when the court was full of willing women without inconvenient husbands. But somehow Merlin doubted that Uther would learn the proper lesson from Igraine's disappearance. Uther had gained his crown far too easily. Now he would reach for anything else he wanted, certain that somehow it would be given to him.

But not by me, Merlin vowed to himself. Tomorrow morning he would ride out of Pendragon and leave Good King Uther to stew in his own juices.

But when Merlin went to the stables to saddle Sir Rupert early the next morning he found the grooms already hustling about, saddling a horse for King Uther. He wondered if Uther knew that Gorlois and Igraine were gone yet. Merlin hurried back toward Sir Rupert's stall, hoping to be away before the king arrived.

So we're leaving? It's about time! the horse said, shaking its head in relief.

"I know, old friend," Merlin said, patting his shoulder. The odd looks he received from the grooms and stableboys didn't bother him in the least. A wizard was supposed to be peculiar and mysterious, and for better or worse, Merlin was a wizard. With a flick of his fingers, Sir Rupert was saddled and bridled. The stableboys gaped in awe, and Merlin smiled quietly to himself. *That* would give them something to talk about for a while!

He rode out into the courtyard, and waited while Pendragon's gates were opened for him. It was not so many months ago that he had been carried in through these same gates a helpless prisoner. Now the king who had imprisoned him was dead, and Merlin had become the reluctant confidante of a new king.

"Merlin!" Uther called, riding up on his own horse. Merlin sighed inwardly, defeated in his hopes to escape another meeting with his liege-lord.

The new king had settled very quickly into his royal entitlements and privileges. He no longer wore his battle armor, dressing instead in costly royal robes of maroon and gold. Large spiral-shaped gold brooches held his cloak to his tunic, and the new crown glittered upon his head. "May I ride with you?"

"Of course," Merlin said, with as much graciousness as he could muster under the circumstances.

"Gorlois has left Pendragon," Uther announced, as soon as the two of them had ridden clear of the castle grounds. "And oddly enough, no one seems to know where he's gone."

Uther seemed content to let Merlin choose their path, but Merlin was by now far too wary of Uther to take any trail that would lead the king toward Avalon and Nimue. Instead, he turned Sir Rupert toward the hills, away from all human habitation, toward a place of power he dimly remembered from his long-ago lessons with Frik.

"Very odd, Your Majesty," Merlin agreed blandly. "But I'm sure he'll turn up."

There was silence for a few minutes as the two men crossed the River Astolat, which was barely a trickle this far north, and then Uther spoke again.

"I believe in you, Merlin," Uther said fulsomely.

"And I in you, Uther," Merlin replied. *Though what it is that I believe shall remain my secret, as I have no intention of returning to Pendragon's dungeons!* It would be easy enough—with Sir Rupert's help—to simply vanish before Uther's eyes, but Merlin held back, hoping to hear something that would tell him he'd been wrong in his judgment of Uther's character.

"How great is your power?" the king asked, keeping his mount close beside Merlin's. "Can you make a woman love me?"

Perhaps he has found someone else and is unsure of himself. "No," Merlin said, more gently. "Magic cannot create love."

Uther leaned toward Merlin as their horses walked slowly, side by side. "Could you kill her husband?" he asked eagerly.

Merlin recoiled, unable to keep the look of disgust from his face. "Igraine." So the king was still after Gorlois's wife.

Uther leaned forward, speaking urgently.

"I want her, Merlin. More than I've ever wanted anything in the world." His brown eyes gazed pleadingly at Merlin, much like a dog begging to be thrown a bone.

"You can't have her," Merlin said briefly.

The king sat back. "Do you know what love is, Merlin?"

Nimue. Our love destroyed her. If she had not risked her life for mine, if she had not been sacrificed to the Great Dragon, her father might be bargaining to marry her to Uther at this very moment. . . . "Yes, Uther. Sad to say, I know what love is," Merlin said ruefully.

"Give me Igraine!" Uther demanded.

"She's not mine to give," Merlin answered evenly. *This is becoming tedious,* he thought impatiently.

"Then I'll take her, even if it means war," Uther answered. The vow had much the tone of a threat.

"It will," Merlin said quietly. It did not take the gift of prophecy to see what would happen if Uther acted upon his own words. When their new king was revealed to be a greedy bully and an unscrupulous thief, the nobles who had flocked to his standard would quickly look to their own causes. The unity of Britain would shatter like a glass bowl dropped on a stone floor.

"So be it! I have Excalibur," Uther said gloatingly.

In that moment Merlin knew what had kept him by Uther's side. He had handed over The Lady of the Lake's magic to the king far too rashly. Excalibur was not meant for the likes of Uther to wield. If left in his hands, the sword of the Ancient Kings would cause untold damage.

"Very well," Merlin said quietly. He forced him-

self to smile as he reined Sir Rupert to a halt and dismounted. "Give me the sword and I'll make a spell."

Unconsciously, Merlin had led Uther to the site
that would serve him best: the Hall of the Mountain
King. He had led Uther here for a reason—this was a
magic place, as magical as the Lake of Enchantment.

The Old Ways taught that the world was composed of Earth, Air, Fire, and Water, each of which had
its ruler, a being who was both divinity and elemental,
drawing their power from the essential nature of the
element they ruled. Legend called them the Elemental
Kings, though two of them were women: Mab, the
Queen of Air and Darkness, ruled the forces of the Air
and the powers of the mind; her sister, the Lady of the
Lake, was the ruler of Water and the heart. Here was
the resting place of the Mountain King, Lord of Earth
and of the will. He had vanished from the world so
long ago that even Frik had not remembered when he
had ceased to walk among mortals. Here the ancient
power of the living rock only slumbered, always on
the verge of waking.

Of the Lord of Fire, lord of the emotions, nothing
was known. Perhaps the Great Dragon had been his
last earthly manifestation, perhaps not—Merlin knew
little of that most tricky and mutable of elements, the
one he hated and feared most.

The power rippled through the air. Merlin could
see the spirit of the wind dancing over the surface of
the grass, see the small bright sparks that were the
lives of the corn-spirits who lived within the grain.
Sprites flitted through the air like drifting blossoms.

He glanced back at Uther. How could he not feel

the magic of this place? But the days when the king's life had been bound up with that of the land were long past. To Uther, the land was only a *thing* that he could do with as he chose, just as he could with the lives around him.

But that was wrong, and today Merlin would do what he could to stop it. He walked over to Uther and reached for Excalibur. Merlin had already given Uther victory and Excalibur; Uther still trusted him. He handed over the sword easily.

Merlin took Excalibur and walked over to the foot of a cliff. The magic all around him made the sword sing to him softly—a seductive song that made him long, momentarily, for what might have been. If only Mab had been a good queen who cared for her people, he would have ruled happily as her champion, guiding the people in the Old Ways in her Triple Name. But it was too late for that. That world had ended with the coming of the New Religion, and now it was too late for them all.

He hefted the sword in his hands. The outcropping he chose was much in the shape of a clenched fist, and for a moment Merlin could almost see the rocks around him transformed into the shape of a sleeping giant, his body sprawled at rest upon the earth. Merlin climbed to the top of the rock, carefully holding onto the sword.

He had not lied to Uther. He would make a spell, but it would not be a spell that Uther would like. Silently, Merlin summoned his power, and then raised Excalibur over his head. With one smooth powerful gesture, Merlin drove Excalibur down into the stone fist.

"No!" Uther cried, but he was too late to stop what had begun.

When its point touched the stone, the sword did not shatter or slide away, nor did the stone chip and crack. The blade sank slowly into the stone, its singing becoming a high wail. Sparks fountained from it and the blade glowed red, but it sank downward inch by inch, until only about a foot of the blade showed above the surface of the rock. Shaken by the power that had flowed through him, Merlin stepped back.

Suddenly the ground began to shake as though it were alive. Flakes of rock showered down from the top of the cliff as the stone woke into life. Now, though still obviously grey and weathered stone, it had become in truth what Merlin had only imagined before— the rough shape of a gargantuan man lying on his side against the earth, his face half buried in the green earth.

The apparition opened one gigantic bloodshot eye and stared at Merlin. "Who dares wake me?" a voice as deep as the earth rumbled.

Uther's horse gave a squeal of fright and bolted, pitching the king to the ground. Sir Rupert, who had seen stranger things, stood his ground placidly.

"I am Merlin." He had not realized that the power of Excalibur would be enough to wake the Mountain King, but if it were, the sword was definitely too powerful to leave in the hands of a weak king like Uther. "And this is Excalibur," he said, gesturing toward the sword. Clasped in the Mountain King's fist, it seemed to glow with a fierce silver light.

"How did you get it?" the Mountain King asked in his slow deliberate way. His voice was so deep that each time he spoke the whole earth shook. Pebbles showered down around Merlin and Uther.

"A gift from the Lady of the Lake," Merlin said.

The Mountain King seemed to ponder for a moment. "She's been a friend of mine since . . . since before the dawn of Time. And if I can remember that, it means I'm an *old* man." The Mountain King gave his rumbling laugh, his vast body shaking, and more showers of stone rained down his rocky face.

"I ask you to hold Excalibur for me till a good man comes to take it from you," Merlin said boldly.

"A good man—then I will be holding it forever, or even longer," the Mountain King said amiably. The rock upon which Merlin stood became a fist again, and the fingers of the stony fist closed tightly around the blade. As they did, the semblance of humanity vanished from the face of the cliff. Even Excalibur's great power was not enough to keep the Mountain King awake in the modern world. In moments, he had returned to his immemorial slumbers and the world was silent once more.

And Excalibur was beyond Uther's reach forever.

Uther stared at the cliff, only now beginning to fully realize what had happened. Merlin had not destroyed Excalibur with his spell, but for Uther the outcome was much as if he had: the sword was buried to its hilt in a boulder, and Uther was no closer to possessing Igraine than he had been before.

"You tricked me, Merlin!" Uther cried angrily. He staggered up the rock toward Merlin, disheveled, crown askew, looking cross and rumpled and unkingly.

"Come, come, Uther. I'm a wizard, that's my business," Merlin said chidingly. He smiled mockingly—he could afford to, now that Excalibur was safe once more. Free at last, Merlin turned away from the king and began walking toward Sir Rupert. "The sword is yours, if you can take it," he called back cheerily.

But that was not something Uther would be able to do, for he was selfish and greedy, and now that Merlin had bespelled it, the sword could only be drawn by a good man. Perhaps the Mountain King had been right, and the sword *would* be here forever.

Merlin reached Sir Rupert and swung himself into the saddle; a simple spell made the two of them as invisible to mortal eyes as the wind.

At the top of the rock, Uther began tugging at the hilt of Excalibur frantically. When he stopped to look around, he was alone.

"Merlin!" Uther cried furiously. "Where are you, Merlin?"

But there was no answer as, unseen by the king, Merlin rode swiftly away from the sword in the stone.

When Merlin at last reached Avalon Abbey, the Father Abbot was able to give him good news: during his absence, the Lady Nimue had continued to recover, and was now strong enough to leave her bed and walk in the Abbey gardens.

"And news has reached us that Vortigern the

Tyrant is dead, and there is a good Christian king upon the throne!" the Father Abbot added.

"A Christian king, certainly—but good? Perhaps someday he will learn to be," Merlin answered. "But I fear I bring bad news for Nimue," he added. The battle in which Uther had gained his crown was less than ten days past, and its full details had not yet reached cloistered settlements like Avalon.

"Lord Ardent," the Father Abbot guessed.

"Is dead," Merlin finished. "It will be best if I tell her at once. Where is she?"

"I believe she is at the Grail Chapel—or what was once the Grail Chapel, before the Grail was lost to us," the Father Abbot amended sadly. He pointed in its direction, and Merlin walked away.

As Merlin traversed the Abbey grounds, he was struck by the beauty he had been unable to notice when he had been caught up in his fear for Nimue's life. The winter ice had turned the old stone buildings into fantastic structures of silver and crystal, and the faint dusting of snow made the buildings look as if they were made of lace. *My mother lived here, prayed here. Elissa must have walked these very paths, seen these sights.*

Merlin did not often think of his mother, killed in the act of giving birth to him. But she had been a postulant here at Avalon, one of the keepers of the Grail, until the night when Mab had used her, ruthlessly, as the vehicle by which she might bring Merlin into the world to be her champion.

Though Merlin did not think it had been Mab's

doing, the Grail had vanished at that same moment, and the small community here, ruled by fear and urged on by Brother Giraldus, had focused on Elissa as the cause of their bereavement, and banished her from Avalon. If Ambrosia had not been with her, Elissa would surely have died then, and not months later in childbirth.

What would these good monks and nuns do, if they knew I was the son of the woman they wronged so sorely? Merlin wondered. *But it was fear that ruled them in that hour; they have been as kind to me—a Pagan wizard—as they should have been to her, and so, in some way, their debt to her is paid. . . .*

He reached the Grail Chapel, and hesitated outside the door. Once it had been the holiest place in all of Britain—when it had held the Grail. Had some force swept the Grail away in the same spirit that Merlin had entombed Excalibur, to keep it from becoming a tool of evil?

First the Grail, now Excalibur. Must all things of goodness and power be hidden away from men to preserve them from misuse? It was a bleak thought, unworthy of this place of hope and rebirth. Despite the fact that their treasure was gone, the religious of Avalon still kept vigil here, and made this chapel the departing-place for all their searches for the Grail. And in their searching, they had spread the message of a gentle and merciful god throughout Britain.

Through the open door, Merlin could see two of the Healing Sisters in their grey and white habits standing before the now-empty altar. Between them a third woman knelt, praying. Though she was so heavily veiled that nothing of her face or body could be seen, Merlin knew instantly that it was Nimue. As he hesitated in the doorway, unsure of what to do, she rose from her prayers, turned, and saw him.

The first gesture she made was to touch her veil, assuring herself that it still concealed her scars. Then she walked slowly toward him, holding out her hands. But Merlin could see that they trembled, for all that she tried to hide their shaking.

"So Vortigern is dead," Nimue said, reading the news in his face. Her hands were warm in his winter-chilled ones. "And Uther is our king."

"Yes," Merlin said. He remembered the hopes Nimue had held for Uther's reign, and what the bitter reality was. "I was there, and . . . I'm sorry I can't bring you better news."

Nimue hung her head. He could see her face dimly through the veiling. "My father defected to Uther, didn't he? He fought against Vortigern."

"Yes," Merlin said. He put an arm around her and led her out of the Chapel. The two Healing Sisters followed behind.

The wind flattened the veil against her face as Nimue stepped outside. She clutched at it desperately to keep it from being torn away. Merlin pretended not to see the gesture, but his heart ached for what she had become.

"Lord Ardent fought for what he thought was right. I saw your father die bravely," Merlin said, once they reached the cloister walk. It was sheltered from the January storms, and long icicles dangled from the roofpeak, glittering in the sun.

"It doesn't matter to me how he died," Nimue said in a ragged voice. "I only know I weep for him."

"I killed Vortigern," Merlin added.

Nimue stopped and turned toward him. He had the sense that she was studying him, perhaps seeing more than he wanted anyone to see. "You say that almost sadly, Merlin," she said.

"No." Merlin's voice was hard. "Not after what he did to you. But when a brave man dies—even one like Vortigern—it leaves a gap." *And one that Uther's unlikely to fill, with his selfishness and greed.*

He took her arm and they continued along the walk. The sound of their feet made loud scuffling sounds against the paving, the sound magnified by all the stone around them. If the center of the cloister walk had not been open to the sky, Merlin would have felt uncomfortably enclosed.

"And Queen Mab?" Nimue asked perceptively.

"That will take longer," Merlin said slowly. Her words reminded him that his task was not over. Uther would not be the shield against Mab that Merlin had hoped for. She would find some way to twist this king, too, to her vile ends. "But I'll do it in the end, I swear."

Once more Nimue stopped and looked at him. "Don't do it for my sake, Merlin. To spend your life on revenge is a waste."

Very gently Merlin put his arms around her, and cradled her head against his chest. *It isn't revenge I seek, but justice—for Elissa, for Ambrosia, for you. Perhaps Mab was a loving mother to her followers once, but those days are long past. She lives only for power, now. She must be stopped.*

* * *

A few hours later Merlin sat with Nimue, keeping her company in her small chamber as they talked of old times. It was not really as dark and grim as he remembered it from the days of her illness; the lime-washed walls were painted in blue and rose with a delicate band of decoration separating the colors. Large windows, their shutters thrown open for the light, looked out over the sea. The room was pleasant and airy, much like the one she had occupied at Pendragon. But there the Princess Nimue had been a prisoner. Here, she was free.

All at once a vast longing to simply *leave* took strong possession of Merlin. The world was wider than Britain—he and Nimue could leave all this barbarity behind—Mab's war, Uther's pettiness—his magic could make Nimue whole again so that she would be willing to leave her seclusion. It would only be an illusion, but no one who saw her would know that, and it would mean so much to her. They could be free, just the two of them, alone together in the wide world. . . .

"Take off your veil," he said suddenly.

Though Nimue had shed the heavy cloak and veil she had worn outdoors, her face was still concealed by a long moss-green scarf that was wrapped concealingly about her head and throat.

"I'm not ready for you to see me," she said, recoiling in fear at his suggestion.

"Let me be the judge of that," Merlin answered, reaching out. Gently he unwound the scarf from about her face and neck, laying it over her shoulders. The pale winter sunlight streaming in through the window shone directly on Nimue's skin. The left half of her face, from the cheekbone to the throat, had been scarred by the Great Dragon's flame. The skin was greyish, shiny, and ridged, like a pool of dirty candle wax. It pulled down the side of her mouth and thickened and coarsened the skin of her throat, making it hang in wattles of scar tissue.

"I'm a monster," Nimue said bitterly.

Merlin didn't answer. He summoned up his power as Frik once had taught him, casting it over Nimue as a fisherman would cast his nets over the ocean. This scarred creature was a false Nimue, and he would restore the true one. He reached out his power. . . .

Nimue caught her breath in desperate hope. She knew what Merlin was attempting. He could cloak her scars in illusion with his magic, give her back at least the seeming of wholeness.

In the weeks Merlin had been gone, Nimue had struggled to heal that part of herself, to become the woman she had once been. Through prayer, through meditation, through the healing powers of Nature she had sought herself, only to be defeated. She could not reach out to remake herself unmarred. And so long as her inner self matched the outer, she could not give Merlin the gift of wholeness he deserved. She would not be his match, his mate.

But she burned with shame each time someone flinched away from the sight of her, and with a greedy, unworthy part of herself, she yearned for Merlin's illusion, though it would cure the body alone and not the spirit. Let her pretend to be what she was not—in this one moment of longing, she would give up all she was, all that she hoped to be, for simple vanity.

But nothing happened. The scars remained.

Nimue watched, desperation making her heart hammer, as Merlin tried again, and again, weaving his Hand-Wizardry, his fingers fluttering in a cage about her face.

It wasn't going to work. The disappointment was as sharp as the relief she felt, as if in this moment she stepped back from the edge of a yawning chasm toward safety.

But inside herself, Nimue wept. How bitter it was to know her beauty meant so much to her! She had even been willing to risk her immortal soul, to accept the taint of the Pagan magic she so feared to restore it. The New Religion taught that magic was a trick that always tainted the recipient. To be given gifts God did not mean them to have corrupted the soul . . . or, worse, blinded it to its weaknesses, allowing them to intensify and grow. She could not recover her wholeness by pretending she was whole already—but oh! when Merlin had failed to grant her the gift she dared not accept, the disappointment had been almost more than she could bear.

In that moment when Vortigern's body vanished beneath the ice at the touch of Excalibur, Merlin had come to an invincible belief in the power of the magic he wielded—and now, even that betrayed him.

It did not work. His magic—the one thing he had always believed in, even when he had rejected it to take vengeance upon Mab—was not strong enough. He'd tried to heal Nimue . . . and failed.

He saw the look in Nimue's eyes as she realized his spell was not working, and in that moment he would have done anything, made any alliance, to have the power to hide her scars. He would have served the Queen of the Old Ways herself.

That thought stopped him. Ally himself with Mab's evil to make Nimue whole again? His hands dropped slowly to his lap as a chill dread enfolded him. Surely that could not be the price of her healing?

If it were, he would not pay it. Not even for the woman he loved more than he loved anything in the world could he serve Queen Mab. And because that was true, all he had done here today was raise Nimue's hopes . . . and not been powerful enough to fulfill them.

"I can't do it. Mab is too strong."

At his words, Nimue got to her feet and walked toward the window. She stopped there, her back to him as she looked out, and carefully wound the veil around her face once more.

"Leave this place and come with me," Merlin begged. Nimue's scars did not matter to him—he loved her. Far from Britain, surely Mab would forget them both.

"I'm not ready to face the world," Nimue said distantly. Her words had the dull finality of tolling bells.

"When will you be ready?" Merlin asked, not moving. If they stayed here at Avalon, Merlin knew that Queen Mab would seek out Nimue once more, and perhaps succeed in destroying her next time. He could not face that. She was too precious to him, more precious even than thoughts of revenge.

This was what Love was. Ambrosia had told him that Love was the strongest power, and he hadn't understood her words until this moment. Stronger than good or evil, stronger than hate, Love swept everything before it in its blind intensity. No wonder Queen Mab feared the power of the human heart. Love truly conquered all.

Oh, dear Lord, thank You for preserving me from this grievous fault! Nimue gasped inside herself. There was still a chance to become whole, at least in spirit— a chance that would have been lost to her if Merlin had succeeded in hiding her scars. This was something that could not be done for her. She must perform this transmutation herself.

"When will you be ready?" Merlin's voice demanded of her.

"I don't know," Nimue said softly. *And until I am whole, I am like a broken goblet; if you try to hold me, you will only wound yourself, my love.* Keeping her voice even, Nimue gazed out toward the ocean and spoke. "Perhaps it would be better if you left Avalon, Merlin. I am . . . I think that I will study to become one of the holy women here. I can spend my life in prayer and healing." *My own and others.* "God does not care what I look like—"

"Neither do I," Merlin said. He crossed the room to her and put his hands upon her shoulders, as if his battle with Mab no longer meant anything to him.

But you must fight her, my love, you must. She has

done so much evil, and you are the only defense we have. Other men would be tempted by her power, as Vortigern was, but you despise it. Oh, Merlin, Merlin—I cannot let you renounce this battle for my sake! It is precisely that thing which I fear most.

"God can find someone else," Merlin said desperately. "Stay with me."

"I must do what my heart commands me, Merlin," Nimue answered faintly. She bowed her head. "And so must you."

The news soon reached Avalon that King Uther had gone to war once more. He said that his vassal, the Duke of Cornwall, had defied him, but everyone in Britain knew the truth. Uther wanted Cornwall's wife.

At first Merlin ignored the feckless king's war. He was tied to Avalon by Nimue's presence there. She'd told him to leave, but he was unable to obey, and no matter how far away he rode, he always ended up returning to Avalon . . . and Nimue.

Sometimes she refused to see him, but Merlin had made friends among the Healing Sisters and he was always able to get news of her. The months passed. Nimue studied and prayed and worked among those pious women, her scars always veiled, while Merlin alternated between hope and despair. His heart told him she loved him still—but what good was that love if they were always to be apart?

But sometimes she would let him come to her again. On those occasions they talked and laughed together almost as freely as they once had, though she would never again let him remove her veil.

* * *

"They say that Uther is mad, like his father Constant," Nimue said to Merlin one day.

It was a Saint Martin's Summer afternoon, one of the warm days that comes after the first nip of frost. Merlin and Nimue were playing chess beneath the apple trees in Avalon's orchard. The trees were in full leaf, and the apples, round and red, were already being gathered in by the young novices.

"Perhaps he is. I don't care," Merlin answered candidly.

White butterflies flitted around Nimue's veiled head. She wore the plain undyed homespun robe of the Healing Sisters, but although she still studied and prayed with them, she had not spoken again of taking binding vows to serve their god.

Merlin studied the board before him, but his thoughts were elsewhere. He knew far better than Nimue the validity of those rumors that reached Avalon in piecemeal fragments. Uther's behavior grew more erratic every day. It was madness to pursue Cornwall's wife, yet Uther did, and Cornwall just as hotly defended her—and the sovereignty of his duchy, for Cornwall had now declared that his lands owed no fealty to a king like Uther.

"But you *must* care," Nimue said earnestly. "If you were there to advise him—"

"He'll take no advice," Merlin said. "From me or from any other. His lords—his bishops—even your Father Abbot—all have begged him to call off this madness. He will not."

"He would do it for you," Nimue answered. He

could tell she was looking at him, even through the concealing veil. "You are his wizard. You gave him victory over Vortigern. He'll remember that."

"And tricked him into giving up Excalibur," Merlin pointed out. "He'll remember that longer. Do you know there is a village there now? Everyone in Britain goes to try to draw the sword from the stone. But only a truly good man will."

After much deliberation, Merlin moved one of his knights out onto the board.

"You do not believe such a man exists," Nimue accused, ignoring the chessboard to argue with Merlin.

"I *know* he doesn't," Merlin corrected her. He had grown cynical after Uther's betrayal of his hopes. Hadn't he said when he trapped Excalibur in the stone that a wizard's business was trickery? All his life, everything he learned had been nothing more than a collection of empty tricks borrowed from Mab, the greatest trickster of all. . . .

"Then you must call a good man into being with your magic," Nimue urged stubbornly. "Surely you can at least stop the fighting between the king and the duke—we see so many of the injured here at Avalon, Merlin. It is hard to see a man die when you know that he has died for nothing."

Merlin nearly did not hear Nimue's last words. What she had suggested reverberated within him as if it were a hammer that had struck the bell of his soul.

She said it as if it were such a simple thing . . . cast forth his magic to trifle with the mysteries of Birth and Death, to summon the rightful wielder of Excalibur into being. Was it as simple as Nimue made it sound? Had someone, once, said those very words to Mab, and set them all on the tangled course that had begun with his conception? And where Mab had failed to create a champion in her own image, could Merlin truly say he would do any better? Dared he even try?

"Merlin?" Nimue was watching him anxiously. "Are you all right?"

"Yes, of course." He smiled at her, but his thoughts were far distant. The temptation to do what she had so lightly suggested was nearly overwhelming, and with a reluctant effort Merlin forced it from his mind. *It's foolish and dangerous. Besides, I wouldn't even know where to begin. I haven't a tenth of Mab's power and learning, and she failed terribly.*

"But you will speak to Uther? For my sake?" Nimue's words broke into his dark thoughts.

"Yes," Merlin agreed reluctantly. "Very well. For your sake, I will do what I can to stop this war." *And pray for me, my love, that I do more good this time than the last time I used my magic for Britain.*

Gorlois had retreated into Tintagel Keep months ago, and the only way to reach his stronghold was along a long, narrow, and easily-defended causeway. Uther's forces had been turned back every time they had tried to take Tintagel, but the king showed no sign of giving up.

Last winter, when his army rested at Winchester, Uther had been content to wait for spring to begin his war against Vortigern. No one thought he would be as careful this winter and wait out the cold season safe behind Pendragon's walls. Uther was a man obsessed.

Uther had made his camp just out of arrow-range of Gorlois's archers. From the doorway of his tent he could see the causeway leading into the keep but he could not approach it. And every night Uther failed to take Tintagel was another night Igraine spent in Gorlois's bed.

Igraine . . . Igraine . . . The thought of her was like a red drumming in his brain, blotting out all else. Uther stared westward toward Tintagel, oblivious to the raw sea wind that blew over the headlands.

"Three months siege and we still haven't taken it!" he groaned aloud.

"There's no way across the causeway, Sire," Sir Boris said. Uther's most loyal knight had supported his master through all the months of fighting, but the faith of even an unimaginative warrior like Sir Boris was beginning to wane. "My advice is to give it up. It's madness," he added, as though that was an explanation.

"I must have Igraine!" Uther moaned. He clenched his fists, staring hopelessly toward the fortress.

"As one who's been to Colchester, as one who knows a few things, I have to tell you, Sire, the kingdom is falling apart while we tear ourselves to pieces," Boris said plaintively. "If this was for money, or love, or power, I could understand it. But all this for *Cornwall's wife?*"

The king ignored the pleading in his liegeman's tone. "You were born old, Boris," Uther said contemptuously. "I've spent all my life fighting. Bloody days

and cold nights with a naked sword as a bedfellow."
And now I want something . . . warmer.

"You'll never take Tintagel," Sir Boris countered
flatly.

What might have become an argument was interrupted as the attention of both men was caught by the
sight of a rider on a grey horse entering the camp. The
newcomer did not wear the armor of Uther's followers. He wore a long dark cloak with silver symbols
embroidered along the hem and a feathered border
studded with the skulls of ravens. He wore no armor,
but on his head was a close-fitting helmet of gold-
washed bronze and deerskin.

Sir Boris crossed himself, as a good Christian
should at the sight of a Pagan wizard.

"Merlin . . ." Uther breathed. Mad hope gleamed
in his dark eyes.

"Hundreds are dead because you have an itch,"
Merlin said brutally as he followed Uther into the
king's tent. The red light of sunset shone over his
shoulders, but most of the interior of the tent was in
shadow, without even a lamp to give it light.

Merlin had not seen Uther for almost a year, and
in truth, it did not look as if the king were suffering
from an itch, but a scourge: Uther was hollow-cheeked
and unshaven, his ragged beard and wild eyes giving
dismal credence to the rumors of madness that surrounded him.

"Will you help cure me of that itch?" Uther demanded belligerently. His face was puffy with inaction
and too much wine, and he glared at Merlin with a

moody distrust that might turn to violence at any moment.

And this is the man that Nimue says I am to persuade to see reason, Merlin thought mournfully. It was as if the ravaged King Uther was as much a victim of forces greater than himself as the lightning-blasted tree was the victim of the storm. For a moment Merlin thought of Mab and her plots, but for the life of him, he did not see how Uther's destruction could benefit the Old Ways. No, Uther had been a weak and selfish king from the very beginning. This was only more of the same.

"You've lost your reputation, Uther, and reputation, like glass, once cracked, can never be repaired," Merlin said pensively.

"Will you help me?" the king demanded again.

"I don't know you anymore. You've become an Ouroboros—You'll destroy the world in your lust!"

Uther took a step toward him. "Will you help me?" he demanded relentlessly.

Merlin could see their words as they chased each other in a golden spiral toward the roof of the tent, to vanish up and out the smoke-hole near the center-pole. "Yes," he said, at last goaded to it against his will. *It's madness.* "I have to be mad to stop this madness."

His words . . . Uther's words . . . bright sparks sailing into eternity. In that moment the dim interior of the tent seemed to glow.

The mantle of prophecy had not descended upon Merlin since the day he had stood before Vortigern for the first time and he had seen the Red Dragon vanquish the White. Dreams of what might be were not the same thing . . . any man might have those. They passed through the consciousness like dim ghosts, inscrutably pointing the way to What Might Be.

Prophecy was a different matter. Prophecy demanded action; it was a call to battle against the forces of chaos.

And now, once again, that summons had come to Merlin.

He saw a golden city, shining in the sun. *This is the dream that is to come.* Its name rippled over him like the notes of a harp: *Camelot.* Camelot, the golden city, city of peace and justice. A glorious city for a glorious king. *Arthur—Arthur of Britain.* For a moment Merlin glimpsed a throne room in which a fair-haired boy raised a gleaming sword—Excalibur—toward the sky. This was the king to be. *Arthur.* The once and future king. The Pendragon.

Uther's son, and Igraine's. *But if Uther goes to Igraine now, this child will be the only child he will ever have. And Arthur will be the greatest king Britain will ever have. He will fight for right, and his name will be remembered for a thousand years.*

Lost in the glorious vision, Merlin still found the strength to wonder what forces had sent him here to assure Arthur's conception by his own aid to Uther. Should he warn Uther of the consequences of this night's work?

Even as the thought occurred to him, Merlin rejected it. He was far too disgusted with Uther's behavior to give the king another warning he would disregard. Let him satisfy his lust without knowing the consequences.

But what of the child, Arthur?

Nimue had told him, half in jest, that he must summon a good man to be a good king, but Merlin did not wish to meddle as viciously in innocent lives as Mab had done to create him.

But this child would be born no matter what he did—was it not meant that he should take Arthur far away from Uther's wickedness and fill him with all that Merlin had ever learned of right and good?

Was that the ultimate reason for Uther's mad pursuit of Igraine, and Merlin's reluctant promise to help him gain his desire? Not to make Uther a better king, or gain him another man's wife, but to get Uther's child, a boy to whom he could teach all that he knew of justice and mercy? A boy who Merlin could shape into a king whose kingship would destroy Mab's evil?

Arthur and Camelot . . . and an end to the Old Ways!

Slowly the last of the vision faded, filling Merlin with hope and resolve. Now, at last, after so many years of fighting, he had something to fight *for.*

"What will it cost me?" Uther growled. His voice brought Merlin's thoughts back to Earth. *You're right to think I will exact a price for this night's work. Perhaps, Uther, you're finally learning wisdom.*

"You will have Igraine, but there will be a child," Merlin said tersely. "A boy. I've seen him, Uther. He's mine." *Arthur. King Arthur. Master of Excalibur; the king who will draw the sword from the stone.*

Even this information was not enough to dissuade the king from the thought of possessing Igraine.

"What will you do with him?" Uther asked incuriously.

"Teach him honor and goodness," Merlin answered shortly.

"I can do that," Uther said, grinning at the thought of the night to come. His eyes burned with a feverish, greedy lust.

Merlin turned away from Uther in disgust. " 'Honor'—'Goodness'—the words stick in your throat! You choke on them, just as you'll choke on your own vomit in the end."

For a brief moment Merlin peered once more into the future, this time to a dark and dirty throne room where a mad king raved on in solitary silence. He turned away from the vision, back to Uther. The king's face was ugly with anger, but his desire for Igraine made him choke down the insults Merlin had given him.

"Very well. I agree."

"Once more: Cornwall will not be harmed!" Merlin said sternly.

"Not by me," Uther said, doing his best to look meek.

The bargain was made, and Merlin steeled himself to do what must be done. At least it was for a good cause: for Arthur, for the king to come, the true master of Excalibur.

"Now, break camp. Withdraw your army. Now—in daylight—so Cornwall can see," Merlin ordered.

The fortress Tintagel was so secure that the upper rooms could have full-sized windows facing landward, instead of the mere arrow-slits that most castles had. From Igraine's chambers, Gorlois could stand in the window and see all of Uther's camp. He'd been watching it for most of an hour. It was unusually active for this time of day.

"Uther's breaking camp," he said at last. It was true. Gorlois could see the tents being struck and bundled into mule-drawn carts. The captains were already marching the men away.

Igraine came and stood beside him. The scarlet-dyed linen of the gold-embroidered Roman gown she wore left her arms bare, and her long dark hair fell free down her back.

"We'll follow him," the young duke decided.

"Don't leave, my lord," Igraine pleaded, taking his arm.

"Why not?" Gorlois asked. His mind was already on tracking Uther. He'd take a small party, no more than a dozen men, and discover what new trick mad King Uther was trying now. Whatever it was, it would not work, Cornwall vowed.

"I have a feeling that—"

"The castle's well guarded," Gorlois interrupted her, having already made up his mind. "You'll be safe, my love." He kissed her rather absentmindedly and walked back inside.

"Look after your mother, Morgan," he said to his daughter.

"I will, Father." The child gazed up at her father adoringly, but Gorlois was already gone, his mind on other things.

*   *   *

Darkness fell as Uther's army rode eastward. Uther, pleading pressing Army matters that needed to be taken care of, rode away from Merlin and searched through the line of marching men until he found Sir Boris. The phlegmatic redheaded knight was riding beside his troops.

"Boris," Uther said, "a word with you?"

Sir Boris turned his heavy-boned destrier aside and rode to where the king waited. "Sire?" he said, with mingled hope and suspicion.

"It's time to tell you my plan," Uther said, looking over his shoulder to see if Merlin was nearby. Satisfied that the wizard was out of earshot, he continued. "When Gorlois sees that the army has gone, he will be certain to follow it."

"Aye, so would any man," Sir Boris said.

"I want you to take some men and wait for him somewhere out of sight. He'll suspect nothing. I want him dead. Do you understand me?"

He had sworn to Merlin that Gorlois would not die by his hand, but Uther could not bear to let Gorlois go free after the Duke had so defied him. If he could not be the one to kill Gorlois, let another do it.

"Very well, Sire," Sir Boris said. If the request disappointed him, his face did not show it. "Cornwall will be dead before morning. But would you not prefer to kill him yourself, Your Majesty?"

"I will be . . . otherwise engaged," Uther said, smiling ferally. By setting Sir Boris after Gorlois, Uther could keep his word and have his revenge as well. He smiled at the thought.

If your business is trickery, Wizard, then so is a

King's. . . . He turned his horse back to where Merlin waited.

After they had gone only a few miles toward Pendragon with the army, Merlin and the king turned again and rode west, cloaked in invisibility, to a hill from which they could see Tintagel. They watched the gates as Gorlois rode out of the fortress at the head of a small troop of men.

"Yes!" Uther cried exultantly.

Merlin studied the man he had once had such high hopes for as if Uther were some disease Merlin was being asked to cure. Would this one night heal the king of his madness and let him rule Britain sanely? Merlin hoped so, but his true hopes were invested in the child to come—in Arthur, who would be king hereafter.

"Remember, Uther, you only have until the morning. Night is your friend. Use it." Merlin gestured, casting his spell, and suddenly it was not Uther who rode beside him, but Gorlois.

Uther looked down at his transformed armor, and felt his suddenly clean-shaven jaw. He crowed triumphantly as he realized what Merlin had done and spurred his horse down the hill, toward the causeway that led to the castle.

Sir Rupert shook his head silently, watching Uther go.

"You don't approve?" Merlin asked the horse.

Of course I don't approve, Sir Rupert said testily. He shook his head again, and the buckles on his bridle jingled.

Merlin gazed off in the direction Uther had ridden.

Tonight Arthur would be conceived, the king to come whose goodness would be worthy of Excalibur. That was what this night was for—that, and for an end to Uther's useless war.

"The end justifies the means," Merlin said.

Sir Rupert snorted derisively. *Where have I heard that before?*

After a moment, Merlin realized the answer. Mab. Those were the very words that the Queen of the Old Ways had used to justify her attack on Nimue.

Had Mab been right all along? Did the simple fact that Merlin used his magic mean that he would become what she was: cold, cruel, uncaring, manipulative?

No! What he'd done for Uther this night was unscrupulous, but he meant only good to come from it. Uther would get over his obsession, and neither Igraine nor Gorlois would ever know what had happened. He must think of the future, of Arthur. Of Britain. Perhaps the end justified the means after all.

Merlin patted Sir Rupert's neck. "Come on, old friend. We must find someplace out of the wind to wait for the morning."

Uther rode down the causeway, toward Tintagel's torch-lit gates already barred for the night. "Open the gates!" he shouted, and silently exulted when they obeyed. It had worked! All of them thought he was the Duke of Cornwall, and their rightful liege-lord. The portcullis rattled up, and Uther rode quickly beneath it and into the castle keep.

* * *

Morgan le Fay sat up very straight in her chair, watching her mother brush her hair at the wavery mirror of polished silver. Her father had told her to watch over her mother, and though she was only eight years old, Morgan was determined that she would not fail him. It was the first time he had ever asked her to do anything, and Morgan knew it was a test. If she took care of her mother properly tonight, then Father would accept her and love her despite her ugliness. He would stop making Mother cry with his accusations of her being tainted by the Old Ways. They could be a happy family at last, just the three of them.

There was an unexpected knock at the door and Morgan's mother looked up from brushing her hair. The door opened. Standing in the doorway was a dark bearded man whom Morgan did not recognize. There was a shimmering blue glow all over him, and his form rippled as though she saw him through water, or smoke.

She looked at her mother, but Igraine did not react to the terrible sight.

"Back so soon, my lord?" Igraine asked calmly.

"Yes, yes. Uther's really gone, and my place is here with you," he said impatiently.

Morgan's eyes grew wide with horror as the apparition stepped into the room. The specter spoke with her father's voice—but it was *not* her father.

"Mother—" she cried. Terror silenced her as the man swooped down on her and lifted her up.

"Time for you to go to bed, little lady. Not another word."

He carried her to the door and set her outside in

the hall. She tried to run back into the room, but the stranger shut the door in her face, shutting her out of the light and warmth of her mother's room and exiling her to the cold darkness of the hallway.

"Mother . . ." Morgan wailed. She banged on the door as hard as she could, but no one came. No one knew the monster was there but her.

Merlin's magic hadn't worked on the brat! Uther cursed silently as he shut the door in her ugly face. It didn't matter, though. She was out in the passageway now, while he was in here with Igraine.

Uther crossed the room in one stride and took her in his arms lustfully.

"Oh!" Igraine said, looking toward the door. "I didn't say good night."

"Good night," Uther muttered huskily, kissing her ravenously. "Good night, good night, and then good night. . . ."

In the Sanctum Sanctorum of her underground palace, Queen Mab stared into her scrying glass, watching. The globe of crystal showed her the tiny figures of Igraine and Uther twined together on the bed. She did not know if the spell she had cast upon him at his coronation would survive this night, but it no longer mattered. The spell had done its work. It had tangled Merlin in its net.

Mab smiled wolfishly. Each day made Merlin truer to his heritage of the Old Ways. No matter how hard he fought against her, he could not escape the fact that he was her son, heir to the Old Ways. He'd broken his oath about using magic, and now he was discovering the joys of manipulating the mortal kind for his own ends.

And soon it would be for *her* ends. Merlin would return to her side, and once more, Mab would reign supreme over all the isles of Britain.

Uther was a clever king, but a weak one, and Mab despised weakness. Still, she had to admire his deviousness. He'd promised Merlin that *he* would not harm Gorlois, but a king had many henchmen. She waved her hand over the crystal, banishing Igraine's bedchamber, and set the crystal to find Igraine's husband. Through the crystal Mab watched as Sir Boris set upon Gorlois and his knights and killed them all, just as Uther had instructed him to.

"So much for your guiltless bloodless victory, dear Merlin!" Mab crooned. "Now your hands are covered with innocent blood, and the child for whom you have done all this will be tainted as well. In the end, Arthur will belong to me!"

The sun rose, turning the walls of Tintagel to silver. Merlin, dozing upon Sir Rupert's back, was awakened by the clatter of horsemen riding across the bridge. They wore Gorlois's livery, but the Duke was not with them.

Hasn't Uther had the sense to leave Tintagel before dawn? The enchantment will not last past sunrise, Merlin fretted uneasily. And if he had already left, where had he gone?

Swiftly Merlin used his magic to transform himself into another of Gorlois's soldiers. With Sir Rupert's help, he caught up with the mounted troop and entered Tintagel's gates with them. He could see that the men had seen heavy fighting. They carried their fallen comrades wrapped in cloaks and tied to the backs of their horses.

"Where is the Lady Igraine! Send for the Lady Igraine!" the captain shouted.

"What is wrong? My lord and lady sleep within and fain would not be disturbed," Tintagel's castellan said.

"Cornwall sleeps a deeper sleep than his lady's, I'll wager," the captain growled. He dismounted from his horse and lifted down one of the wrapped bodies, laying it on the flagstones before the castellan. "Here he is." He flung back a fold of the cloak to expose Gorlois's death-pale face.

Uther, you have betrayed us all! Merlin thought in anguish. He had no doubt that somehow Gorlois's death could be traced to Uther's plottings. He broke away from the others and ran up the stairs, thinking that at least Arthur would now be born—and that Britain must have a king, even if a bad one, to hold the throne for him until he was old enough to take it.

The others were close behind him. At the top of the stairs, Merlin ran down the hall to the lady-bower where Igraine slept. A simple gesture unbarred the door, and Merlin swung it open.

But he was already too late. Uther sat upon the edge of the bed, regarding Igraine with baffled disgust, as if he could not imagine how he had come here. The morning sun showed him as he truly was, and Merlin wondered if there was enough time to cast another spell of disguise and hope Uther could bluff his way out. But Igraíne was stirring, and as Merlin entered the room she sat up, and looked toward the man whom she thought to be her husband.

Her eyes grew wide at the sight of Uther, and she screamed.

The king snatched up a sword to defend himself, and Merlin quickly banished his own disguise, lest Uther strike at him. But Gorlois's men were only seconds behind, and in the moment Merlin saw Uther recognize him as an ally, the first of them rushed in.

"An intruder!" the soldier cried, rushing at Uther.

"No!" Merlin shouted, but it was already too late.

Uther flung up his sword and cut at the soldier. He no longer carried Excalibur, but the king's blade was sharp. The trooper went down, dying as he fell. Igraine screamed again, in horror and pity.

In desperation, Merlin cast the first spell he could think of, closing his eyes and drawing his fingers across them, then flinging the spell out into the room. In that instant, everyone there was struck blind. Their cries and screams filled the hall and chamber, breeding chaos and confusion.

"Uther!" Merlin whispered, taking the king's arm. The king startled and swore at the touch, but he recognized Merlin's voice. "Come with me."

"Damn you, Merlin, what have you done to me?" Uther demanded, staring sightlessly toward Merlin.

"It will pass," Merlin said shortly. He was angry at a blindness of his own—once more Uther had managed to transcend Merlin's low opinion of him. "In the name of heaven, Uther—come now or stay and die."

Reluctantly, the king allowed himself to be led away. The doorway was choked with blinded guardsmen, but Merlin led Uther toward the window . . . and through it. A second spell brought the sea-mist boiling up beneath the tower, to solidify into steps that allowed the two men to reach the causeway unobserved.

With another gesture, Merlin canceled both spells. The mist began to fall away from the tower, and Uther blinked, owl-like, at the dim light of day.

"Where's my horse?" he demanded.

"Where's your army?" Merlin shot back. "I told you Gorlois was not to be harmed!"

"By me," the king amended, smirking. "You said I wasn't to harm him, Merlin, and as God is my witness, I kept that vow."

Merlin turned away with a groan of disgust. All his ideals, all his good intentions, turned to naught by the banal spitefulness of a dissolute king. Despite his care, despite his vows, Merlin's hands were red with innocent blood.

Uther began to laugh, a harsh bray of triumph.

"Not so high-and-mighty now, are you, Merlin? You're just as easily fooled as any other man!"

"Get away from me!" Merlin shouted, filled with revulsion. Mab's mocking laughter seemed to ring in his ears—from the very beginning, she had known it would come to this, that Merlin would become a pander to a lecher, and an executioner for a tyrant. All his ideals were dead, murdered with Gorlois.

"Get away from me!" Merlin shouted again. He turned away from Uther and began to run through the morning mist, but no matter how he fled, he could not outstrip the wild laughter that filled his brain.

Fool—fool! Merlin the butcher, Merlin the fool. . . .

CHAPTER FIVE

THE THRONE OF BETRAYAL

T he room was filled with candles, rack upon rack of them, until the chamber blazed with light like the cathedral on a feast day. Their flame made the warm summer air stiflingly hot, but neither of the chamber's occupants complained.

One, because he had no choice but to be here. The other, because he wanted light at all costs—light to drive away the shadows that filled his waking dreams with terror.

On the morning he had awakened in Igraine's bed, Uther had felt as if he had roused from a fever dream. His lust for Cornwall's wife had vanished like dew in the morning sun, and he could no longer remember why it had ever seemed so important to him to possess her.

But he remembered everything else very well. How Merlin had tricked him and stolen Excalibur.

Had tricked him again, giving him a woman he no longer wanted. Tricks, all tricks, and Pagan wizard's lies. . . .

"Tell me, Yvain. How many kings have you served?" Uther asked. Beads of sweat rolled down his face, and his linen tunic was soaked through with perspiration, but despite the heat, King Uther lounged at his ease upon the Pendragon throne, drinking brandy from a blue glass cup that had come all the way from Byzantium. Once it had belonged to the tyrant Vortigern, just as the man before him had.

"More than one," Yvain the Fox answered, "but all of them well." He was a slender man with greying hair and a narrow beard, such as had become the fashion at Uther's court. The thick gold hoop that he wore in his left ear sparkled in the candlelight.

"A good answer," Uther said genially. He drank again, his eyes darting about the room nervously, and wiped his forehead with the edge of his tunic. It was night, and Uther hated the darkness. "And will you serve me well?"

Yvain the Fox bowed silently, imperturbable even in the oven-heat of the King's throne room, and waited for Uther to come to the point.

"I want you to go to Tintagel," Uther said. He leaned forward and lowered his voice, and Yvain took a step closer to the throne. "The Lady Igraine—Cornwall's widow—is with child."

Yvain nodded. All the world knew the story of how Uther had pursued the lady, laying siege to her husband's castle for months in a hopeless attempt to possess her. And at the moment of her husband's death, Uther had seemingly lost interest in his prize.

"I want you to wait there until the child is born, then take it and bring it here to me," Uther continued. "It will be a son."

"The lady may object," Yvain said cautiously.

"I don't care," Uther enunciated slowly through gritted teeth. "Bring me that child!" And then, unexpectedly, the king began to laugh.

"Frik . . . what are you doing?"

Mab sat upon her carven throne in the room where Frik had once tutored Merlin, staring intently into the polished surface of a dark, misshapen crystal. Into it she poured all the unchanging nature of stone, the inertia and passivity of rock.

Frik sat behind her at a high desk. He was writing in a large book with a very long quill pen.

"Writing fairy stories. So you'll be remembered," he answered in a hoarse, quavery voice. He was wearing a scholar's hood and robes, and the gingery hair and whiskers of this persona fluffed wildly about his face. Crooked wire-rimmed glasses balanced on the end of his nose.

"You don't need to do that, Frik. I'll not be forgotten," Mab said confidently.

"Well . . ." the gnome said doubtfully.

"Well?" Mab demanded, turning in her seat to glare at him.

"For us!" the gnome improvised hastily. "Things are going rather well—for us!" He cringed, hoping to avoid one of his volatile mistress's painful reprimands.

"I'm going to make sure," Mab said. She gazed into the black stone a moment longer, then tossed the crystal over her shoulder in Frik's direction.

"See to it."

Merlin and Sir Rupert stood once more on the ridge that overlooked the causeway that led to Tintagel, waiting for the birth of Igraine's child. He had last been here on the night that child had been conceived, and his memories of that night were not happy ones. Uther had never returned to marry the woman he had lusted for so disastrously.

Uther betrayed me . . . and I betrayed Igraine by helping Uther seduce her, by luring Gorlois into that ambush, by not distrusting Uther as much as I should have, even after all the warnings he gave me. The Wheel of Life turns, one betrayal leading to another, and another. And the innocent die. . . .

These days, King Uther kept court at Pendragon in Londinium just as his father had, and there were rumors that he was also growing as mad as Old King Constant had been. But even that did not matter very much to Merlin, not now that Arthur was about to be born. Everything Merlin had done to get a good king for Britain would be justified once Arthur ruled the land. And the blood on his hands would at last be washed away. . . .

During the past several months as he awaited the baby's birth, Merlin had prepared a place for the baby Arthur with Sir Hector of the Forest Sauvage, far to the north. There he could teach Arthur all he would need to know to be both a good man and a good king.

And everything would be all right at last.

In her lady-bower within the walls of Tintagel Keep, Igraine writhed upon her bed in hard labor, choking back her screams. The priests said that the pain of childbirth was woman's price to pay for her betrayal in the Garden of Eden, and that the pain of childbirth suffered now limited the pains of Hell later.

Igraine did not believe it. She knew that God was punishing her, that her soul was damned by what she had done. The agony she suffered now was only a foretaste of the suffering to come. God had given her Morgan as a warning of her wickedness, and she had not listened. Now Gorlois was dead and Igraine was an adulteress, and for that she would surely burn.

The midwives bustled about the bed, doing all that they could to soothe her. They said it would not be much longer, but Igraine knew the truth. This was only the beginning. The pain would go on forever.

The stabbing pangs began again, harder than before, and Igraine screamed.

Morgan le Fay sat at the table in the nursery, listening to her mother's distant cries with a certain gloomy relish. Her father was dead, and, since the night the king had come to Tintagel, her mother had grown cold and distant, sitting alone for hours, staring at nothing. No one had any time to spare for her, and she was lonely.

Morgan's nursery was a large barren room. Her outgrown toys were scattered about, intermixed with newer ones—like the rocking unicorn in the corner—

that had been bought for the new baby. Morgan's old cradle stood by the door, waiting for its new occupant, the baby that was even now being born in the room at the end of the hall.

"Hello, Morgan," an unfamiliar voice said.

Morgan turned toward the door. Standing in the doorway was a peculiar creature dressed all in close-fitting black. His long pointed ears curved upward like horns, and his goggle eyes were pale yellow, like a cat's.

Morgan was startled but not afraid. She had never been afraid of the unknown, even as a baby. "Who are you?" she asked curiously.

"I'm a gnome," the gnome announced.

"You're tall for a gnome, aren't you?" Morgan asked suspiciously.

"Gnomes do indeed come in all shapes and sizes. I'm the tall kind," the gnome said proudly.

"Can you do magic?" Morgan asked. She'd never given up hope of finding someone who could. Magic, she knew, was of the Old Ways, and her father had said that the Old Ways had made her, so perhaps that meant she could do magic, providing she could find someone to teach her.

"Of course," the gnome said, as if it were the most natural thing in the world. "Watch."

With a sweep of his hand, Frik transformed himself. No longer was he crooked and dark and ugly— no, now Frik was tall and golden-haired, a dashing adventurer wearing a voluminous white shirt and tight black leather pants and carrying a very sharp rapier.

"Ah, beautiful lady!" he cried, bowing, and now even his voice was beautiful, a rich, deep, heroic voice. "I am at your service! Your wish is my command."

Morgan laughed delightedly, clapping her hands.

"Watch me swash a buckle!" Frik cried, leaping to the table. He engaged in a fierce combat against a nonexistent opponent—a combat which he, of course, won. He bowed again and leaped lightly down from the table, reverting to his original form once more.

"That's weal magic, not twicks!" Morgan lisped in delight. Frik knew exactly what the girl was thinking: Just as she had always suspected it would be, magic was fun. With magic, she would not have to be alone and ugly and forgotten. Magic could transform her life. She could have friends and adventures and everyone would love her.

It was a popular mortal fantasy, and exploiting it was Frik's chief stock in trade. But the sort of magic Morgan wanted to do—the big, flashy, powerful illusions—could not be done by those of mortal blood.

Still, they never stopped asking and trying, and believing anyone who said they could if only they worked at it hard enough.

"Will you teach me how to do that?" Morgan demanded excitedly . . . just as they all did, down through the centuries.

"I certainly shall," Frik lied, "*if* you do something for me. Your new baby brother will be born soon—how terribly exciting, don't you think?" Frik added confidingly.

"He's not my weal brother," Morgan said coldly. "The man who made him wasn't my weal father."

Frik was momentarily taken aback. In his limited experience, all mortals loved babies, noisy disgusting tiresome things that they were. But somehow Morgan was different.

"Well. I mean, that's clever, Morgan. You'll make a wonderful pupil for the fantastic things I can teach you." *Such as not to trust strange gnomes, but that's one mortals never get the hang of, isn't it?*

"What do you want me to do?" Morgan asked eagerly. Glowing with excitement and the effect of Frik's praises, she was almost pretty, despite her disfigurement.

Frik produced the black gem that Mab had given him.

"Just put this stone in the baby's crib," he said, offering little Morgan Queen Mab's dark crystal.

It was Mab's gift to the baby Arthur. He had only to touch it for Mab's gift to flow into him. As he grew, it would first appear to be maturity and integrity, but what it would really be was stubbornness and the unwillingness to change his mind. For the rest of his life, Arthur would always do the first thing he thought of, not the best thing, and he would never set aside the first idea he had for a better one. Such a gift could not harm a humble farmer, but it could destroy a king, and Mab knew that Merlin meant Igraine's baby to be king.

Morgan took the stone. Frik smiled and bowed to her.

"Wait!" Morgan said. "What shall I call you?"

The gnome bowed, a handsome blond cavalier. "Dear lady, you may call me anything you like. My name is Frik, and I am at your service."

And then he vanished.

He would not return for more than sixteen years.

Merlin, waiting on the cliffs above the shore, heard the baby's first wailing cry. In his mind he heard the midwife's triumphant shout: *It's a boy!*

"Arthur is born!" Merlin cried in triumph. "At last! A good man—a good king!"

"You're easily fooled, Merlin. . . ."

Queen Mab appeared upon a spire of rock a few yards away. A deep chasm, through which the sea hissed and foamed, separated her from Merlin. She was a terrifying archaic figure dressed in black and silver, her long black hair and filmy black robes streaming out behind her like scraps of ocean mist. Her eyes were wild dark pools and her mouth was a dark red scar in her pale stricken face.

"Uther fooled you when he killed Cornwall!" Mab cawed. "Now his child is damned!"

Mab gestured, and suddenly the clouds began to race by unnaturally fast. The sky darkened and the wind began to howl as the Queen of the Old Ways showed Merlin the power that was still hers to wield . . . power greater than his own.

"The boy is mine!" Merlin shouted defiantly.

"He'll be his father's son!" Mab gloated. "Because of him, the chaos of blood will go on and on and out of it the people will come back to *me!*"

The storm she had raised tore at Merlin's robes,

threatening to pluck him from the cliff and hurl him into the sea below. The ocean threw itself at the rocks like a maddened predator, its spray breaking over both figures, until it took all of Merlin's strength simply to stand where he was.

"I'll see you fade into nothing!" Merlin shouted into the sky. He stared into the fairy queen's eyes. *See my determination, Mab. See my strength. I have made many mistakes, but I will never surrender to your evil—and neither will Arthur!*

"Poor Merlin," Mab crooned in mock sympathy. "Wrong again. *I'm winning. . . .*"

And with her words still echoing in his ears, Mab was gone. The wind dropped, the foaming sea slowly became calm. The clouds overhead broke apart to reveal the pale sky of a midsummer evening. It was just sunset, and a full pale moon was rising in the east, shedding its creamy golden light over the peaceful Cornish landscape.

Could Mab be right? The question tormented Merlin. He was no longer sure of the purity of his own intentions, nor did he still believe that he could look into men's hearts with any degree of accuracy. He had thought Uther would be Britain's savior, only to find that Uther was a venal, fallible, greedy man. What if he were wrong about Arthur's future as well?

No. My visions never lie. Arthur will be the king Britain needs. There is no darkness in him. But I must keep him safe until he is a man.

Merlin had told Uther that there would be a child from his night spent with Igraine, and though Uther had sworn to give him up, Merlin did not trust the vow the king had made that the child would be Merlin's to raise. He and Uther had parted enemies, and enemies they would remain. Now Merlin must hide young Arthur to keep him safe from the taint of the king's evil.

Merlin turned and walked down from the cliff. Toward Tintagel, to claim Uther's promise.

Silent and invisible as a wraith, Merlin passed into the castle. Everyone was celebrating the birth of a fine healthy boy; Merlin saw kegs of ale being rolled into the forecourt so that all the castlefolk could drink a health to the newborn child. Few of them knew that Uther had ever even been here, let alone suspected that Uther was the father of Igraine's child. Merlin was content to have it so until the time came to make Arthur king, but that day would never come unless Merlin took the child now.

Merlin crossed the courtyard and entered the tower keep where Igraine's rooms lay. No one saw that he was there. Merlin did not wish them to see him, and he was, after all, a wizard.

Morgan le Fay sat silently in a corner of the nursery, holding the black crystal Frik had given her in her small hands, thinking of the day when she would be the beautiful and adored liege-lady of Tintagel and the name of Morgan le Fay would be feared throughout the land. Frik would teach her all the magic in the universe and everything would be wonderful.

Morgan sat so still that Brisen didn't see her when she came in to put the new baby in his crib. Brisen had been Morgan's nurse when she was a baby, and now she was *his*. That was one more thing her half-brother had stolen from her.

Morgan looked down at the black stone in her hands. Perhaps if she put it in his cradle the stone would hurt her brother. Frik hadn't said, and Morgan didn't really care. When Brisen was gone, she tiptoed over to the cradle and looked in.

Her new brother looked like any other baby: red and wrinkled and smelly, wrapped in a blue blanket. Morgan quickly tucked the dark crystal under the blanket against the baby's body and stepped back, but nothing happened. Perhaps it would take a while.

She reached down and took the blanket out of the cradle. It smelled faintly of her mother's perfume, and Morgan wrapped it around herself as the baby fussed. Then she retreated to a corner to wait for something to happen.

Merlin opened the door to the nursery. The light from the nursery windows fell upon the cradle, where baby Arthur lay sleeping, uncovered to the air. Merlin quickly bent over the cradle and picked up the baby, tucking him into a fold of his feathered cloak. He did not notice as a small black stone fell from a fold of Arthur's swaddling-clothes.

As unnoticed as he had come, the wizard left Tintagel, carrying the child who was the hope of Britain with him. Behind him the runestone, its power expended, lay in the cradle.

*   *   *

Silent and invisible, Queen Mab watched Merlin go, carrying the baby in his arms. It didn't matter what Merlin did with his little Arthur now. She had already set her mark on the baby, and was confident that he would not become the good man that Merlin hoped for. Besides—Mab glanced toward Morgan, who stood staring after Merlin with a mixed expression of hope and shock—she had more than one string to her bow. Uther, Morgan, Igraine: all of them were her puppets, and in the end, they would give her Britain.

But now, there was one last loose end to tidy up.

Igraine awoke suddenly. She was alone in her bedroom. The windows at the far end of the room stood open, and the red sunset light shone through them. She reached for her baby, but he was not beside her in the bed.

She sat up painfully, reaching for her shawl. Brisen must have put the baby in his cradle in the nursery, but Igraine wanted to see her son. If she could hold him in her arms, she would not feel quite so lost. Since Gorlois's murder, the baby had been the one spark of light in Igraine's life, even though Igraine knew that he was Uther's child and not her husband's. She needed to touch him, to reassure herself of his existence.

"Merlin has taken the baby," Mab crooned in her ear. *"He has hidden him away. You will never see him again."*

Igraine looked around wildly, but she could not see the source of the whispering voice. Perhaps she had only imagined it.

"It was Merlin . . ." Mab said again.

Merlin! It was Uther's foul Pagan wizard who was the cause of all Igraine's unhappiness. He had tricked her into adultery with his sorcery and destroyed her husband. Igraine crept from her bed, pulling her shawl about her thin shoulders.

Once she had been a beautiful woman, but the last year's happenings had not been kind to the young duchess. The first streaks of grey had appeared in her dark hair, and her sunken eyes burned feverishly bright. If Uther saw her now, would he be tempted into profane lust by the sight of her?

Igraine laughed soundlessly at the thought, knowing the answer. She had sinned, however unknowingly, and God had taken her comeliness from her in punishment. But he would not punish her child, her perfect, beautiful child. . . .

"Merlin has taken him . . ." whispered the voice.

Afraid now, Igraine ran down the hall to the nursery and threw open the door. The cradle was empty except for a small black rock.

"My baby!" Igraine cried. She did not see Morgan standing in the shadows.

"He's gone," Mab hissed. *"You know that, don't you? Merlin has taken him, just as he took everything else: your husband, your reputation, and now your son. You're lost, you're alone, you have nothing left to live for, do you . . .?"*

With a wild despairing cry, Igraine fled the nursery.

*   *   *

Cornwall's duchess stood on the parapet of Tintagel's highest tower. In the twilight she could see a lone rider on a grey horse riding away down the causeway far below. Merlin.

"He has taken the only thing you have left, hasn't he?" Mab said. She stood on the air a few feet away, and held out her hand to Igraine. *"You have to stop him. Come to me. . . ."*

"Mother, wait!" Morgan cried. She ran after her mother, but Igraine did not hear her. Morgan reached the top of the stairs leading to the tower. She saw her mother and a strange woman whom she did not know—a glittering, magical woman who stood on thin air as if it were stone. As Morgan watched in horror, Igraine stepped out to join the stranger, but the air did not hold her up as it did the other woman. Igraine screamed in terror as she fell and Morgan covered her eyes, shuddering in horror as the sound stopped.

When Morgan looked again, the strange woman who had stood on the air was gone. She ran to the edge of the tower and looked down. Far below, she could see Igraine's lifeless body tangled upon the rocks.

I am all alone, now, Morgan le Fay thought. *I am the mistress of Tintagel. No one else is left.*

Yvain the Fox was not a stupid man. It had been easy enough to infiltrate Tintagel disguised as a visiting priest. The duchess had been delighted to have a holy man available to baptize her child when it was born. Taking the child would be easy—a sleeping potion in the nurse's ale, and Yvain could slip from the castle with the baby and no one would be the wiser.

And so, when Igraine had gone into labor, he had been prepared to wait patiently for his chance. When the birth of a fine boy had been announced, Yvain had drunk the child's health along with the rest of the castle. But before another hour had passed, Tintagel's lady had leaped to her death from the highest tower, and the child she had borne was nowhere to be found.

Uther, Yvain was sure, would not welcome this news. And rather than return to Pendragon to tell it to him, Yvain thought he would travel.

To Ireland, perhaps. Or France. Or even Rome . . . somewhere far, far away from Uther and Britain.

As Merlin rode away from the castle he heard a faint wild scream cut through the dusk behind him. Turning, he saw a white figure fall wailing from the highest tower of the castle onto the rocks below.

Igraine.

The sudden horrible realization of what he had done was like a knife in his heart. Blinded by altruism, he had thought only of Arthur, of Britain. He had never thought of Igraine, of what it would mean to her to mysteriously lose the child.

What can one more death matter among so many? Merlin thought bleakly. But he knew the truth: every death mattered. And he had caused so many. . . .

But it ends here, Merlin thought with desperate hope. *All the blood, all the pain, all the betrayal. Arthur will be free of it, and of the Old Ways. Nothing of them will touch him, nothing!*

As if aware of Merlin's inner turmoil, the baby woke and began to cry. Merlin tucked the cloak around him gently, and rode away from Tintagel—north, toward the Forest Sauvage.

By the following morning Merlin had reached the Forest Sauvage where Sir Hector lived with his good lady Hermesent. Though they followed the New Religion, Sir Hector and his wife were not afraid of the Old Ways, for all who lived close to the land possessed an innate understanding of its powers. Sir Hector was a good-hearted man more interested in farming than in fighting, and Hermesent was a kindly woman who had long wanted a large family of her own, though they had only one child, Kay, a boy about three years old.

Hermesent had found Merlin and nursed him back to health when Merlin had wandered the land, reckless with despair, in the months after Cornwall's death. Merlin did not think she would turn away a foundling child.

Or the wizard who brought it.

The dogs began to bark as Sir Rupert approached the comfortable old manor house where Sir Hector and Hermesent lived. The horse threw up his head and stopped as the dogs galloped in circles around them, yelping like mad things. A few moments later Sir Hector came out to see what all the noise was about.

"Merlin!" he said with pleasure. "Come in—come in—you know you are always welcome here."

Perhaps I am welcome here, Merlin thought as he dismounted, careful not to wake the sleeping baby, *but there is nowhere else in all Britain where that will be true once Uther learns of this night's work.* He patted Sir Rupert on the shoulder and walked toward his host.

"Eh?" Sir Hector said, noticing Merlin's burden. "What's that you've got there?"

"A baby," Merlin said. "He has no mother, and his father is a thoughtless and cruel man. I want him to grow up somewhere that he can be safe and loved."

As Sir Hector stared down at the child in astonishment, Lady Hermesent came out of the house. As if sensing help was near, Arthur awoke and began to cry hungrily.

"It's a baby," Hermesent said in surprise, scooping Arthur from Merlin's arms and folding back the blanket to inspect him. "Wet and hungry, poor mite." She studied Merlin critically. "And how did you come to have a baby, Master Merlin?

"Never mind," she said, before he could answer. "I'm not sure I want to know. I'll take care of him for you, never fear. No man ever born, wizard or not, ever knew the first thing about children. There, there, child. Don't fret," she said to the crying baby, turning away from the men and walking toward the house.

"His name is Arthur," Merlin called after her.

"Arthur," said Sir Hector. "Arthur. Well, well. A good name. And good lungs, as well," he added, for the baby's cries were still audible in the distance. "I'd say you've done a good day's work to bring him here, Master Merlin."

"I suppose I have," Merlin agreed, looking off toward the house. "I hope this won't cause you any trouble. Or at least, not too much of it."

"Nonsense," Sir Hector said, putting an arm

around Merlin's shoulders and leading him toward the house. "How much trouble can one boy be?"

It would be several years before Arthur would need him again. Following his heart, Merlin rode south and west again, toward Avalon Abbey and Nimue. But along the way, he stopped to revisit an old familiar locale that lay only a few hours from Sir Hector's manor house.

The round hut nestled in the clearing in the center of Barnstable Forest seemed unchanged, as if he had stepped away from its door moments—not years—before. Leaving Sir Rupert to graze on the lush summer foliage, Merlin dismounted and walked inside.

It was hard to believe that it had been less than two years since he last stood before this hearth. So many things had happened to him in that time, things both good and bad—Vortigern, Nimue, Uther. He had slain one king, and discovered that another was greedy and weak. He had found his lost love, only to have her taken from him again by Mab's plotting. He had killed, betrayed, lied, murdered, stolen—and all for the king to come, the good king who would lead Britain out of the terrible darkness into which the reigns of three bad kings had plunged her.

If he could. If anyone could.

Shaking his head at his black thoughts, Merlin turned to examine the hut. All the food that had been stored here was gone, of course—stolen by mice and birds and squirrels—but his herbs and oils were safe in their sealed stone jars. He had lived here simply, and most of his simple possessions were intact—the bed, the stool, the table, the horn cups and wooden plates. An afternoon's cleaning and Merlin could take up residence here once more.

But was that what he wanted?

Merlin sighed wearily, rubbing his jaw. In truth, he no longer knew what it was that he wanted. He had fought for so long against Mab that it seemed he had forgotten to fight *for* anything. And when he had tried, all he seemed to do was cause more suffering. The only thing that was still shining and pure in his life was Nimue.

And even she did not belong to him wholly. There, it seemed, his rival was the god of her New Religion, the one that Queen Mab hated so much, the one whose priesthood sought to put an end to the Old Ways for all time.

Once Merlin had believed that the enemy of his enemy was his ally, but Uther had taught him what a delusion that was. Merlin did not hate the New Religion, but he did not love it, either—and he did not know how to fight it. If Nimue loved her strange foreign god more than she loved him, then Merlin would lose his love to prayers and chanting and the stone walls of Avalon. The only way to halt that for certain was with magic—and if he stooped to using magic simply for his own convenience, Merlin would have become as vile as Queen Mab.

No. There must be another way. Merlin knew that he had done great evil in the name of good, but he must put both his guilt and his blame behind him. Now more than ever Merlin must strive to be a good man— to renounce the flashy, easy tricks of magic not because of Mab, but for his own good, and seek the deep hidden wisdom to be found in the contemplation of the natural world, the wisdom that lay in prophecy and in dreams.

Arthur's birth had changed him more than he knew—now Merlin realized that he must be good to teach goodness, and he wondered if he was still capable of what he had once thought was so simple a thing.

Perhaps Nimue could teach him.

If she loved him still.

It was high summer once more, a few weeks after Arthur's birth, and at Avalon Abbey, all drowsed beneath the shimmering heat. Merlin had managed to coax Nimue to walk in the garden with him, but she had found it was too hot even for that, and they sat at the foot of a tree, resting in its meager shade.

The Father Abbot, there to chaperon Nimue, was frankly asleep at the window that overlooked the close, and the only one watching the lovers was a marmalade cat that lay half-dozing upon the slanting Abbey roof.

Everything is regimented and orderly here, Merlin mused. *They try to shut out the outside world, that disorderly place full of magic and wonder, but try as they might, some part of it always sneaks in.* He plucked up the blown dandelion that had invaded Avalon's gardens and studied its downy white puffball. Even though his touch had been gentle, seeds lofted from the white silky head in clouds of fluff, soaring into the sky on the gentle summer breeze.

"You can't believe that you truly belong here,"

Merlin continued persuasively. "Locking yourself away like this. You've committed no crime. It's foolish and wrong."

Nimue hung her head, and pulled her scarf protectively closer around her face. "I can't stand the thought of people peering, whispering, pointing at me . . ." she said, looking away.

"We'll live in the forest. Animals don't point and whisper," Merlin argued.

"But it's a dream, Merlin," Nimue protested.

My dream—but not yours? Merlin wondered, not for the first time. "I want to make it real," he said, taking her hand. He was a wizard, trained in the Old Ways. Surely his magic would give him the words to convince her.

But Nimue shook her head, though she did not withdraw her hand. "I've found a peace here in prayer and meditation. It is a peace I've never known before. It passes my understanding."

"To be honest, Nimue, it passes my understanding, too," Merlin answered, faintly cross. "Why do you shut yourself away here?" He asked the unanswerable question despite himself, knowing that they were drifting once more into the helpless, circuitous arguments.

"To be nearer my God," Nimue whispered.

Merlin shook his head. "The nearer you are to Him, the further you are from me," he protested. He had been raised in the Old Ways—to him the gods were real and tangible, as objective as rain and bread. He did not understand how anyone could draw comfort from the Christians' silent god of the spirit. "Will you take off that veil?"

Nimue cringed away as Merlin gently unwound the kerchief from her face. Her scars were purple-grey and rigid against the living skin of her face, their presence turning a beautiful woman into a monster.

But Merlin loved them, because he loved her. Only Love did not conquer all, as the poets insisted. Love solved nothing at all. Gently, Merlin kissed her cheek. Nimue wept silently. Once again there were no answers, and no solutions.

CHAPTER SIX

THE THRONE OF REBIRTH

The slanting rays of the afternoon sun shone through the door of the room Sir Hector had designated as the schoolroom. Sir Hector himself discussed weighty matters such as the coming harvest and the price of flour with two of his tenants at the back door. Through the door that had been left open because of the heat came the interesting smells of the kitchen where Hermesent was overseeing the preparation of the evening meal for the residents of the tiny farm holding.

Arthur and Kay were at their lessons—Kay bored and fidgeting, Arthur doing his best to listen to his tutor's words. The heat, the quiet hum of voices, and the smell of baking pies all made it very hard to concentrate.

"Consider the moon. In her fullness, she is a perfect circle, but what constitutes her perfection? It is the fact that in a circle every part is equal, and no part is more important than the rest. Thus we may state that equality is perfection, for the attempt to gain supremacy over another directly convenes the natural law which the moon shows to us. . . ."

It was amazing how much all this brought back his own days as a student in the Hollow Hills, Merlin thought. What an ungrateful pupil he had been—and how Frik had suffered with him! It hurt to look back at those days of his long-vanished childhood and think about how happy he had been. Even though it had been a joy founded on ignorance of terrible truths, those now seemed to him to have been carefree, innocent days, days when his future stretched before him as a wonderland of bright possibility.

But while his own childhood was long dead, those of his pupils had just begun.

Merlin had presented himself as a tutor for the boys three years ago, when Arthur was seven and Kay was ten. Despite Hermesent's misgivings, Merlin had no intention of passing on to either boy the magical curriculum that he'd learned in the Hollow Hills, but rather, the things that his own first teacher, Blaise, had taught him when he'd lived in the forest: ethics, morals, how to choose the right path through life.

As well as a little reading, writing, and good plain Latin.

"The Golden Rule: Do unto others as you would have others do unto you. Now by 'others' I don't mean your family or your friends, because it's easy to do the right thing for them. But for strangers or enemies, people you would ordinarily turn aside from—"

Arthur had raised his hand to ask a question. "But if you do right by them, why are they your enemies? Ow!" he added, because Kay had kicked him.

"You may as well ask why those who know us well misbehave toward us," Merlin said, frowning discouragingly at Kay.

"Because he's a little wart," Kay muttered. The older boy had little patience with Merlin's lessons and showed it frequently. His disinterest did not worry Merlin. Kay would not grow up to be the next king.

And Arthur would.

"Master Kay, if you are having such trouble with the lesson, I'll ask you to copy it out on your slateboard now. Ten times, please, Master Kay."

The older boy glared rebelliously at Merlin before bending to his work with a sigh.

"And you, Master Arthur, may oblige me by translating the Golden Rule into Latin and writing it out in a fair hand in both Latin and English. If you would."

Arthur reached for the large Latin grammar without complaint.

It had been ten years since the boy's birth, and in those years, King Uther had become ever more moody and withdrawn. Though the king did not seem to mourn Igraine, he also had not married, as every king had a duty to do, to secure an heir. As Uther retreated behind the walls of Pendragon Castle, rarely venturing outside, he left the business of running his kingdom more and more to his lieutenants. Rumors began to spread across the countryside that Uther, disappointed in his wizard's powers, had turned to dabbling in magic of his own, summoning the devils and dark angels to do his bidding through the satanic necromancy of the New Religion.

If the rumors were true, Merlin had seen little evidence that any demons of the New Religion answered Uther's call. But the fact remained that all dark sorcery was drawn from the same wellspring of anger and envy, and Merlin worried that Uther's meddling might be enough to draw Mab to him.

Did she still exist? Or had she faded away into nothingness just as she had always feared? Each year the New Religion gained more of a hold over the minds and hearts of the people of Britain. Each year more of the old magic slipped away. When he had been a boy, Merlin had spoken freely to the animals of field and forest. Now when he did, few of them answered him. And each year the farmers worked a little harder to bring in their crops as the soil forgot more of the fertility magic that had once belonged to it.

But though Merlin grieved for the magic that was gone, part of him felt it was for the best. Many of the Old Powers had been meddlesome and cruel—the power of magic bred arrogance in even the gentlest heart—and Mankind was all the safer for not being at their mercy. But was the security they had gained worth the wonders they had lost? It was hard, sometimes, to say.

Abruptly Merlin realized he'd been woolgathering. Kay and Arthur, their lessons completed, were exchanging kicks and pinches beneath the table, hoping he wouldn't see. Merlin cleared his throat meaningfully and the scuffling stopped.

"That's enough for today. Why don't you boys go

and play? You can run off some of that excess energy before dinner."

Kay did not have to be told twice. He ran from the room, sandals clattering, whooping with delight at his freedom. Arthur followed more slowly, but no less eagerly. He was only a boy and sometimes found his lessons very dull.

It would be good practice for him, Merlin thought. A good and conscientious king must often find the work of governing dull, for it would not always be a matter of fighting wars and going on quests. Yet the goodness Merlin saw in Arthur encouraged him to hold to his task, shaping a good king to rule over Britain.

Faintly, he could hear the boys yelling outside. Merlin sat down at the table, pushing aside the books and slates they had left behind. From a pocket inside his robe Merlin withdrew a tightly-rolled scroll, bound with ribbon and sealed. The seal bore an image of a shining Cup—the seal was that of Avalon Abbey, and it was a letter from Nimue.

"My dearest Merlin, I am always sad that I cannot write the words I know you long to hear from me. . . ."

She wrote to him often, to tell him of her days. They were much like his own, occupied with caring for others in the long uneasy peace that Uther's troubled reign had brought. Nimue spent her days in prayer and healing; Merlin spent his trying to instill a moral sense into two young boys.

Sometimes he wondered which of the two of them had set themself the harder task.

*　　*　　*

And so the years passed. When Arthur was fifteen, Merlin moved back to his hut in Barnstable Forest so the boy could come and visit him there. Kay no longer took any interest in their lessons, and spent all his days with his father and his father's knights, learning the ways of war. For it had been nearly eighteen years since the midwinter battle that had seen Vortigern slain and Uther set in his place, and without an heir to the throne of England, everyone knew that there would be war when King Uther died.

It was spring. Snow still remained in the shaded hollows of trees, and each morning silvered the fallen leaves with hoarfrost, though the winds held a hint of warmth. Snowdrops, irises, and daffodils pushed up through the mulch of last autumn's leaves, covering the land in bright flowers.

Everyone knew that Merlin, the old hermit, lived here—though he was not all that old, and though some people remembered the days when he had been a young man and a seer. The countryfolk knew, also, that Sir Hector's younger boy, Arthur, visited Merlin frequently—but Sir Hector was well-liked and Arthur charmed everyone he met, so no one minded where he rode, so long as it was not through the crops.

For Merlin, these were quiet, peaceful years, during which he lived close to the land and its rhythms. There were only two things that marred his complete contentment: the fact that Nimue still refused to leave Avalon, and his dreams.

He knew that they warned him of what was to come, or told him of things happening elsewhere in the land, but Merlin did not like them. The news, these days, was never good.

Again and again, the visions showed him Uther, in a black crypt beneath the cathedral he'd had built for the New Religion, praying to darker, older powers. Merlin did not know what Uther hoped to gain from these incantations, but in each dream the king looked older, more haggard, more like his mad father Constant. When Merlin dragged himself out of these dreams, the little forest cottage stank of blood for hours afterward. Blood for a king whose reign had begun in blood . . . and wizardry.

He had not dreamed last night. Still, when he awoke this morning Merlin knew that something very important had happened last night while he slept. But what?

If it would not come to him, Merlin would seek it out. He filled a small stone bowl with water from the spring and set it before himself, gazing intently into it.

Many things could be used to *scry* with: the flames of a candle, a polished crystal ball, a mirror. Merlin preferred the oldest and simplest of these aids to seeing: a bowl of water. As he stared down into it, he focused all his will on being as the water was, empty and serene and still. And as he gazed into the water, slowly it seemed to darken, until it seemed that he was gazing through a portal that looked elsewhere.

Merlin saw the crypt that he'd seen so often in dreams. Almost he could hear the chanting of the monks at prayer, smell the incense used in the Christian rite, feel the dampness of this hidden place beneath the high altar. As the vision sharpened, he could see

Uther kneeling at the base of a massive cross carved from black stone, his lips moving as he conjured harm to his enemies.

But this time there was a dagger in the king's hand, a dagger already wet with blood. As Merlin watched, knowing that what he saw was already in the past, Uther began to weep painfully, and then stabbed himself through the heart.

Merlin recoiled, and the water in the bowl trembled, cutting off his sight of what had been. Still numb with what he had learned, Merlin got to his feet and carried the bowl outside. He poured the water out upon the ground and then, almost as an afterthought, broke the bowl. He didn't think he could ever bring himself to eat his morning porridge from it again.

So Uther was dead. Merlin had known the day must come, but like all men, had hoped it would not come this soon. Arthur was not yet seventeen. Though in many ways he was a fine young man, in some ways Arthur was a boy still. Was he ready to take Excalibur and do what must be done? Or did Merlin expect too much of him?

He is the vessel of all my hopes. He has to be ready—and so must I.

Briskly, Merlin made preparations to be away from the cottage for a long time. He made up some simple remedies to take with him on the journey, and put out the food that would not keep for the forest creatures. He summoned Sir Rupert, and made sure the fairy horse was saddled and ready to travel.

He must be ready to greet Arthur when he came.

*   *   *

Whooping, Arthur urged his bay gelding to even greater speed. Startled pheasants fled from beneath his charger's hooves, and crows called rudely after him from the trees.

The messenger had come to Sir Hector only a few hours before, bearing the unbelievable news that the King was dead. The old knight had immediately begun making preparations to travel to Winchester, because no one knew who would be king after Uther, and there was certain to be war. Of course, both Arthur and Kay had demanded to accompany him, but Sir Hector had said that Arthur must stay behind with Hermesent, while Kay, only three years older, would get to see the sights and wonders of the outside world.

Arthur had fretted over the unfairness of that, until he realized that he could at least bring the news to someone who had no other way of knowing it: his old tutor, Merlin. He'd saddled Boukephalos, his fastest horse, and ridden the animal *ventre-à-terre* for the forest hut. His black cloak flowed out behind him, the fabric tugging at the two round silver brooches that held it fixed to his ring-mail jerkin. The saffron tunic with gold embroidery that he wore beneath his armor was the finest one he owned, saved for feast days and other special days—and this was certainly the most important day Arthur could remember.

As he sighted the hut, he could see Merlin was already standing outside it. Arthur pulled Boukephalos to a halt.

"Arthur, don't charge around like that, the horses don't like it," Merlin said crossly. "And don't get off. We're leaving right away."

But Arthur was too excited to pay much attention to what Merlin was saying. "Merlin, have you heard the news? King Uther's dead."

"Rupert," Merlin said. A horse that Arthur had never seen before came trotting out from behind the hut. It was a fine-boned grey, a princely steed, and Arthur wondered how his fusty old tutor had come by such a fine animal.

"Didn't you hear what I said? The king's dead," Arthur repeated.

"I know," Merlin said.

"Know? How could you know out here in the woods?" Arthur demanded, sure that Merlin was teasing him.

But it did not seem as if he was. "A little bird told me," Merlin said. He swung into the saddle and began to ride away.

"Where are we going?" Arthur asked, following.

"To make you king."

Of course Arthur did not believe him—who would believe such an outrageous claim, especially one who had grown to manhood as the foster son of a small landholder in the shelter and protection of the Forest Sauvage?

"Merlin, tell me! How can I be king?" Arthur cried after him.

Merlin rode on without answering. He hadn't realized how hard it would be to tell Arthur the truth about himself, for it would involve telling him much of the truth about Merlin as well. The truth about Arthur's father was the truth about the death of Gorlois of Cornwall, the deception of Igraine, Merlin's part in the

Merlin: the King's Wizard ✳ 173

whole squalid plot. The ancient ghosts of his treachery had slept for many years. Telling the truth to Arthur about his parentage would reawaken them, and Merlin found he dreaded the very real possibility of forfeiting Arthur's good opinion of him. Somehow Merlin felt that if he disappointed Arthur it would signal an end to all his attempts to choose the good over the expedient.

"Merlin!" Arthur called again.

"Because you were born to it," Merlin answered shortly.

They rode south, along the bank of a rushing river. The day was bright and the sun shone, but for all the attention Merlin paid to his surroundings, the two of them could have been riding through the densest fog. The hopes he had cherished for years were about to become reality—or be destroyed forever. And if Arthur failed, Merlin did not think he had the strength to go on with his fight. Mab would win. And victory or defeat lay in the unknowing hands of one slender golden boy.

Arthur.

"I've no royal blood in me! *Merlin!*"

It had been nearly two decades since Merlin had given the sword Excalibur into the keeping of the Old Man of the Mountain, and in that time its legend had proliferated. Over the years, a village had grown up around the stone, filled with tradesmen and craftsmen and merchants all attracted by the endless stream of knights and princes who came from near and far, each one hoping it would be *he* who was fated to draw the sword from the stone and become the next ruler of Britain.

Excalibur Village was filled with all the excitement of a market fair. Vendors selling meat pies, gingerbread, tankards of ale, and small knots of tinsel ribbon that one could buy to prove he'd been here and at least seen the magic sword moved through the crowd of Britons and Saxons who had come to watch the latest attempts to draw Excalibur from the rock. Now that Uther was dead, the crowds—and the number of contenders—were larger than ever.

"You try, Father," Kay said, draining the cup of ale he had just purchased and handing it back to the ale-seller.

Sir Hector shook his head. They had stopped here on their way to Winchester. Sir Hector hoped for a few last moments of peace before joining the council of nobles, and Kay had wanted to see the sword.

"Even if I were fortunate enough to be able to pull Excalibur from the stone, I do not think I could be a good king."

"Well, *I* could!" Kay said impulsively. Without waiting for his father's reply, the young knight ran through the crowd of curious bystanders, up the hill, and grasped the golden hilt of the sword.

It had been sunk into the stone before he had been born, but Excalibur was still as bright and gleaming as if it had just come from the swordsmith. When Kay clasped the hilt, he imagined that he heard a faint singing, as if of angel voices. He quickly made the sign of the cross to protect himself from any Pagan magic that might still cling to the sword, then took a firm grip on the hilt and pulled.

Nothing happened. Kay strained harder, unable to believe the sword would not move. It was as if he dragged at the rock itself.

"Stand aside! This is a job for a *man*!" Sir Boris said.

Kay staggered back, panting, his palms stinging from the effort he'd made. Sir Boris—red of hair, red of face, and circular of girth—swaggered up to the sword.

"Is that windbag back again?" Kay heard someone say. Shaking his head and trying to hide his smile, Kay trotted back down the hill to where his father stood.

"I hear that Sir Boris has come every feast day for the last ten years to try to free Excalibur," Sir Hector said to his son.

"If he isn't careful, he'll do himself an injury," another of the villagers said.

Kay watched as Sir Boris strained, growing alarmingly purple with the effort, before collapsing, out of breath, at the foot of the stone. The villagers hooted and jeered, and Kay was glad to have at least escaped their ridicule, if he couldn't draw the sword.

"Father," he whispered. "If no one can pull the sword from the stone, what then? Who will be king?"

Sir Hector looked worried. "Someone must be king, Kay. And if no one can draw Excalibur, I fear that there will be war."

Arthur had finally fallen silent, even his persistent questioning failing to draw more answers from a distracted Merlin. The path Merlin had chosen led through another forest, and the boy and the wizard now rode quietly, side by side. Spring had not yet come to these woods; all the trees were winter-barren, and the crunching of the horses' hooves on the dead leaves of the forest floor was the only sound. It was as if they rode through a world outside of Time, a world that contained no living things but themselves.

There is something terribly familiar about this, the wizard thought.

Mab had not had a hand in Uther's destruction. She had not needed to involve herself, as the seeds of Uther's own madness had blossomed without additional help. But she had been aware of his death, and known, too, that Merlin would soon make the next move in their private little war. He would thrust his protégé, Arthur, into the forefront of events . . . if he could.

How much simpler things would be if the boy died here. The jewel on Mab's forefinger glowed blood-red as she stroked the hooded head of her companion. The blind-hood hid its eyes, for gryphons were sight-hunters, and it would attack the first prey it saw.

There were four of them, all hooded, crouched expectantly in the trees around her as Mab, too, awaited the signal to begin the hunt. At last she heard the sound of approaching horses.

Mab drew the hood from the first gryphon's head.

Merlin drew his sword. The uneasiness he felt had no perceptible cause, but he had long ago learned to trust his instincts. Something terrible was about to happen.

A moment later, it did.

"Gryphons!" Arthur shouted, pointing.

Gryphons were creatures of the Old Magic, once used by the fairy court to hunt their prey. The creatures were about the size of large dogs, with brown-feathered hawk heads and dun-colored bodies. They had the clawed feet and tufted tails of lions, and gliding membranes that stretched between their forelimbs and their ribs allowed them to fly for short distances. They preferred to hunt in packs, and were savage and dangerous adversaries.

"Arthur!" Merlin cried. Merlin caught a glimpse of the boy struggling to keep his seat as two of the gryphons attacked him. The bay gelding reared and snorted, fighting his rider.

"There's another one! Look out!" Arthur shouted.

When one of the gryphons jumped onto his neck, Boukephalos bucked frantically, tossing Arthur to the ground. Two of the gryphons, snarling and slashing, circled the boy where he lay helpless on the forest floor.

Merlin struck out with his sword as Sir Rupert backed and sidled, trying to keep the creatures from getting behind him. Sir Rupert did not react as Boukephalos had, but Sir Rupert had been foaled upon the plains of Annwn, and lived his life among creatures of magic and wonder. The gryphons were dangerous, but they did not terrify him as they did Arthur's mortal horse.

But Sir Rupert's cool head was not enough to save

them. Without help, all four of them were doomed. Merlin cast about for something that could aid them, and saw a wasp's nest clinging to the branch of the tree above him.

"Arthur! Keep still!" Merlin shouted. Fending off his attackers as best he could, he gestured toward the mud nest, asking with his magic for their help.

Wasps came boiling out of their home, heading for the gryphons. They buzzed around the animals' heads, stinging and tormenting them. Though their stings were small, their numbers were great, and it seemed only a few seconds before the gryphons had enough of an enemy they could not fight. The pack took flight, screeching its dismay as the gryphons loped off into the forest.

"Thank you," Merlin said to two of the small stinging insects. They hovered before his face for a moment longer before retreating back into their mud-nest home.

"I did nothing," Arthur said aggrievedly, staggering to his feet. His left arm was red with blood, the tunic sleeve torn by the gryphons' pecking beaks.

"I wasn't talking to you," Merlin said absently. He dismounted to see to Arthur's injury; one of the salves he'd made up this morning would do to make sure the scratches healed cleanly.

"What was that?" Arthur asked, holding out his arm so that Merlin could tend to it. His blue eyes watched his old tutor warily, and Merlin knew Arthur was adding together all the strange events that had taken place since this morning and beginning to wonder if Merlin was really who he had seemed to be through all the years of Arthur's childhood.

"That," Merlin said in answer, "that was a message from an old friend." *And you're right. I am both more and less than you have thought me, my young friend. As are you.*

In her sanctum deep under the hill, Mab gazed into a deep amber crystal, a repository of the Old Magic. As she watched, its dark honey color paled, until it was white and crumbling—useless. She tossed the crystal into a pile of similarly drained ones.

My power is fading.

Mab hated to admit that truth even to herself. She hated the fact that it *was* the truth. But the long interregnum while Uther reigned and Arthur grew into his destiny had been years that had seen Mab's power slowly dwindle. The great feats of her past could not be repeated. The last dragon was dead. And Merlin—who was to have been her greatest champion, her greatest achievement—worked tirelessly to bring a final end to the Old Ways.

But I have magic enough to prevent that, my Merlin. If I cannot bend you to my will, I can at least destroy all that you love. Beginning with the boy. . . .

Through all the rest of the day Merlin had felt Arthur's eyes upon his back, wondering, questioning, assessing. It took them several hours to catch and calm Boukephalos after his fright with the gryphons, and afterward—though he was a splendid animal—Arthur's bay gelding could not match Sir Rupert's magical speed. A journey that would have taken Merlin and Sir Rupert only a few hours at best found the travelers still on the road to their destination when darkness fell and Merlin called a halt for the night. As Arthur unsaddled the horses, Merlin gathered together some stones and heaped them in a small pile. It would only take a simple spell to turn the bare stones into a fire that would burn all night without needing to be replenished, but Merlin hesitated.

Fire was the easiest magic, the first magic, but in Merlin's mind it would always be associated with his earliest doubts about Mab, the first painful moments when he had begun to suspect the motives of the Queen of the Old Ways whose magic had given him birth. More than a quarter of a century separated Merlin now from the innocent boy he had once been. He had become more like his great enemy than he would ever have dreamed possible, but he still battled on, hoping that his heritage—half-fairy, half-mortal—did not doom him to become as evil as Mab.

"Shall I go gather some wood for the fire now?" Arthur asked. He looked doubtfully at the pile of stones.

"It isn't necessary," Merlin answered. He drew a deep breath, and passed his hand slowly above the stones. *Only a Hand-Wizard.* It was surprising that after so many years, his failure to achieve all that Mab had asked of him still hurt.

The stones began to glow, and a wave of heat swept out from them. Another moment passed, and they burst into flame.

Arthur sprang back from the flames with a yelp of surprise, staring at Merlin in shock.

"You're a *wizard*," the boy said. His voice held accusation, and he reached out to touch the fire, as if unsure of its reality. "Ow!" He sucked on his scorched fingers.

"Fire always burns, young Arthur," Merlin said severely. "No matter its source."

"Now will you tell me everything?" Arthur asked, shaking off his wonder at Merlin's magic and sitting down on a large stone beside the fire.

"Yes, it's—it's time," Merlin said reluctantly. *The boy is young—too young to know that explaining everything settles nothing. I can only hope he'll understand my part in it, and be as merciful as a king must be.*

"Arthur, you should know that Sir Hector isn't your real father."

For a moment Merlin became a child again, hearing Ambrosia explain the truth about his mother—and his parentage—to him for the first time. He knew how important his next words would be, and chose them carefully.

"Your father was King Uther, and you are the true heir to the throne."

He seated himself next to Arthur, savoring the last moments of the time when the two of them could be merely tutor and pupil. When Arthur drew the sword from the stone, that time would end. Arthur would be king. Merlin's king.

"King Uther," Arthur said, marveling. "But who was my mother?"

"She was the Lady Igraine," Merlin said reluctantly.

"The Duke of Cornwall's wife?" Arthur asked. Merlin nodded reluctantly. "Then I'm illegitimate."

Arthur had been raised in the New Religion. Such things mattered to them.

"It will not matter to Britain," Merlin said. "You are Uther's only son. You are the true king, now that Uther is dead." He watched Arthur's face, as it settled into new lines of knowledge and regret. He had gained his real parents and lost them in the same moment, and as Merlin knew, that was a bitter thing.

"Then you aren't my tutor at all. You're the wizard Merlin, the one who killed Vortigern and put Uther on the throne."

"Yes," Merlin said quietly. "I am that Merlin. But I was also your tutor."

"Why didn't you teach me magic?" Arthur demanded.

"A king does not need magic to rule—a king needs a good heart and a clear head. They are more important than magic. But rest assured, there is also magic involved, and tomorrow you will see it."

Arthur studied Merlin's face for a long moment, trying to understand all he had been told.

"Did my father—did Sir Hector—know?"

"That you were Uther's son? He may have suspected it, but I never told him. Though I brought you to him to foster, he loved you as if you were his own."

"Didn't Uther want me?" The anguished question was like a knife in Merlin's own heart. He reached out to pat the boy awkwardly upon the shoulder.

"That wasn't how it was. Listen now, and you shall have the whole story. Many years ago, when your grandfather Constant was king, a wicked queen named Mab plotted against him. Mab was no ordinary woman, but a Fay, the Queen of the Old Ways. . . ."

It turned out better than Merlin had hoped. Arthur heard the whole story and did not give way to anger or temper as his father and grandfather might have. Instead, he was thoughtful, saying little as he rolled himself into his cloak for sleep that night. The following morning he was quieter than usual, but did his share of the chores willingly before he and Merlin rode on.

Finally, in the late afternoon, as they stopped to rest on a ridge overlooking a lake valley, Arthur spoke about what Merlin had told him the night before.

"If I am Uther's only son," he said, "I want what is mine. I want to be king." He turned his horse down the trail, taking the lead for the first time.

"And if you are king, what then?" Merlin asked neutrally, though inwardly he was rejoicing as he followed Arthur. Until that moment, it had been possible that Arthur would reject the crown, been unable to see himself as king. But he had accepted his royal destiny.

"Well, I —" Arthur began.

"Whoa, whoa," Merlin interrupted, taking Boukephalos's bridle.

"What! What is it now?" Arthur half-drew his sword, expecting another attack like the one the day before.

Merlin pointed at a snail crossing the road before them. "He has the right of way."

Arthur looked bewildered, but accepted the rebuke meekly enough. Carefully, he rode around the snail.

"You were saying—if you were king," Merlin prompted him as they waited.

"I'd do all the things you taught me," Arthur said dreamily. "I'd build a golden city devoted to peace and charity."

"What the world needs is justice and compassion more than charity," Merlin said, thinking of the vision that had told him this day would come. "Still, Camelot sounds like a dream worthy of a king. Come on, Rupert," he said as the snail had passed.

Obediently, Sir Rupert moved forward, but Arthur stayed where he was, transfixed by the vision of his golden city.

"Camelot," he murmured to himself, tasting the name. "Camelot. . . ."

"Come on, Arthur!" Merlin called back.

Merlin had purposely chosen a route to their destination that would keep them away from main roads and villages, for the country was in a state of great unrest following Uther's death. Mab did not attack them again, and so, just as he had planned, they arrived at Excalibur Village near midnight.

The full moon shone high above them. The rim of Arianrhod's Silver Wheel was a silvery slash across the heavens, and the stars were bright pinpricks in the sky. The villagers and sword-pilgrims were asleep in the small village of tents and more permanent buildings that had grown up at the foot of the mountain. No dog barked, no nightbird cried, no person spoke, as Merlin and Arthur rode up to the base of the cliff where Excalibur waited.

There were candles stuck in the clefts of the rocks, their flames wavering in the wind. They had been left there as prayers by members of both the New Religion and the Old Ways, for everyone knew that the sword Excalibur had great magic, and Britain's need was equally great.

The hilt of the sword glowed golden in the moonlight. Arthur dismounted and walked up the hill toward it like a young man going to his bride. But when he reached it he hesitated, looking back at Merlin.

"All the knights in Britain have tried to take it, but it is the sword of the king. It's yours, Arthur."

Merlin saw Arthur summon up all his courage as he grasped the hilt of the sword in both hands. But before he could pull on it, a voice spoke from behind him.

"Merlin? It seems you were only here a moment ago," the Mountain King rumbled.

Arthur looked behind him. The boy's eyes widened as he saw the enormous face that had been a cliff only the moment before.

"My lord, this man claims Excalibur," Merlin announced.

"Who is it?" the Mountain King rumbled in his slow, deep voice.

"I am Arthur, the only son of Uther and rightful king of Britain!" the boy cried.

"Why give him the sword?"

One of the boulders on the hillside seemed to split

as Mab issued forth from it. Moving with a flickering motion, she positioned herself a few yards away. Her skin sparkled like crystal, and her eyes were dark fathomless pools. The Queen of the Old Ways glowed, as though the fires of earth were consuming her from within. Her dark robes glittered as if they had been woven from the light of black stars. She pointed one sable-taloned finger accusingly at Arthur.

"He'll betray the people, just as his father did!"

Arthur glanced at her, then looked back at the Mountain King, his hands still upon the hilt of Excalibur.

"I don't know what I'll do or what I'll become—only what I am!"

"A wise answer," the Mountain King said.

"I had a wise teacher," Arthur said with a faint smile. Merlin's heart swelled with pride; with every second that passed, Arthur became more a king, and less the wild, good-hearted boy who had been Merlin's pupil. But kingly or not, Mab would try to smash both him and the sword the Lady of the Lake had given into Merlin's keeping.

"He will try to destroy the Old Ways!" Mab raged. "You'll be forgotten like the rest of us!"

"That is your fear, not mine, Mab," the Mountain King said in his slow rich voice. "I cannot die. I am the Rock of Ages; I'll live forever, on the edge of dreams."

Mab recoiled as if the Mountain King's words were blows.

"Now, Arthur!" Merlin cried. "Now is the time!"

Arthur hesitated for only a moment. Tightening his grip upon the sword, he began to pull.

"The sword is yours," the Mountain King said, releasing his grip.

But Mab had not yet conceded defeat. She gestured, her robes flashing in the moonlight, and as she did, the sword in Arthur's hands began to glow with heat.

His face contorted with pain, but his determination didn't waver. Slowly, with a shrill scraping sound, the blade began to move against the rock as it was released from its prison. Blood oozed from between his fingers and dripped down the hilt, and still Arthur pulled, drawing Excalibur from the stone. As the sword's magic was freed, the Mountain King closed his eyes, settling into sleep once more.

The sound had awakened the village. As Merlin watched, lamps were lit in the tents and houses, and the voices of the villagers could be heard, blending in a growing babble of sound as each of them asked what was happening. At that moment, the blade slipped free from the rock, its magic flaring with a blinding light.

With a flourish, Arthur raised the sword above his head. "Excalibur!" he shouted as the cooling blade flashed in the moonlight. Blood from his wounded hands dripped down his wrist, spattering his face like some unholy baptism. "Excalibur!"

"Look at him, Merlin," Mab jeered. "His reign begins in blood and it will end the same way."

But Merlin knew the key to contending against Mab now. Mab drew her power from faith, from belief. The greatest defense against her destructive magics was hope.

"No, Mab," Merlin answered, smiling triumphantly. "You're wrong. Arthur will heal the land."

Mab hissed in defiance, but Merlin's conviction was too much for her. With an angry gesture, the fairy queen vanished, leaving the young king and his wizard alone in the moonlight. Arthur had come into his power at last . . . and so had Merlin.

The villagers were coming from their tents and huts now, heading toward the sword-stone. When they saw Arthur standing on the hill, they stopped, milling about in confusion.

Arthur raised the sword high once more. The light from the candles massed at the base of the rock cast a deep amber glow over the young king, but the sword's light was the bright silver of starlight.

"He has the sword!" one of the villagers shouted. "He has Excalibur!"

"He's the king!" another said. There was a loud murmur of voices as the message was passed through the crowd to those too far away to see. *The king—the king—the king. . . .*

"Long live the king!" someone shouted, and in a moment the cry was taken up by every voice. *"Long live the King! Long live the King!"*

Merlin watched Arthur, and saw the moment when the boy—the king—realized that the crowd was shouting for *him.* He swung Excalibur over his head. It flashed blue in the moonlight and Arthur laughed, his joy melding with the song of the magic sword.

And Merlin laughed with him, certain of Arthur's goodness, certain at last that the future would be bright.

*   *   *

The land under the hill had neither sun nor moon to mark the passing of the days, and its sleepless inhabitants did not miss them. Hindered only slightly by the cloud of curious sprites that flitted about his head, Frik went about his daily chores.

It seemed only moments since young Master Merlin had been his pupil, and Frik found that he still missed the boy—though consciously he knew that time passed differently in the Lands of Men, and the half-mortal boy he remembered was many years older now. Those had been the days! Her Majesty had been happy when Merlin was with them, looking forward to a future in which she would have regained all her ancient influence.

But since Merlin had left them, life seemed to consist of nothing but a series of setbacks. Though Mab schemed and plotted as tirelessly as she ever had, it never seemed to gain them anything.

And it seemed that Time itself had turned against them. The magic that Mab expended was not repaid in the form of belief—the New Religion had made too many inroads on the numbers of those who had once followed the Old Ways. More and more often these days, Frik came across drifts of crystals drained of power—power that now was gone forever.

And when enough power had vanished, that would be the end of everything. They—Frik, and Mab, and all the creatures of magic that filled her dominion—would fade away like morning mist, to have no more reality than the dreams that mortals dreamed. Fussing under his breath, the gnome began to pick up the colorless, crumbling crystals: the residue of expended magic.

Someday, when the mortals realized what they'd lost, these fragments would be revered as if they still held great power, but by then he, and Mab, and all their enchanted world would be long gone, vanished in the mists of Time.

Lost in his dire thoughts, Frik did not notice when Mab appeared beside him—though he did notice as she sent him sprawling with a well-placed kick. The debris he had gathered up scattered across the floor once more.

"Don't you ever tidy up, Frik?" she hissed.

Frik risked a cautious glance at his mistress. She was in a towering rage—he could tell that much easily. But why?

"Oh, I try, Your Majesty, but I'm terribly overworked—and I can't use imps, gnomes, or fairies—they're utterly useless with anything practical. I mean, I have so much to do!" he said obsequiously as he picked up the crystals he'd dropped. Groveling usually worked to dull the edge of Mab's temper.

But not this time.

"And you'll have more! I've totally given up on Merlin!" Mab said, sweeping her cape around herself as if she were some furious bird of prey. "I thought that, despite everything, he might come round in the end," she added, and there was almost a note of dejection in her harsh, toneless voice.

Given up on Merlin? Frik was stunned. But Merlin had been Mab's pet project for so long—she had been so certain he would rejoin her at last! Even though Frik had suspected Merlin was far more stubborn than Mab had dreamed, to hear his mistress admit failure—!

"Well I mean he's a stubborn creature, isn't he?" Frik offered tentatively, trying to gauge her mood.

"I wanted him to join me, so I fooled myself!" Mab's perfect face was harsh with regret.

"I've never known you to do that before over anyone," Frik said quietly, getting to his feet. He had never seen the Queen of the Old Ways so shaken, so unsure of herself. What had happened to challenge Mab's certainty that she could someday bend Merlin to her will? Why, she almost seemed vulnerable!

But if Mab had been disillusioned, it had not made her soft. Hissing her displeasure at Frik's effrontery, she slapped him across the face hard enough to make him stagger back yelping.

"Enough!" she said, brusquely dismissing her moment of weakness. "Oh yes, Arthur's cursed. I want everyone to know in good time—and that will be your job, Frik!"

Arthur . . . that was the baby Merlin had once had such hopes for, the one with the ambitious half-sister, Morgan. Frik wondered what had happened to her . . . he supposed the girl must be all grown-up, if her brother was causing such trouble. Still, it might be amusing to go and see. It had been a long time since Frik had done anything for fun.

"Yes, Your Majesty. Of course, Your Majesty," Frik said, fawning and kowtowing as he bowed and backed carefully out of reach.

*   *   *

Uther's will had specified that he was to lie in state and be buried at Winchester, not Pendragon. Perhaps he felt that he had sullied the cathedral at Londinium with his blasphemies, or perhaps at the end of a failed reign he had thought longingly back to the days of struggle and victory that had been his at Winchester in his youth. Whatever the reason, it was here that his body lay upon its bier of state, robed in scarlet, crowned in gold, surrounded by candles, with monks chanting prayers day and night for the repose of King Uther's once-troubled soul.

But if the late king was now at peace, his kingdom was not. Everyone knew that Excalibur had vanished from the stone in which it had been imprisoned for so long—but no one knew who had drawn it forth.

It was spring, and the fancies of men across Britain turned to war.

"Uther was my cousin! I claim the throne by right!" Lord Lot shouted across Uther's body. The grey-bearded noble was dressed in the Briton style, with a gold collar about his neck testifying to his connection to royal blood.

"You did not pull the sword Excalibur from the rock!" Lord Leodegrance roared back. All the dukes and princes of Britain were gathered in that room, united by one thought: that each of them was worthy to be king.

"Nobody did!" Lord Lot cried.

"You all failed. My father is king by right of blood!" Gawain shouted. Lord Lot's son was a warrior in his prime. Tall and fair like all the members of the

Iceni tribe, he was loved by his people as much for his
gentleness as for his formidable prowess in battle. The
Iceni were a rich people, their lands far from those
overrun by the Saxon hordes, and Gawain wore a
fawn-colored cape embroidered in the Celtic style
over well-worn British plate mail ornamented with
pure gold. While he supported his father's claim to the
throne, every man there knew that Gawain would not
demand the crown for himself. All the Iceni prince had
ever asked of life was the chance to be loyal to a worthy man.

"I am nearer to Uther than you," Lord Leodegrance said, reopening the old argument. The ties of
blood that linked all the noble families of Britain had
become a net to ensnare them in, as each one weighed
his connections to Uther to gauge his acceptability for
the kingship.

"His sister was Uther's niece," Sir Hector said
slowly. "I pledge my army to Lord Leodegrance."

"Listen to Sir Hector!" Lord Leodegrance urged
his fellow nobles.

"I have a claim, too!" Sir Boris interrupted, his red
face darkening with exasperation.

"Nobody's going to follow a bearded blowhard!"
Gawain jeered.

The rotund old knight's flaming hair was thinner
now and streaked with grey, but he still wore the
banded armor and *tunica virilis* of a Roman soldier,
and was a warrior in his heart. With a roar he flung
himself at Lord Lot's son. Standing candle trees filled
with rings of lit candles rocked dangerously, spattering
the shouting men below them with hot beeswax.

Though they had all left their weapons outside this holy place, tempers ran hot and fast. The princes of Britain surged back and forth, trying to decide with their fists what could not be settled by any reasoned argument, while unnoticed by everyone, the old king's body slipped from its bier to the floor.

Merlin and Arthur had set out for Winchester at first light. Arthur was very quiet on the journey, thinking of what it meant to be king. Merlin knew that the battle was far from over; though Excalibur conferred the true kingship, the race of men was as foolish, stubborn, and petty-minded as ever.

When they reached the cathedral, Merlin began to suspect his estimate might have been too charitable. The sound of shouting voices could be heard even through the door. Arthur glanced uneasily at Merlin.

"These are the men you must rule," Merlin said as he opened the door.

The sounds of shouting and inarticulate anger rolled over the two men like an ocean wave. There was no way for them to be heard over it.

Merlin drew his fingers across his lips and then cast the gesture out into the room. At once there was silence. The men continued to shout, but there was no sound. As they realized what had happened, they slowly fell silent, staring at each other in wonder.

Merlin led Arthur into the middle of the room.

"That's better, isn't it, my lords?" he said ostentatiously. "Now you can listen instead of fighting. It should be a novel experience for most of you." With a flick of his left hand, Merlin returned their voices to them. "Uther had a son. I give you Arthur, true King of Britain."

There was a moment of silence as they stared at Merlin, then most of the nobles burst out laughing, discovering by this that they could speak again. As the laughter died, Lord Lot spoke.

"Uther had no son. Everyone knows that."

Arthur's cool blue gaze swept the room, stopping where the body of King Uther—his father—lolled from the dais. Ignoring them all, he went to the bier, gently lifting his father's body in his arms and arranging it decently once more upon the scarlet pall.

"He did." Sir Boris looked stricken, as if he spoke in spite of himself. "Uther did have a son. When Uther conquered Tintagel, he took the Lady Igraine. A son was born. It's true. I was there."

"Arthur?" Sir Hector spoke wonderingly, reaching out his hand to the boy he had raised from infancy. "Is Uther's son?"

"If he is, let him draw Excalibur from the stone," Gawain said with simple practicality.

"I already have!" Arthur announced proudly. He drew Excalibur and flourished it, and once more Merlin heard the high, sweet song of the sword.

Gawain looked stunned as he gazed upon a sight he had plainly never expected to see. "Well, prove it!" he said, nearly stammering. "Prove that this is Excalibur!"

Without a word, Arthur swung the sword about his head in a great arc. The crowd flinched back, though the sword came nowhere near them. No living man was Arthur's target. Instead, Excalibur sliced the flames from two of the nearest branches of candles.

But the magic did not end there. The flames, still in two perfect rings, floated up to the ceiling, slowly dissolving as they rose. All those assembled watched the spectacle in stunned silence. Slowly, Gawain went to his knees, as much out of shock as in reverence.

"You do have Excalibur and you are Uther's son. I acknowledge you as my liege-lord and King," Sir Boris said dogmatically. With grave ponderousness, the elderly knight walked to Arthur's side and knelt to do him homage.

"And so do I," Sir Hector said. Kneeling, he kissed the hand of the king who had been his foster son.

"He has the sword," Lord Leodegrance said simply, kneeling and bowing his head to Arthur. "Accept him, Lot . . . Arthur is king."

"Never," Lord Lot bellowed. "I'll not bend my knee to a boy—nor will my son!" He turned to go.

"I can speak for myself, Father," Gawain said sharply. "He has Excalibur. He is the king."

Lord Lot froze where he stood, staring at his son.

"Gawain! You'd go against your own father?"

"If the cause is just," Gawain said evenly.

"And if it's not—and you're wrong?" Lord Lot demanded.

"Then you will have to kill me in battle," Gawain said softly. "I am the king's man, Father." Slowly Gawain knelt again among the others.

"So be it!" Lord Lot said coldly.

"Shame on you!" someone cried.

"My Lords, hard as it may be for you, think for a moment," Merlin said coaxingly. "We have all seen too many wars."

Some of the nobles standing with Lord Lot wavered at Merlin's words, but Lot himself was too outraged by Gawain's defection to think calmly.

"My mind's made up! All with me, follow me!" he stormed from the room, followed by half a dozen other lords. The sound of the door as it slammed behind them was the loudest sound Merlin had ever heard: the sound of his hopes for peace crashing down into nothingness. Across Uther's body he gazed at Arthur, and found that Arthur was staring back with the same emotion in his eyes—despair.

CHAPTER SEVEN

THE THRONE OF FATE

Tintagel Keep stood as it always had, a solitary citadel upon the Cornish headlands. Within its walls, Morgan le Fay ruled as sole overlord, as she had from the time when she was eight years old.

It was a lonely life. Since the day that Uther had taken the castle and Gorlois had died, there had been an aura of ill-luck surrounding Tintagel's walls like the grey sea-mist. When Igraine died and her newborn son vanished, the curse was complete. No one went to Tintagel if they could avoid it.

Morgan told herself she didn't mind, but it wasn't true. She hated the loneliness, the isolation, the way her own servants—-the few that remained—turned away from the sight of her disfigured face. But there was no remedy for any of these things. No man would willingly marry Cornwall's cursed and ugly daughter.

If only her father had lived to defeat Uther! Gorlois had been the true king of Britain, the rightful heir to the throne. Royal blood ran in Morgan's veins; she should have been a princess instead of a lonely and forgotten outcast.

But Uther had used Merlin's magic and trickery to destroy Cornwall and take their lands for his own. And Gorlois's forgotten daughter had nothing.

So Morgan amused herself with toys and with reading the ancient books in the castle library. From those books, she had learned to build something the old Romans had called a *kite*. When she carried it up to a stairway overlooking the sea, it took flight easily in the wind, and Morgan watched it soar, free as she could never be.

"Hello, Morgan. My, how you've grown."

Morgan turned around to see the oddest creature she could ever remember seeing. He was dressed all in close-fitting black. His skin was pale, and he had goggling, yellow-green eyes. He wore a close-fitting cap that made his long pointed ears all the more obvious, and stood in a half crouch, rubbing his hands together.

"Who're you?" Morgan said belligerently. Whoever he was, she was certain he'd only come here to make fun of her. She knew what she looked like—an ugly woman whom no one wanted, wearing a shabby, badly-made gown. Her hands clutched the kitestring tightly.

"Don't you remember me?" the stranger said. "I used to visit you when you were very young. . . ."

He turned around, and suddenly he was a tall blond man, too handsome to be real, in a flowing white shirt. His long blond hair floated in the breeze and there was a laughing devil in his gaze.

"Fair lady!" he cried, saluting her.

There were several barrels on the landing that were in the process of being winched up into a tower from the landing stage below. With a carefree laugh, he kicked the one still roped to the pulley over the side, and grabbed the other end of the rope. As the barrel fell, it became a counterweight to raise him to the highest tower of Tintagel. Drawing his sword, the swashbuckler capered back and forth, doing battle against imaginary foes while Morgan laughed for joy.

"I wemember you!" she cried. "I thought you were a dweam!"

"I'm real," Frik said, bowing and smiling from his perch upon the wall.

"You lied to me," Morgan said accusingly. She remembered the nights of heartbreak that had followed her mother's death, when she had wept, not for Igraine, but for the dashing, magical cavalier who had never returned to keep his promises to her. "You told me you'd make me beautiful and you never did."

Frik pranced down the stairs until he stood before her.

"Did I?" he asked. "Then I will. But first you must put away childish things." With a flick of his rapier, he severed the kite string. With a cry of dismay, Morgan watched it sail away, off into the endless blue.

"Why so sad?" Frik asked. "It's only a toy."

Morgan turned back. She flinched when she saw that Frik was holding out a mirror, then approached it, breathless with hope.

Her heart sank when she saw her reflection—marred, bucktoothed, plain—but almost before she could register her disappointment the image began to change, as if the morning mists were vanishing to reveal the beautiful golden face of the sun, and what appeared was almost too dazzling to behold.

"I'm beautiful!" Morgan gasped. She snatched the mirror from Frik's hand and inspected herself closely.

Everything had changed. Her straight mouse-brown hair was now piled high upon her head in a mass of auburn ringlets, her teeth were even and white, and her *face* . . . her face was beautiful, her eyes perfect, her muddy, spotty skin a rich cream, her new beauty expertly enhanced with cosmetics.

"Very, very beautiful," Frik agreed proudly. "I think clothes cut in the Roman style are the only gowns for a lady of fashion."

Gone, too, Morgan realized, was the dowdy makeshift dress she had been wearing only a moment ago. In its place was a glorious sky-blue gown trimmed in gold.

She was beautiful. More than that, she was perfect. He'd done all he'd promised, and more than she'd dared dream of asking for.

"It's wonderful," Morgan whispered. "Now get me the thwone!" she demanded abruptly.

Frik looked regretful. "That's beyond my powers," he said. He put an arm about her shoulders, leading her back into the castle. "But I do have one or two other little tricks that I'd be delighted to show you. . . ."

* * *

Humans, Frik mused, were very strange. Take Morgan, for example. He'd showed up after a particularly long absence to grant a simply enormous number of her dearest wishes, and did she think to ask him why? Certainly not. She simply took all his gifts and never asked what he might ask in payment.

It hadn't taken Frik long to remember Morgan when Mab gave him the task of discrediting Arthur. With the power of the Old Ways waning so disastrously, Frik had known he'd need a mortal ally. And Morgan had always been so ambitious. . . .

For hours the two of them wandered through Tintagel, transforming the castle from a barren hulk to the most opulent palace Morgan could imagine. Frik filled rooms with exquisite furniture, closets with beautiful gowns, and chests with jewels. It was all trickery, of course, but it *looked* real, and Frik suspected that Morgan didn't care about anything beyond appearances.

Last of all, they reached the Great Hall. With a wave of his hand, Frik covered the walls with banners and the floors with furs. He lit a crackling fire in the great fireplace at one end of the hall, and with a gesture covered the table with a rich cloth, brilliant candles, and a lavish banquet served up on plates of pure gold—all stolen from others, as illusory food wasn't very tasty. For an encore, he created a throne at the far end of the table, a throne big enough for two. Seated beside his creation, Frik exerted himself to the utmost to charm her. His plan was to lull any inconvenient mortal scruples she might have, but Frik was already beginning to suspect that Morgan didn't have any.

Still, the wine was good. And having someone

look at him adoringly made quite a welcome change from Her Majesty's tantrums. Morgan hung upon his every word, delighted to hear everything Frik could tell her about the Land of Magic and its enchanted inhabitants.

"I can tell you from personal experience: elves are so short, when it rains they're the last to know," Frik murmured confidingly.

Morgan gazed at him for a startled moment, then she got the joke and went off into gales of tipsy laughter.

"Stop enjoying yourself and get on with it!" a too-familiar voice hissed. Frik jumped, staring down at his winecup. Mab's face appeared as one of the four ornamental faces on the cup's outer rim. The tiny golden face was contorted in an expression of wrath. A moment later, it was gone.

Frik sighed inwardly. He always hated this part. If it was hard, it was a lot of work, and if it was easy, it was somehow disappointing. Broodingly, the transformed gnome got to his feet and began to pace.

"I've been thinking, Morgan," he said, as though it had just occurred to him. "There *might* be a way of giving you what you want. Your *son* could be king."

"Well, how?" Morgan said blankly. Her speech impediment had been the last thing to fade, but now she possessed no more than a charming lisp. "If Arthur defeats Lord Lot he'll be king. And I can't marry him." Her voice held a faintly aggrieved tone as she crossed the room to join him.

Frik smiled. "You don't have to marry him . . . to have his son."

"But we have the same mother." Morgan's impression of patronizing indignation would have been a good deal more convincing if she hadn't been distracted by her new comeliness. She gazed at her slender hands with their painted oval nails, then began to stroke and admire her coiling auburn locks.

Vain as a cat, Frik thought. Of course, Frik liked cats.

"And underneath this charming and devilishly handsome exterior, I'm a crabby . . . old . . . gnome." He put his hand on the back of Morgan's neck and kissed her passionately.

It was obviously a new experience; Morgan purred contentedly and wreathed her arms about his neck.

"Does it matter?" Frik asked, smiling down at her.

"Not a bit," Morgan sighed, then giggled coquettishly. "Well, that depends . . ." Then abruptly she was all business, turning her face away from him and sitting down on the throne once more. "You don't have to seduce me to win me over. Like everyone else: I want the crown." Her brown eyes stared past him, fixed on a glory Frik couldn't see.

"I like you, Morgan le Fay. You're a truthful young woman," Frik said, seating himself beside her.

Morgan shrugged, dismissing the only honest compliment Frik had yet paid her. "And I like you. Whoever you are." She smiled and reached for him again.

As she did, her elbow struck her cup and knocked it over. The scarlet wine flowed across the table like a river of blood.

*   *   *

It had been six weeks since Arthur had pulled Excalibur from the rock. The Romans had held this day sacred to Apollo. The Christians celebrated the Feast of St. John. But those who followed the Old Ways knew it as the day that the sun passed into the House of the Lion: Midsummer.

And on this day, the kingship of Britain would be decided.

The two armies were gathered at Badon Hill. The plain before it was green and smooth and even. By nightfall, it would be none of these things. The grass would be red with blood, churned to mud by the gouging hooves of the warhorses, and the empty plain would be littered with the bodies of the dead.

"The army's almost ready, Sire," Sir Boris said. "It's going to be a bonny fight!"

Arthur looked at Merlin as Sir Boris rode away along the line. Neither of them shared the old warrior's enthusiasm for what was to come—Merlin, because he had seen it before, and Arthur, because of the lessons Merlin had taught him: that might did not make right, and a king who ruled by force was just a bully with a crown.

Arthur looked around at the empty tents behind him, then at the line of men who would risk their lives for him this day. Here were the grey horses of the Royal Guard, there the black horses of the King's Companions. Welsh archers with their longbows stood proudly by dressed in Lincoln green beside wild Scots painted blue with woad and armed with enormous claymores. Behind the soldiers, a plume of incense smoke rose toward heaven, and Arthur could see the gleam of the golden croziers. Even the Holy Church was on his side, and for his own standard, he had taken the image of the Blessed Mother. The king's standard was blue, with the Lady's image upon it in silver.

He looked across the field, to where Lord Lot's army was gathered, at the top of Badon Hill. All his knights were there with him. Only one was missing. Lot's son. Gawain fought at Arthur's side.

In a few short weeks, Arthur and Gawain had become the closest of friends. Gawain stood beside him, wearing a red cape and his fine bronze helmet ornamented with the Iceni's totem beasts. Gawain looked every inch a king, and had no desire to be one.

Today I kill the father of my best friend, or he kills me. Either way, this will be a dark day for Britain. No! I will not accept that. Merlin taught me to use my mind, not my sword.

"We're ready, Sire," Sir Boris said, returning.

Suddenly Arthur knew what he must do. "Wait for my signal," he said. Gawain and Merlin, both standing near, nodded. He strode through the ranks to where a foot soldier held his horse and mounted Boukephalos in one smooth motion. Then Arthur rode forward alone, out onto the battlefield.

"He'll be killed!" Sir Hector said. "Merlin!" he said, turning to the wizard.

Merlin stood where he was, saying nothing. His feathered cloak fluttered softly in the morning breeze, and the midsummer sun glinted off the bronze of the conical cap he wore.

"What the devil's he doing?" Lord Leodegrance

demanded, but no one answered. All eyes in the army were upon Arthur. Their king looked very small and alone as he rode across the battlefield, into the swords and spears and arrows of an army that had sworn to kill him.

Lord Lot's face was impassive as he watched Arthur ride toward his army. If there had been the least sign of a threat, he would have ordered an attack, but Arthur rode alone, without even a helmet on his head. Not even his wizard was with him.

Lot kept his face impassive as Arthur reached him. The boy reined his horse to a stop and dismounted, walking the rest of the way up the hill. He faced Lot without flinching, and Lot tried to remind himself of how unsuitable the boy was to be king. Never mind his parentage; the boy was too young. Why, Arthur was about the age of Lot's youngest daughter, Guinevere! But child or man, Lot would have to kill him if Arthur wouldn't see reason, because the war could not end until one of them was dead.

"There's no reason why men should die today, my Lord. The quarrel is between us," Arthur said in a clear, carrying voice.

"It is," Lot said grudgingly. Without his intent, his gaze was drawn to the sword at Arthur's hip, the sword from the stone. But a sword wasn't enough to make a man king—look at Uther. Or Vortigern. . . .

Suddenly Arthur drew the sword. Lot and his men scrabbled for their own weapons, but in a moment it was clear Arthur did not intend to attack. Instead he held out the sword to Lot, hilt first.

"This is Excalibur," Arthur said. "It is the sword of the true king. If you believe you have a right to it, take it . . ."

Was it to be as simple as that? Had the boy decided to surrender? Lot took the sword into his hands, feeling its lightness and balance, the way it almost seemed to sing softly to him as he held it. The sword was everything the bards had said it was, forged of steel as fine as silver, sharper than lost hopes.

". . . and cut off my head," Arthur finished, kneeling for the blow.

Lot steeled himself not to recoil. It was this or war, Lot told himself. Arthur's death, or Gawain's, and many others' as well. He lifted the sword.

But he could not strike. The song of the sword filled him. He could hear it, because Lot was of the Blood Royal, but hearing it, he knew the song was not for him. The song and the sword were both for Arthur—a youth so kingly he was willing to humble himself and die so that those innocent of his quarrel should not be harmed.

Arthur was the true king.

Lot lowered the sword slowly.

"Forgive me, Arthur," he said hoarsely. "I can feel it. The sword is yours. You are the true king."

He held the sword out to Arthur. Still kneeling, Arthur took it.

"The war is over!" Lot cried, so that all his men could hear him. He held out his hand and raised Arthur to his feet. The shining look of approval in those grey eyes was all the reward Lot needed. Here was a king he could follow into the halls of Death itself.

As he handed Excalibur back to Arthur, his entire army burst into wild cheers. "Arthur is our true king by blood and right!" Lot shouted, and this time it was loud enough to be heard by both armies. Arthur raised the sword into the sky, and the midsummer sun flashed from the shining blade. Arthur's army roared with delight at the sight.

There was a thunder of horses' hooves as the Royal Guard—led by Gawain—thundered across the field, cheering wildly. The rest of Arthur's army followed, whooping and yelling with joy.

Gawain reached Lot first. He leaped from his horse and ran up the last of the hill, catching his father in a fierce embrace. "Father—oh, Father!" he gasped, hugging Lot so tightly that the old warrior pounded his son's back with a mailed fist. In moments the two armies were commingled upon the slope of Badon Hill, so that it was impossible to separate them—one force, indivisible, in the service of Britain.

Merlin had not stirred from where he stood. Today was Arthur's victory, not his. This had been the last test of kingship, and Arthur had passed it. He had won the day without shedding a drop of blood, and made Lot love him for it. Arthur was both a good man and a good king; he would bring the New Religion to all of Britain through peace, not by the sword. The days of madness, pain, and blood were over, and the future was sanctified by Arthur's goodness.

I've done myself out of a job, Merlin thought to himself with pleasure. It was the day he'd worked for, hoped for, for the last twenty years, since that long-ago winter's day when he rode into Winchester to give his aid to Uther. Constant . . . Vortigern . . . Uther . . . each had been a bad king. Constant had loved his god too much; Vortigern had loved his own way. Uther had been ruled by greed and fear both. But Arthur had none of the faults of his predecessors: he was strong where they had been weak, tolerant where they had been fanatic, gentle where they had been ruthless.

On what would have been their battlefield, the two armies were gathered in a ring about Arthur. Excalibur flashed in his hand. He spoke, and Merlin heard the words quite clearly.

"Here in this circle, let us give thanks to our Savior for this deliverance. And let this circle be a symbol of our purpose; each man in it is equal to the other, each has a voice, each will strive to fight for truth and honor. Let us pray."

He knelt, and all the others, Pagan and Christian, knelt with him to receive the blessing of the Church. Merlin smiled wistfully. For all its intolerance, the New Religion was a gentler shepherd than the Old Ways had been to the people of Britain, and yet Merlin could not give himself to it, any more than he had been able to make himself into Mab's champion. His birthright had condemned him to stand forever between, wholly a part neither of mortal world nor fairy realms.

But at this moment, his own isolation did not matter. This time Merlin's hopes had not led him astray. He had forged a true champion of justice to rule over Britain. His work was over. Now, at last, he could live his life for himself . . . for Nimue.

A few hours later, Merlin had said his good-byes and tied up his affairs. Quietly, unnoticed by anyone, even Arthur, Merlin mounted Sir Rupert and rode away from the rejoicing camp into the soft dusk.

With Sir Rupert's magical help, Merlin reached Avalon quickly. It was still dusk as he rode up to the gates, and he could hear the church bells tolling for Vespers.

It had been twenty years since he first saw these walls. He had come here filled with hate, a dying girl in his arms. But as the years had passed between that moment and this, Merlin had found far more cause for love than for hate, and now his patience and his hope were to be rewarded. Now he and Nimue could be together.

He was well-known by now in Avalon, and the gatekeeper passed him without a challenge. He rode into the inner courtyard and dismounted. The monk whose duty it was to receive all visitors to Avalon came forward to greet him, and Merlin sighed inwardly. It was Father Giraldus, an unfortunate coincidence. Merlin and Giraldus did not get on—Giraldus blamed the Old Ways for the disappearance of the Grail from Avalon, and thought that no Pagan should ever be allowed to set foot in its holy precincts.

"What is it?" Father Giraldus said grudgingly.

"I've come to see Nimue," Merlin said. Even Giraldus's surliness could not dampen his high spirits.

"*Sister* Nimue is at her prayers," Giraldus said. "As are all good Christians. When they are over, you must ask the Novice Mistress if you can see her."

"What?" Suddenly all Merlin's good humor vanished. "But Nimue is a lay sister among the Healers—your Church has no dominion over her."

"*Sister* Nimue has taken her first vows. Soon she will be wholly apart from the world," Giraldus said with an angry look of triumph.

"Pride," Merlin said tightly, "is the greatest sin, the one by which Lucifer fell from heaven. You should look to your soul, Father." With a flick of his fingers, Merlin made himself invisible, running toward the Grail Chapel before Giraldus could stop him.

He could feel the faith of the nuns gathered here like a bright beacon in the night; though faith was not the same thing as magic, it could work as many miracles. He stood outside the door as the nuns chanted their prayers, and when they filed out, returning to their cells, he saw that Nimue was with them, dressed as one of them, though still veiled to hide her scars.

Unseen by everyone, Merlin followed Nimue back to her room. Even when she thought she was alone, he saw, she did not remove her veil. She hummed softly to herself as she circled the room, lighting candles.

"Hello, Nimue," Merlin said.

She gasped, spinning around to see Merlin standing beside the door. "Merlin! What are you doing here?"

"I came to see you. Nimue, why didn't you tell me?"

Nimue hung her head. "I wanted a life. I couldn't go on forever, suspended between you and God."

"And you chose God," Merlin said, trying to keep the bitterness out of his voice.

"God needs me!" Nimue answered. "And you don't! I waited, Merlin. I truly did. But when we all heard that Arthur had been made king, and you didn't come. . . ."

"I came as soon as I could," Merlin said, crossing the room to stand before her. "Nimue, these vows are not binding. The Father Abbot has been my good friend for years. He will release you if you ask. Come away with me. Arthur is secure upon his throne; he doesn't need me anymore."

"And was there ever a king who did not need advisers?" Nimue asked bitterly.

Merlin reached out to take her by the shoulders, but Nimue turned away. He let his hands drop.

"I came back for you, so that we could be together. I know I've put my life—our life—on hold for too long, but Britain needed me."

"Britain will always need you, Merlin. There will always be another crisis that needs you to mend it. Please understand—" She turned to face him, tears glittering in her dark eyes. "I love you for that most of all. You will always be my perfect gentle knight. But I cannot be a part of such a life. It frightens me too much."

This time she did not resist as Merlin drew her toward him. He kissed her gently upon the forehead.

"I am done with that, Nimue. I swear to you, that part of my life is over. I dedicated myself to Mab's destruction, but she cannot be defeated by her own methods—they only make her stronger. It is Arthur who will put an end to her, by building a world in which she can no longer exist. My part is ended."

Nimue studied his face for a long moment, then flung herself into his arms, weeping.

"Oh, my love!" She pressed her face against his chest. "How I've hoped you would someday be able to say those words. I will go to the Father Abbot tomorrow. I know he will accept my decision. I only hope God will understand how much I love you. . . ."

The prayers on the battlefield had led to a celebration, as the consolidated armies raided the supplies brought to sustain a war for the means to make a feast.

Now he was truly King, Arthur thought to himself. No sword, no coronation, could mean more to him than the praise and thanks of men who were alive tonight because he'd done the right thing. He'd visited as many campfires as he could, and at each he'd been offered wine, or mead, or the potent *hrolka* that the Saxons had introduced to Britain. Finally he'd adjourned to his own tent for a quiet party with his closest companions. They'd talked for hours about Britain's future, of the golden city of Camelot that Arthur would build upon the site where he had drawn Excalibur from the stone.

"And the Grail!" said Kay, leaning sideways in his chair. His cheeks were flushed with wine. "If *you* can be King, surely that means you can restore the Grail? Camelot won't be complete without it."

"Kay!" Sir Hector said, embarrassed at his son's plain speaking. Arthur held up a hand.

"No, he's right. The Grail left Britain because our

people were unworthy of so great a treasure. How better to prove how far we have come from those dark days than to bring the Grail back to Camelot? I shall build a special church at Camelot to house it—and when it is there for all men to see, it will prove that the ages of darkness and sin are passed, that we are worthy once more."

All of them cheered him, even Lord Lot, who still followed the Old Ways. Only Gawain looked troubled. Arthur was about to ask him why, when an increase in the commotion outside made him step outside his tent.

An astonishing sight greeted his eyes. Making its way slowly through the camp was a long cortege of white horses. Every other rider was carrying torches, and those who did not carry torches led pure white pack mules heavily laden with chests and packs of all description. Every rider was sumptuously dressed, and even the tack of the mules gleamed with gold.

Riding at the head of the procession was the most beautiful woman Arthur had ever seen. Her long hair was a deep chestnut, piled high upon her head and set with jewels. The opulent gown she wore left her arms bare; it was woven of a fabric the like of which Arthur had never seen, seeming one moment to be red, another gold, the next a royal purple. Her fingers were jeweled and her white arms gleamed with gold.

"Your Majesty."

The man who rode beside her dismounted and presented himself to Arthur, bowing low. "May I present my lady . . . Marie, Queen of the Border Celts, who comes to pay you homage."

The speaker's long blond hair fell forward in a

curtain that could not quite hide his gleeful smile. Despite his claims of Celtic blood, the man was as fair as a Saxon. His only half-concealed mirth made Arthur wonder if he were being made the butt of some rude joke. He might have pursued the matter, but at that moment Marie herself came forward and Arthur forgot everything else as she curtsied deeply, her dark eyes never leaving his face.

"You are most welcome, my lady," Arthur said. He raised her to her feet and led her into the tent.

The others—Lot, Hector, Boris—had already come outside, curious about the new arrivals. Queen Marie's servants had already begun unloading the mules, and through the cloth walls of his tent Arthur could hear his knights exclaiming over the gold, the jewels, the silks and spices that Queen Marie had brought. But it seemed to Arthur that the lady herself was the richest gift of all.

"Lady, we are overwhelmed by your gifts," Arthur said. He could not think of what to say next. He knew he was blushing, and was glad that the soft light of the tent disguised the fact.

"Well, perhaps I—and my servants—can join you for the night," Morgan whispered softly. She kept her face smooth, though inwardly she was laughing at how easily Arthur was taken in. Frik's enchantment had worked! "We've had a long, tiring journey, and would like to rest before we return home."

But there would be no rest for Arthur, not if Morgan had her way. The young King did not suspect that there was no Marie, that she was his half-sister Morgan, and all the gifts she had brought would vanish in the morning light like the fairy gold they were. By then she would have what she wanted. Look at him— the boy was already tripping over his own tongue.

"Of course!" Arthur said eagerly. "We could spend some time together. You can tell me about your people."

I can think of better things to do than talk! Morgan jeered inwardly. "It will be a pleasure, Your Majesty," she said aloud. She stared at the wine-jug on the table until Arthur got the hint.

"Uh, some"—he tripped over a stool—"some wine, Lady Marie?"

"Thank you," she said, taking the opportunity to move farther into the tent. Only a curtain separated her from Arthur's bed, and only a few hours from being the mother of the next King of Britain. She did not fear that they would be interrupted—Frik would see to that, her golden-haired dream lover, the only one she'd ever known who had treated her as she deserved to be treated. Her father had abandoned her, and so had her mother. Her brother had forgotten her—look at him, panting after her beautiful illusion. Had he ever once sent to Tintagel to see how she was?

He deserved everything she was about to do.

Merlin awoke with a start. The candles had burned down to nubbins, the wick guttering in the middle of a wide lake of liquid wax. He straightened up, wincing slightly—a chair was no place to sleep, not at his age. Beside him, Nimue slumbered chastely in her bed.

But something had awakened him—what?"

Merlin stared into the candle flame. The wax bubbled and seethed, and as he watched in horror, it molded itself into human figures, figures that writhed and coupled and intertwined unmistakably.

"What are you showing me, Mab?" he demanded.

The figures appeared in the wax again, and this time he knew them. One was Arthur.

The other was Morgan le Fay.

Eldritch laughter filled the room, soft and chill as winter's snow.

"What have you done?" Merlin cried in horror. *Arthur.* He must go to him at once. If he could not stop this disaster, perhaps he could soften its effects. He got to his feet and ran from the room.

He did not look back.

Mab laughed, loud shrieks of laughter as inhuman as the storm that raged outside the throne room at Pendragon Castle. The castle was deserted—Arthur was in the field, with his army—and Mab felt it was a fitting site for her ultimate triumph. She skipped along the flagstoned floor, Frik behind her. The gnome made sure he was smiling when she looked at him, but frankly, he'd never felt less like frolicking. Morgan was *his*—his creation, his greatest achievement, his biggest fan, and he'd been forced to hand her over to that pimply boy Arthur. What use would she have for him now that she had Arthur's child?

Mab glanced at him suspiciously. Frik smiled dutifully.

* * *

The morning sun shone on Nimue's face, awakening her. She did not open her eyes. She wanted to savor this moment. Today she would leave Avalon—not as she had the last time, a frightened child traveling to the court of a mad king, but as a woman going to her lover. There was a strength in Merlin she had never sensed before—strength enough for both of them, strength enough to make everything all right at last.

"Merlin?" Nimue said.

There was no answer.

She opened her eyes and stared at the empty room. There was the chair he had slept in; there was the melted wax that was all that was left of the candle that had lit their conversation as they had talked together, long into the night.

Merlin was gone. She'd been right to pledge herself to God after all—and wrong to believe in Merlin.

Nimue covered her face with her hands and wept.

Merlin rode as fast as he could, but all Mab's power was arrayed against him. He reached Badon Hill only to discover that Arthur had left there at dawn. One of his servants thought that Arthur had ridden to Winchester. Merlin followed, but Arthur was not there, and it was another day before Merlin reached Pendragon Castle.

I can't take many more expeditions like that one, Sir Rupert complained as he cantered over the drawbridge at Pendragon. Arthur was here—Merlin could see his blue standard flying from the tower.

"There won't be any more, old friend," Merlin

said, patting Sir Rupert's shoulder. "This may be the end of everything."

As he walked toward the Great Hall, Merlin summoned his wizard's staff, a slender rowan sapling with a round ball of clear crystal embedded among the tangled roots of its tip. It would make him look more impressive, and after two days on the road without sleep, he needed it to lean on as well. He was filled with a bone-weariness; Mab had reached out from the ashes of her greatest defeat to destroy them all. She had forced him to betray Nimue as well, and that injury was the one Merlin felt most keenly. Aching inside, he flung open the doors of the Great Hall.

The room from which Vortigern and Uther had both ruled was filled with shadows and the ghosts of other days. It seemed to Merlin that even the walls whispered together, mocking his hopes of a better life. One faint ray of sun streamed into the room, haloing Arthur's golden hair as he sat upon his throne surrounded by his chief knights. Exhausted and angry, Merlin's heart swelled with rage—all these men counted themselves as Arthur's friends. Why hadn't any of them kept him from the fearful mistake he had made?

"Out, my lords!" Merlin shouted. He banged his staff on the floor for added emphasis.

Only a few weeks ago, they would have left without question. Now they looked to Arthur, and only rose to go when he nodded his assent.

"And close the door behind you!" Merlin shouted as they left. He saw Sir Boris make the sign against evil, and for a moment he was glad that they resented and feared him.

"Merlin, what is it?" Arthur asked, coming to his feet and moving toward his old tutor. His face showed only concern for Merlin's obvious distress. He was dressed all in deep russet, his tunic trimmed with large flat circles of gold that matched the color of his hair, but for all his kingliness, Arthur did not yet wear a crown. Uther's crown had been buried with Uther, and a new one had not yet been made.

"Tell me the truth, Arthur. Two nights ago you slept with a woman." Merlin held back his anger with an effort.

Arthur's face reflected bewilderment and a touch of kingly temper. "Yes, if you must know, I did. Though I don't see why I need to tell you."

"That was Morgan le Fay," Merlin announced.

"Who?" Arthur said blankly.

"Her mother was the Lady Igraine," Merlin answered. "*Your* mother."

Arthur's face went grey with shock as the significance of Merlin's words sank in. Incest was as great a sin in the New Religion as illegitimacy, and as he realized the enormity of what he had done, Arthur fell slowly to his knees beside his throne and buried his face against his arm.

"I didn't know," he groaned. "I swear I didn't know. . . ."

"There will be a child. Mab will see to that." As the first shock of his defeat wore off, Merlin began to understand the game that Mab played here. As Merlin had taken Uther's child, Mab would take Arthur's, and mold him into the death of all their hopes.

If only he had stayed beside Arthur that night—if only he had warned him to be more suspicious—or sought a vision of the future. Against his will, such a vision came now. Merlin saw armies careening through fog, saw Arthur die at the hands of a bat-winged warrior whose symbol was the eclipse, as a burning comet overshadowed half the sky, turning the day to blood.

All their dreams for a golden city of peace and justice had been undone by one careless act, made possible because once again Merlin had underestimated his great enemy. But he had been thinking only of Nimue.

Nimue had told him the truth long ago, and she had been right, as always. As much as their love drew them together, Duty pulled them apart. Arthur was a good king, but he could not do battle against Mab. Only Merlin could do that.

"He'll be the future, and he'll destroy us," Merlin said inexorably. But Merlin would be there, watching over Arthur, to postpone that future for as long as he could.

He would not go to Avalon again.

It was late, after midnight prayers. For hours Nimue had wept and prayed, trying to understand how Merlin could have left her again after he had begged her to set aside her holy vows.

It wasn't his choice. Something terrible must have happened to call him away.

Mab. Merlin's great enemy, Queen of the Old Ways, yet still, in some strange way, his mother as well. Mab was the force that the New Religion prayed in the night to be defended from: it was Mab who sent nightmares and evil thoughts, who twisted lives into disorder and pain. She would not be easily defeated. Merlin had been wrong. His work was not over. He was still needed in the world.

Oh, let me be strong enough to bear it, to lend him my strength until the day we can both be free! Apart we are stronger than we are together; I will pray to keep our love alive, though this parting is the bitterest yet.

Nimue bowed her head, at peace with herself now even though her heart still ached with loss. The years she had spent within these walls as her soul healed into acceptance had not been in vain. She knew what Merlin was, and accepted him with all her heart—and accepted his destiny as well. She knew without question that they deserved their happiness, and that someday they would be together. But for now, if Merlin returned to Avalon, she would find the courage to send him away again without seeing him, and pray that someday the time would come when they could both be free.

She was about to return to her cell when suddenly a bright light shone full upon her face. It was coming from the garden. Curious, Nimue walked toward it, wondering who else wandered abroad tonight. But when she reached the spot, she realized it was the full moon's light she had seen, shining up at her from the ground.

"A mirror," Nimue said wonderingly, reaching for it. The mirror was large and ornate, its reflective surface made of fine silver polished smooth as oil. "But there are no mirrors in Avalon."

She picked it up, knowing without the strength to resist that what she was about to do would harm her. Throwing back her veil, she gazed into the mirror and saw her own face.

It was as bad as she'd feared. The scars had not faded and softened with age. They still covered her cheek and throat, the reminder of the Great Dragon and of Mab's wickedness. The reminder of the danger of magic—and the holiness of the war Merlin waged.

Suddenly there was a rumble of thunder from the clear night sky, and a flash of lightning enveloped her, searing her flesh to the bone. Before Nimue could gather her wits to scream, it was gone.

And so were the scars.

Nimue stared into the mirror, unable to believe what she saw. Then, realizing whose work this must be, she slowly lowered the mirror.

Mab was standing before her in the garden.

The Queen of the Old Ways had been a force in Nimue's life since she was sixteen years old. She was now nearly forty, and this was the first time Nimue had ever seen Mab in the flesh. She was a tiny woman, dressed in fantastical dark robes that seemed to be woven from cobwebs and shadows. Her skin glittered as if she were not made of flesh, but of moonlight and crystal.

"You see how I can change you?" Mab asked. Her voice was a toneless hissing. She spoke carefully, as if human language were foreign to her, as if her native tongue were something else entirely.

"You've changed me already," Nimue said evenly. "You've scarred me." No good could come of talking to Queen Mab. On this subject Merlin and the New Religion were in complete agreement. Nimue turned away.

"I know," Mab said to her back. "It's so unfair."

"Unfair?" Nimue said incredulously, turning back to face Mab. "That was *evil.*"

"With evil all around me, I can do nothing but evil—to survive!" Mab put on a show of contrition, but Nimue knew the fairy queen felt nothing. Merlin had told her that Mab's heart was a stone.

"Oh," Nimue said in angry mock sympathy. "That's too easy. You can fight it, like Merlin."

Mab watched her unblinkingly, as if she were the raven that was her totem.

"It's because of Merlin that all this came about," Mab wheedled.

"That's not true!" Nimue said, stung by the accusation. Once again she reminded herself that even talking to the Queen of the Old Ways held a thousand hidden dangers. "Why are you here, Mab?" she said sternly.

"To make you an offer," Mab hissed in her graveyard voice. "I'll restore your beauty if you take Merlin away to a place I've created for you. You can live with him there to the end of your days."

Nimue glanced at the perfect reflection in the mirror she still held. *This* was her true self, not that travesty Mab had forced her to wear all the days of her life. "And be happy?" she asked.

"And be happy," Mab agreed quickly.

But no. If God had delivered her into Mab's hands to be scarred by the dragon, she must try to accept her fate, and not use it as an excuse to do evil herself. If she did, she would be as wicked as Mab.

"He has a destiny, Mab. It would keep him from his purpose," Nimue said.

"It would keep him from wasting his life," Mab retorted.

Nimue wavered. Wasn't that as true as its opposite? Merlin had placed Uther on the throne and seen him destroy all hope for peace. Now Arthur faced some new trouble—for why else would Merlin have left her? Didn't his absence mean that Arthur was doomed to fail, too? What if Mab was right?

No. If Mab was right, the Queen of the Old Ways would be arguing with Merlin, not with her. Mab was trying to get her to betray Merlin.

"He believes that fighting for what is right isn't a waste," Nimue said. "I wouldn't do that to him. I love him."

"*I* love him," Mab asserted, taking a step closer to Nimue. Now they stood face-to-face.

"You hate him," Nimue countered.

"I hate him . . . too," Mab admitted reluctantly. "What's your answer?"

"No," Nimue said baldly.

Mab seemed surprised by her response, as far as Nimue could read any expression on that inhumanly beautiful face. "I'm . . . sorry," Mab said slowly. She stepped back. "If you change your mind, just call my name. Out loud." She flung up her arms, and there was another flare of intolerable brightness. The thunder rumbled, and Mab was gone.

Nimue put a hand up to her face, and felt once more the roughness of the scars. She flung the silver mirror as far from her as she could.

CHAPTER EIGHT

THE THRONE
OF LOVE

A full year passed before Merlin saw Arthur again. He could not bring himself to return to Avalon; though Merlin came to realize that he had not betrayed Nimue, he *had* failed her. Instead, Merlin went north, but even his beloved forest held no peace for him, and so the king's wizard roamed the length and breadth of Arthur's kingdom, listening to what was said of the new king, and using the simple healing arts he had learned long ago from his foster mother Ambrosia. He made no secret of who he was and where he was, and one day, word reached him that Arthur wanted to see him again.

As Merlin rode along the bank of the Astolat into what had once been Excalibur Village, he could see that much had changed. On the place where Excalibur had been buried in the rock, a great city was rising to spread along the shores of the lake into which the river fed: Camelot, the golden city. Arthur's dream.

As Merlin rode slowly through the piles of stone and scaffolding shrouding the rising buildings, he heard someone call his name.

"Merlin!" Arthur ran to his side.

Arthur had changed in the last year, the king Arthur had become erasing the last marks of the boy Merlin had left behind. But it was still with his old joyousness that Arthur came up to his old tutor, smiling as though there had never been any rift between them.

"What's all this, Arthur?" Merlin asked.

"A promise made flesh. I'm building the city of Camelot." He took Sir Rupert's bridle, and began to walk toward the architect's pavilion. "It's a new beginning," he said, a little diffidently. "I made a mistake that night, but I can't believe I'm condemned for all eternity for one mistake."

"Not by me," Merlin said warmly. He recognized the gentle teachings of the monks of Avalon who took their teaching from Pelagius and not Augustine, and was happy that Arthur had found a way to transform his guilt into something constructive. "I'll never condemn you, Arthur."

The young king smiled, but Camelot was not the reason he had summoned Merlin back.

"I hope to marry Lord Lot's daughter," Arthur announced.

Merlin had heard that Gawain and his father had both accepted the New Religion and been baptized last winter, and this must mean that the rest of the family had as well, for Arthur would never marry someone who clung to the Old Ways. And each day there were fewer of the Old Believers in the land, as Arthur's sincerity and genuine humility won converts where fire and the sword had been unable to.

"Ah," Merlin said. Marriage would be the best way to banish the last lingering specter of Morgan's trickery. "Do you love her?"

"She'll make a splendid queen and a good wife. We hope to be married here at Camelot." Arthur grinned, looking around at all the half-completed buildings. "I don't care if it's not finished. Will you be there with me?"

"I'll be honored," Merlin said warmly. "What's her name, your bride?"

"Guinevere," Arthur said.

Guinevere of the Iceni was Lot's youngest daughter. She and Arthur had set the date of their marriage for autumn, at harvesttide, and a few weeks before, Gawain brought her to Camelot.

The city was still unfinished, but it was growing fast, thanks to the army of workers engaged in every facet of its building. Arthur had found a use for the great army that Britain had been afflicted with since Vortigern's time—he had them taught a trade. Camelot was to be only the first of Arthur's projects; when it was complete he meant to remake Londinium as well. His grandfather's old fortress, Pendragon, was already being torn down, its stone used to build the golden city.

The cathedral would be finished first, then the castle, but at the moment, neither structure was complete.

Guinevere had an elaborate pavilion set up outside the city for her use. The first night she was there, Arthur invited Merlin to supper to meet her.

Arthur's tent was still the same one he had used in his brief military campaign against Lord Lot, but now it had been transformed into a kingly palace. The floor of the main room had been covered with thick carpets brought from the east, and the walls were hung with tapestries showing scenes of hunting and war. Massive pieces of furniture that would someday grace the halls of Camelot filled the tent—a long oak table whose legs were carved with griffins and acorns, a sideboard that glittered with silver goblets and decanters of Roman glass. The chairs were carved and painted, softened with embroidered cushions that had been stuffed with goose down, lavender, and myrrh. The chamber was lit by a dozen candelabra, each taller than a tall man and made of solid fine-wrought silver.

The table was laid for the meal to come with plates of silver and gold brought from Uther's treasury and laden with the delicacies of Britain: partridge, goose, swan-cased pies, and fruits in syrup lay on the gleaming white cloth.

Merlin paused for a moment in the doorway, dazzled by the splendor that filled the little tent. It seemed that all that was good in life had been gathered together in this one place, and the wonder of it was like an assault on the senses, or like rain after a long drought. The last kings of Britain had been greedy and miserly, and Arthur was nothing like them. He spent money for the pleasure it gave both others and himself, and saw no reason that the court at Camelot should not be as lavish as anything known in Rome itself.

It was a small private occasion—of all of Arthur's inner circle, only Gawain was there with his sister.

"This is Guinevere," Arthur said, leading her forward.

She was dark-haired and dark-eyed as Igraine had been, but Merlin, who had seen both women, thought Guinevere was the more beautiful of the two. She did not have Igraine's self-possession, though that might be simply because she was a year younger than Arthur. She regarded Merlin with apprehension, her eyes wide.

"Your ladyship," Merlin said.

Guinevere glanced at Arthur, unsure of whether she should curtsey to Merlin. When she married Arthur she would be Britain's Queen, but Merlin was Arthur's wizard. At last she extended her hand, spots of bright color high on her cheeks. Merlin bowed over it.

"Now I have you both beside me," Arthur said. "My dearest friend, and my dearest love."

Merlin glanced at Gawain, but the prince's face reflected nothing but happiness and approval. Guinevere blushed, lowering her eyes modestly. It should have been a perfect moment of happiness, but at that moment Merlin felt a faint thrill of warning, as though this golden moment held the seeds of its own destruction.

What was Morgan doing at this moment? The child she had conceived with Arthur would have been born by now, but she had sent no word, content to wait within Tintagel's walls like some malignant spider.

Suddenly the happy scene before him took on an ominous overtone. Such moments of happiness were not meant to last, and Arthur had already sown the seeds of his own destruction.

Less than a month later, Arthur and Guinevere married. Though the cathedral still lacked a roof and windows, the wedding ceremony was held there just as Arthur had wished. The ceremony was attended by all the nobility of Britain—lords and ladies dressed in their finest gowns and jewels. Even the weather had cooperated, for the September day was clear and bright, gilding the stones of the church with the sun's own gold.

It was somehow fitting, Merlin thought, gazing up at the heavens, that Arthur should be married under the open sky. The best of the Old Ways and the New Religion were blended in him and in his reign. Perhaps they could outface Mab's ill-wishing and Morgan's curse after all.

Beside Merlin, Arthur fidgeted nervously. The king was dressed all in white brocade—bareheaded, for the much-promised crown still was not ready—and waited at the altar.

"You weren't this nervous facing Lot across a battlefield," Merlin reminded him.

"This is Lot's *daughter*," Arthur replied, as though that made a difference.

There was a stirring at the back of the church and the bride appeared. Guinevere was dressed all in white silk samite, and wearing her dowry jewels, a pearl-studded coronet and necklace that had come all the way from Byzantium. Pearls hung down like tears in veils on both sides of her face.

Gawain led her forward, his face bright with pride, and suddenly the nervous young girl Merlin had met was gone. Guinevere walked proudly, head high, every inch a queen.

The ceremony was brief. Arthur and Guinevere clasped hands over the holy fire and swore to obey all the laws of marriage. The priest pronounced the blessing in a good Church Latin, and then it was over. Britain once more had a Queen.

The feast that night was a great marvel, providing every delicacy the realm could offer. It went on for hours, with every noble vying with his fellows to be the one who presented Arthur with the costliest and rarest wedding gift.

Sir Ban of Benwick gifted Arthur with a tiny boat made of gold and silver that was small enough to fit in the palm of his hand. The boat was named Pridwen, and when it was set in the water it would grow to its full size, and hold enough provisions to keep ten men for a journey of ten weeks. Sir Palomedes, a Saracen who had left his far lands and journeyed to Britain because of a prophecy, gave Arthur a spear he had won in a joust with the Red Knight of the Red Lands. The spear, Rhongomyniad the Roaring, could pierce through seven stones at a cast, and would not rest until it tasted the enemy's blood. But it was Lord Lot's gift that Arthur valued most.

Since Badon Hill, Arthur had been turning over in

his mind the idea of an order of chivalry that would bring to an end all the fighting among the lords of Britain. Within the order there would be no degrees of rank, and each knight would be pledged to come to the aid of any of his brother knights who called for his help. Such an order would be vital to Britain's peace and safety when Arthur undertook the quest he had planned. He had decided to call this new order The Round Table, because a round table had no head or foot, and all who sat around it would be equal, just as Arthur wished all his knights to be.

Lord Lot had caused such a table to be made, and tonight he presented it to his new son-in-law. The table was carried in at the end of the feast, and everyone marveled at its size. The table was thirty feet across and decorated in alternating bands of green and white radiating out from the center. Along the outside edge was a space where each knight's name could be painted as he joined The Round Table. Arthur's name was already there, and he stood, raising his golden cup in salute.

"You see before you my promise that justice and right shall rule in Britain, and all shall be treated fairly, no matter whether they be of high degree or low. Who will join me to protect the weak, defend the innocent, and bring peace and prosperity to our land?"

Every knight in the room was on his feet in an instant, shouting his promise to join Arthur's Round Table.

"And I promise all of you that the Ages of Chaos are over forever! The light of goodness shall once more shine over Britain, and its token, the Holy Grail, shall be brought to Camelot to heal the land. I myself shall go in search of it—this I swear!"

They all cheered him, but Merlin, watching from a corner, felt a twinge of unease. This quest Arthur proposed would leave the realm undefended, and Arthur would leave deadly enemies behind him who would be happy to work mischief in his absence . . . enemies like Morgan le Fay.

"Your announcement came as . . . quite a surprise," Merlin said.

Arthur was showing him the latest work on the city. As the masons rushed to put roofs upon the buildings before the first snows, it seemed that the city changed hourly, coming closer to the fulfillment of a dream.

But whose dream?

"It must be done," Arthur said soberly. "While the Grail is lost to us, the harm done to the land by Queen Mab cannot be healed. In finding the Grail, I can both heal the land and atone for my own foolishness."

"Who will you send on this quest?" Merlin asked.

"I will go myself, and as soon as a suitable champion for Britain can be chosen. There will be a tourney at Easter, and the knight who wins it will be my deputy and Guinevere's champion while I am away."

"But, Sire—" Merlin protested. Six months! Though Arthur worked long days conscientiously setting Britain in order, that was not enough time to appoint qualified advisers and deputies to all the kingdom's vacant posts even if the king had meant to stay home. To leave so quickly, with so many things unsettled, would plunge the realm into chaos once more.

"My mind is made up, Merlin. The Grail is basic to Britain's spiritual well-being. Until it is found, nothing else matters. And only when it has been found will I be worthy of my queen," Arthur told him firmly.

Merlin had heard rumors that Arthur and his new Queen slept apart, but he had not had the heart to seek confirmation of them. He had feared the worst, and it seemed to be true: betrayed by Morgan le Fay, Arthur did not believe in his own worthiness to rule.

As the days passed, Merlin realized that nothing he could do would change Arthur's mind. He could only trust that Arthur's instincts were sound, and do what he could to support Arthur's wishes. And so, Merlin's next course of action was clear: he must go to see Morgan le Fay, and learn what he could of her plans for the future.

As he rode up to the gates of Tintagel Keep on that late October day, Merlin saw that the castle's towers were enshrouded in an enchanted mist that shielded Tintagel from the world. If Arthur had ever searched for his half-sister, he would have searched in vain. Only someone versed in the Old Ways could penetrate this wall of witchery and gain the keep.

As he guided Sir Rupert through the gates, Merlin discerned something he had not sensed for many years. The very air was filled with magic, just as that of Mab's domain had been.

He dismounted in the courtyard, and stablehands came to take Sir Rupert. With his otherworld Sight,

Merlin could see what they really were—not human men, but mice transformed by magic into servants. They did not wear, as one might expect Morgan's servants to, the silver and green livery of the Duchy of Cornwall. Instead, their tabards were black, with a silver eclipse upon the breast.

The sign he had seen in his vision.

With a sinking heart, Merlin went to call upon the mistress of Tintagel Keep.

Morgan le Fay was happier than she had ever been in her life. She had everything she could ever have wanted—a dashing cavalier to keep her company, clothes and jewels and wealth beyond price, and a beautiful, perfect, child.

"Mordred," she cooed to the redheaded toddler seated with her on the bearskin rug before the fire. "My little Mordred."

The child crowed and clapped his hands. Though he had been born only a few months ago, Mordred was already a well-grown toddler. Magic had seen to that, the same magic that had brought Morgan so many good things.

At that moment a lady's maid—she had previously been, if Morgan recalled correctly, a chicken—opened the door to the Great Hall. "Merlin is here to see you, my lady."

Merlin! Queen Mab had promised Morgan that she would be able to humble the wizard who had destroyed her family. Let him see that he had failed to destroy her.

"Send him in," Morgan said disdainfully. "You

hear that, Mordred?" Morgan said to her child. "There's a wizard come to see us. Won't that be fun?"

As soon as Merlin entered the Great Hall he received another unpleasant shock. It had only been a year and some months since the aftermath of Badon Hill. The child Arthur had begotten should still be in swaddling clothes. Instead, he was the size of a child nearly two. Oh, Mab had meddled most terribly in Morgan's life!

"My lady Morgan," Merlin said with grave courtesy. "Do you know why I'm here?"

"Say hello to my son, Mordred," Morgan interrupted haughtily. The light from the windows fell full upon her face where she knelt on the fur beside her son, and Merlin saw Morgan's compensation for her aid in Mab's wickedness. When he'd last seen her, she'd been an ugly child. Now she was beautiful as only those granted fairy gifts could be.

The unease he had felt riding up to Tintagel's walls ripened into horror. Mab did not bestow her gifts lightly, but she had lavished magic upon Morgan and Tintagel. What measureless repayment of her favors did she anticipate—and what did Morgan have?

"Master Mordred," Merlin said with a tiny bow. The auburn-haired child was dressed in a tunic the color of dried blood. Silvery symbols of the Old Ways gleamed through the fabric, and the scent of magic was strong in the air.

Mordred made a face at Merlin and stuck out his tongue, jeering impudently.

"That was rude, Mordred," his mother admonished him dotingly. "You can do anything you like, but you must never be rude! 'Rude' is being weak." She got to her feet and came toward her guest. "You were saying, Merlin?" Morgan said insolently.

"Do you know why I'm here?" Merlin repeated patiently.

"H'm." Morgan pretended to think deeply. "It has to do with my son. Hasn't he grown?" She smiled sweetly.

"Yes he has—and more than is natural, I'm sorry to say."

"Yes of course: it's magic," Morgan said happily. No regret was visible in her beautiful eyes.

Was this how his own life would have gone if Merlin had not had Ambrosia to care for him, teach him, love him? If Blaise and Herne—and Bran and all the other animals of the forest—had not been there to guide his first stirrings toward a code of ethics and morality? What would he have become without them, once Mab had begun to guide him in the ways of magic?

What would little Mordred become now? Genuine concern for the boy filled Merlin's next words.

"Morgan, I beg you. For the sake of the country, you must not teach him the Old Ways."

Now Morgan's facade of superior politeness shattered. Her face was contorted with fury. "This country means *nothing* to me!" she raged. "A bastard sits on the throne that should be mine—a bastard begotten in blood when his father, Uther, seduced my mother and killed my father!"

"It's the future that I'm thinking of," Merlin said.

"You *would* think of the future, Merlin," Morgan mocked, "because the past is too painful. *You* chose Uther to be king; *you* helped him seduce my mother and destroy me. In the end, you begot Mordred just as surely as Queen Mab and Arthur!"

How Morgan's words hurt—it was as if she could see into his secret soul and touch on all the most painful memories.

"I know that, but I can live with it," Merlin said quietly. If he had not given in to Uther and done what he wished, the whole country would have been drowned in blood, and Arthur would never have been born. Arthur's victory paid for all the transgressions of Merlin's life.

"Just as you'll have to live with the fact that *Mordred* will be king," Morgan cooed poisonously.

A child raised and molded by Mab, created out of the Old Ways to be its tool and hers? "No," Merlin said soberly, "that can never be."

Mordred, growing tired of listening to the adults talk, wandered over to the long table that stood in the center of the Great Hall. There was a knife upon the table, its bronze blade shining brightly in the sun. With an intent look upon his face, Mordred grasped the knife in his chubby hands, and then flung it with preternatural strength toward his mother's visitor.

Merlin caught it bare inches from his heart, but if Morgan was alarmed at Mordred's behavior, she showed no sign of it. She knelt beside Mordred and kissed him upon the cheek.

"Mordred, Merlin is a guest," she said with arch reproof. "Don't be naughty. He just wants attention," she said in an aside to Merlin. "You'll get all the attention you want when you're king, dear. And he will be, Merlin," Morgan added. "He's Arthur's son."

But not the son of Arthur's wife, and Britain is now a Christian realm; such matters as legitimacy will mean more to the people with each passing year. As they did to your father, Morgan—Gorlois was a staunch defender of the new faith. How he hated it that Uther accepted my help; I think it was that, more than Uther's lust for Igraine, that drove him into open rebellion. . . .

"What about the Old Ways?" Merlin asked Morgan. *You are Gorlois's daughter, and he lived every day of his life in concern for his immortal soul. Surely what you have done to get Mordred weighs heavily on your soul as well?*

"You're in no position to lecture me on what I can or cannot do," Morgan said haughtily, rising to her feet. "The Old Ways have been good to me. They've given me a son and made me beautiful."

"Oh, Morgan." Merlin crossed to where she stood and cupped her face in his hands. "It's only an illusion."

She stared up at him, her eyes mocking and bitter. "Beauty is always an illusion, Merlin. Didn't you know that?"

Suddenly there was a grinding shattering sound. Merlin whirled in the direction it came from, and as he watched, Mab and Frik pushed through the door in a shower of splinters.

"We thought we'd come in the traditional way, through the door," Frik said.

"It's traditional to open it first," Merlin said dryly.

"Mordred, look who's here! Your Auntie Mab and Uncle Frik," Morgan cried delightedly.

It was obviously not the first time Mab and Frik had visited Tintagel Keep. With a cry of delight, Mordred flung himself upon Mab, who swung him around and around, cackling with delight. Inside himself, Merlin shuddered. It was like watching a baby play with a cobra—only it was Mordred's soul that was in danger, not his life. All the aversion he felt for Mab and the Old Ways was reborn anew as he watched her with Mordred. The Queen of the Old Ways was a poisonous flower—nothing wholesome could flourish in her shadow.

And to see her here, flaunting her welcome at Tintagel, so openly a presence in Morgan's life, and the child's. . . .

"It's been ages, Merlin," Frik said. He'd changed his gnomish form from that of the pedantic scholar Merlin remembered. Now Frik was tall and handsome, with flowing blond hair and a sword upon his hip. "Do you ever think of your old school where I tried to teach you the fundamentals of magic?" Frik crossed to Morgan and kissed her hand. She hung on his arm, staring triumphantly at Merlin.

"He could have been my star pupil," Frik confided to Morgan, "but he proved . . ."

"Disappointing," Mab hissed. "But *you* won't, will you, Mordred?" The baby giggled in delight.

"Isn't he handsome?" Morgan gloated.

"Handsome is as handsome does," Frik said, with a little of his old schoolroom pendantry showing through the swaggering gallant. "What does that mean? I've never really understood the phrase."

Morgan laughed and kissed him.

Mab had brought little Mordred a golden crown and scepter, and a brown-and-white pony just his size. "Toys, Mordred," she said, placing the crown upon his head and lifting him onto the pony. "Auntie always brings you lots of lovely toys. . . ."

"You see, Merlin?" Morgan said. "You took my family away from me, and now I have a new one." Frik kissed her hand, and then her wrist, playing the courtly lover.

"It won't last, Morgan," Merlin warned desperately. He knew Mab's tricks—she and Frik could be charming when they chose, but it was all an act, a show put on until the need for it was past.

"Nothing does," Morgan said simply.

Merlin took one last look around the room—the amorous lovers, Mab doting on her hellborn babe—and turned to go. There was nothing he could do here. It was too late. Mab had made herself too completely at home. Morgan was selfishly blind to the consequences of her liaison.

"Don't you see it—feel it?" Mab said. "I'm winning, Merlin! I have the precious gift of patience; it will be years before Mordred can claim the throne but I can wait. Time means nothing to me!"

If that were really true, then Mab would not plot so desperately to retain her power. But just as time was running out for Mab, it was also running out for Arthur's golden city. While Arthur quested for the Grail, Morgan and her son would be free to work their mischief freely in Britain. If Arthur could not be persuaded to forsake his quest—if he were gone when Mordred reached out for the throne—then there was nothing Merlin could do to save Camelot.

Nothing.

"You'll be the death of Arthur and the end of all poor Merlin's dreams, won't you, my sweetie?" Mab cooed to the baby.

Merlin turned and stalked from the room.

"Oh, look!" Morgan cried. "The big bad wizard can't do a thing! Run, Wizard!" she cried, and the others took up the chant: "Run, run, run—"

Merlin slammed the door behind him, cutting off their mocking laughter.

Just as it had been the last time Morgan was involved, Merlin's business with the king was urgent, but this time he made sure not to burst into an important countil. If Mordred's existence were to become public knowledge, it would undo all of Arthur's good works before they even began.

Merlin found Arthur in the royal mews, among his birds of prey. The Master of Hawks was on an errand elsewhere, and Arthur was alone. All around him, hawks and falcons huddled on their perches, the bright leather of their hoods like jewels in the musty dimness.

"Your Majesty?" Merlin said.

"Merlin!" Arthur turned around, his smile welcoming. It faded as he studied Merlin's face. "You look tired."

"I have had some . . . difficult news." Merlin hesitated. Should he tell Arthur what he had learned? He must. It was secrecy that had doomed them all in the first place. Arthur, of all men, deserved to know the whole truth. "I have seen your son. His name is Mordred."

Arthur flinched at the words. Merlin could see the hopeful need in his eyes, the desire to ask about Mordred. Arthur was by nature a loving man, and if only things had been different, he could have welcomed Mordred into his life eagerly.

"I . . . see," Arthur said at last. "Merlin, what have you come to say to me?"

"I have come to ask you—no, to *beg* you—put off this quest until matters here in Britain are more settled; until you have an heir—"

"I have an heir," Arthur said bitterly. "Mordred, begotten in sin and treachery, out of the Old Ways. There can be no other heir to my crown until the Grail is found. When I have achieved it, the Grail will wash me clean of all sin and restore the land."

Arthur's grey eyes stared levelly into Merlin's, as if to try to convince him by that alone of how certain Arthur was of the truth of his words. But it was not necessary. If this was what Arthur believed, then it was true. If he would not consummate his marriage to the queen while the weight of his sin lay so heavily upon him, he would beget no other child than Mordred.

"You told me once," Merlin said, "that you did not believe you could be condemned for all eternity for one mistake."

"God will not condemn me," Arthur said, "but I am not alone in this sin. There is Morgan, and now Mordred. I seek the Grail for them as well as for

Britain, so that we can all escape the failures of the past into a joyous future of hope. Only when the Grail is returned to Britain will I know that God has truly cleansed us all."

Merlin's shoulders slumped. Arthur was as fixed in his course as Morgan was in hers. There was no hope of turning Arthur from his quest—and the worst of it was, this journey was inspired by the best of reasons, the purest idealism. How could Merlin argue against it, when to do so would be to argue against every lesson he had ever taught to Arthur?

"I suppose you are right, Sire. And I suppose I had better go and seek you a perfect champion, someone who will guard the kingdom while you are far away."

Once again Merlin stood upon the shore of the Enchanted Lake. He had come here in many seasons, but never before in autumn. The birches on the shores of the lake were crowned with gold, and the very blueness of the sky seemed to speak of the impermanence of all things. Autumn was the dying time, when the land prepared itself for the long sleep that was both a death and a rebirth.

Out on the lake some ducks, about to embark upon their migration southward, bobbed upon the surface. A gentle touch of Merlin's magic set them diving beneath the chop. A moment later, the Lady of the Lake appeared from beneath the surface of the water.

It was the first time Merlin had seen her since he had come to beg Excalibur from her many years ago, and it seemed to him that her beauty was more ethereal, less of this world, than it had ever seemed before.

"Merlin?" she whispered, and her silvery voice echoed back from the wind and the water. "You're troubled again?"

Merlin smiled ruefully. "It's still the same cry for help, Lady. Your sister, Mab, grows more powerful."

"And I grow weaker," the Lady of the Lake sighed. Her hands moved gently at her sides, holding her position in the lake of air. Her collar of shining fish flitted about her throat like tiny spots of light.

"What can I do?" Merlin asked urgently. "I have to find a man to guard the throne while Arthur goes questing for the Holy Grail. The temptation will be to seize the crown while he's gone."

"You need a man pure in heart," the Lady of the Lake told him gently.

"I've tried to find him before," Merlin said. "He doesn't exist."

The Lady of the Lake blinked slowly as she regarded him from glowing blue eyes. In a voice even fainter than before she told him, "The answer is at Joyous Gard. My ship will take you. . . ."

As Merlin watched, the silvery figure shimmered out of sight. And in the distance, Merlin saw a ship sailing toward him across the lake.

It was like and yet unlike the ship that had carried the young Merlin to the Land of Magic so many years ago. This slender craft had a hull the same pale blue as the Lake, and a tall mast with a painted sail. From these hints, Merlin knew that Joyous Gard was far away. But the Lady of the Lake had always stood his friend. Without hesitation, Merlin climbed into the boat and set sail.

*   *   *

The ship sailed into the bank of mist that was a gateway between worlds, and when it came out again, there was no land to be seen in any direction and the air smelled of the open sea. The bright sun of summer, and not the cool light of autumn, beat down upon Merlin, warming his bones, and Merlin realized that the boat sailed not only through space but through time, to that enchanted land, the future. It was as if he voyaged through a dream and more than a dream—a dream of a dream. *One day they'll describe me, Arthur, Guinevere, and Camelot as a dream,* he thought to himself. A shimmering vision danced before his eyes, of Joyous Gard with its golden towers, and Merlin knew that this dream was alive, as all good dreams are. That no matter what the future held, Arthur's dream would live as well.

The warm sun and the gentle rocking of the enchanted boat did their work, and soon Merlin, weary from so many long journeys, could stay awake no longer. His eyes closed, and he slept, stretched out full-length upon the bottom of the boat.

It seemed as if Merlin had slept centuries, until all the world he had known had passed away. When he awoke, the ship was still, the sail half-furled, and a small boy was standing beside the vessel, staring down at Merlin gravely. The boy's hair was the white-blond color that seldom lasts beyond early childhood, and he wore a coronet of gold and royal purple.

"Who are you?" the boy asked.

Merlin groaned a little as he sat up. Magic ship or

not, the stiffness of age was beginning to touch his bones. "I'm Merlin," he answered. "The wizard."

But instead of being impressed at that declaration, the boy laughed. "There aren't any wizards left," he scoffed.

"I'm the last of them," Merlin answered, knowing somehow that it was true. He got to his feet. "And who are you?"

"Galahad," the boy answered. "My mother is the Lady Elaine and my father is Sir Lancelot." He stared at Merlin a moment longer, then seemed to remember his manners. "I bid you welcome to Joyous Gard, Merlin the wizard."

"I thank you, Master Galahad," Merlin answered absently.

Sir Lancelot must be the good man the Lady of the Lake had sent Merlin here to find. He stepped out of the boat and looked around.

The Lady's boat had landed on a crescent-shaped beach of glittering white sand. Beyond it, upon the headland, stood Joyous Gard, as beautiful as it had been in his vision.

If only Arthur were here to see it! Lancelot's castle was everything Arthur had dreamed Camelot would be; a castle forged from the fabric of dreams. Stone carved to seem as light as air and as lacy as sea foam rose up to form towers taller than the tallest tree. Its steep conical roofs were plated in pure gold, and pennons in a thousand colors flew from every spire. If this were a dream of the future, then it was a future that Arthur had helped to create.

"It's . . . beautiful," Merlin whispered.

"Joyous Gard is dedicated to honor and chivalry," Galahad said proudly. "It is a place where the strong defend the weak."

"Then it is the place I have searched for all my life," Merlin said. "Pray take me to your father, Master Galahad."

Galahad took Merlin through the castle courtyard and led him not to an audience chamber, but toward the forge. Everything Merlin saw in Joyous Gard was bright and clean and airy, and he felt like a revenant, like a dark ghost from a time of blood and battle who had somehow strayed into an era of civilized good fellowship. No one in Joyous Gard even wore armor. It was as if this land had been at peace so long it had forgotten all the arts of war. But when they reached their destination, Merlin saw that one man, at least, was still a warrior.

"There he is," Galahad said, pointing.

Lancelot was a tall fair man. He was bronze where Arthur was golden, but in Lancelot, Merlin thought he saw a shadow of the man Arthur would become. Lancelot wore a dark tunic trimmed in silver Celtic knotwork, and wide silver bracers that gleamed in the sun. As Merlin approached, Lancelot was holding a sword to the grinding stone, honing its edge as the smith turned the wheel.

He stopped as Merlin and Galahad approached. Striking the sword against an anvil, he held the blade to his ear, gauging its tone.

"What does it say?" Merlin asked.

"It says, 'I will prove strong and true in battle'—

and to be wary of strangers," Lancelot added, regarding Merlin.

Well, I suppose I do look a bit out of place here, Merlin thought to himself.

"Father," Galahad said, "this is Merlin."

At once Lancelot's manner changed. "Merlin? Ah, well, then. You're no stranger. I've heard of you, and you are certainly welcome to Joyous Gard. Galahad, run and tell the Lady Elaine that we have a special visitor."

The boy sped off on his errand, his bright hair flashing in the sun.

"Now tell me, Merlin, what brings you to Joyous Gard," Lancelot said. He flung his arm companionably over Merlin's shoulder and the two men began to walk toward the main castle keep.

"It is a magnificent place," Merlin said, still looking around.

"As close to heaven as we could find on earth . . . though I sometimes wish there were a few more dragons to slay."

"I cannot offer you dragons, Sir Lancelot, but I can offer you a great adventure," Merlin said as they crossed from light into shadow. Lancelot was about to reply, when he was distracted by the arrival of the Lady Elaine.

The lady of Joyous Gard wore a silvery gown sewn with pearls, and her rich auburn hair cascaded down her back, swept away from her face by a gold and pearl diadem in the antique style.

"Elaine!" Lancelot said heartily. "Look! Merlin the wizard has come to offer me adventure."

"Master Merlin." Like Lancelot, she seemed to know Merlin already, at least by reputation, but unlike her husband, what Elaine knew did not seem to cheer her. She regarded Merlin with troubled eyes. "What sort of adventure brings you to Joyous Gard?"

"I've come here to find a man to defend King Arthur in his kingdom. But he must be a good man, pure of heart," Merlin said.

"You've found him," Elaine answered. Her expression lightened as she crossed to her husband and took his arm. They gazed at each other lovingly. "My Lancelot has slain dragons and overthrown tyrants. He is the best knight in the world, and there is no other that is his match. But it must have been a long journey that brought you here, Master Merlin. Surely you will rest and refresh yourself before you return to Camelot?"

Merlin hesitated. "I fear, Lady, that every hour I am away from Camelot brings disaster closer."

"Then we will leave at once," Lancelot said decisively. "But it will take some time to gather together my arms and to saddle Bayard. At least take a cup of wine before we depart."

"Gladly," Merlin answered.

Elaine conducted him to the Great Hall and ordered a servant to bring wine and cakes. Lancelot went to see to his equipment, and there was a spring in his step that had been absent before.

"You seem troubled, Lady Elaine," Merlin said cautiously, when he had gone.

"I shall miss him," Elaine said simply. "But Lancelot is a valiant heart. He was not made for peace, but for war. If adventure beckons, he must go. It is his nature."

Merlin wanted to tell Elaine that her husband was in no danger, but he dared not say something which might not be true. As much as Joyous Gard seemed to promise that the defeat of the Old Ways and the triumph of Good would surely come, the land the magic ship had brought him to was not the only future that might befall. And so he drank the wine, when it came, and said nothing.

Much later, long after the knowledge could do him any good, Merlin realized that while Elaine had been right to say that Lancelot had all of knighthood's virtues, it was also true that the best knight in the world had every one of its failings as well: impatience, temper, and overconfidence. But on this sunny day in Joyous Gard, as Merlin sat drinking sweet wine and listening to the music of the sea through the windows of the Great Hall, that realization was far in the future.

It was nearly an hour before Lancelot returned. He was garbed now all in silvery chain mail that shone like the scales of a fish, and carried under one arm a plumed helm of an unfamiliar design. In his other hand he carried a swordbelt wrapped around a sword and scabbard, and Elaine hurried to him to buckle it about his waist. Merlin could see the name of the sword written on the scabbard: *Joyeuse,* named for Joyous Gard itself.

"Are you sure this is what you want?" Merlin heard him ask Elaine in a low voice.

"It's not what *I* want," she whispered back. "It's

what *you* want. I can't hold you back. It's your chance for one last great adventure."

Lancelot smiled and kissed her fondly. "I'm ready!" he called to Merlin.

"Then let us be off," Merlin said.

The servants were already leading Lancelot's great black warhorse down the beach to the magic ship when Merlin and the others arrived. Elaine stood stoically, refusing to weep; young Galahad glanced from one parent to the other, not understanding why his mother was so sad when his father was so happy.

Despite Merlin's misgivings, the black Bayard stepped daintily into the ship without any trouble. Lancelot followed, and Merlin came last of all. The moment he had clambered into the boat, its sail filled with an unfelt wind and it began to slide gently off the sand. Elaine and Galahad stood upon the shore, waving good-bye.

"Galahad!" Lancelot called. "Protect your mother while I'm away!"

The boy waved harder, but the boat was already too far for his reply to reach them. It sailed swiftly, and soon the mist rose up around them once more.

Merlin had done well to be so hasty in his visit to Joyous Gard. Though the journey seemed to him to have been only a matter of hours, six months time had passed in Britain. When the boat grounded on the shore of the Enchanted Lake and Merlin was able to ask questions of the citizens of nearby villages, he found that it was spring, and the Eastertide tourney that would choose the champion of Britain was about to begin.

As Merlin and Lancelot rode for Camelot, they heard about it in every village they passed, for Arthur had declared there would be a holiday throughout the kingdom while the tourney was fought.

"Everything moves too fast," Merlin muttered to himself.

"What's that, Sir Wizard?" Lancelot asked. The knight was in high spirits at the prospect of a tournament.

"Nothing," Merlin answered. It was enough that Lancelot had come to champion Arthur while Arthur went upon this quest. He did not need to know about Mab, and Mordred, and Morgan, and the whole sordid tangle of the Old Ways that shadowed Arthur's reign.

CHAPTER NINE

The Throne of Chivalry

The opening day of the tourney dawned bright and cloudless. Knights had come from all over Britain, and from as far away as Armorica and the Languedoc, to vie for the honor of becoming Britain's champion.

The cathedral at Camelot was close to being finished; and Arthur, Guinevere, and all the knights who would fight today had gone there at dawn to hear the Easter Mass read. After Mass, the knights had retreated to their pavilions to arm themselves and prepare for the day's fighting, while the King conferred with his councilors, making plans for his upcoming quest.

The tourney field had been laid out upon the shore of the lake, and the sun glittered off the surface of the water. When the hour at last arrived for the tourney to begin, the rows of seats that faced the lake along the side of the tourney field were filled with the cream of Britain's nobility. Their clothing and jewels glittered in the sun like a vast rainbow ocean.

King Arthur was the last to arrive. He had filled out over the last few months, looking now less like a gawky boy and more like an assured, self-confident king. He was dressed all in royal red, his tunic sewn with thin plates of pure gold and his scarlet cloak brilliant with golden interlaced knotwork. The king's crown had been finished at Christmastide, and it glinted upon his brow like the rays of the sun. He took his place in the stands upon the elaborately painted and carved throne beside his Queen.

Guinevere was dressed as splendidly as he, and standing around the Royal couple were the first nobles of the realm: Sir Boris, Lord Lot, Lord Leodegrance, Sir Hector, and the rest.

Arthur raised his hand, and the knights rode forward to salute him. Here was Gawain, with his brothers Agravain, Gaheris, and Gareth; Arthur's foster brother Sir Kay; Palomedes the Moor; Accolon of Gaul; the Eireish brothers, Balin and Balan; Bedivere of Wales and his cousin Culhwch; the woman warrior Bradamante; Sir Sagramore and Sir Dinadan of the Round Table; Sir Tristan and Sir Hoel . . . two hundred dauntless knights, the full flower of chivalry in the West, were gathered upon this field to fight for the honor of Britain.

At Arthur's signal a trumpet sounded. The knights raised their swords in salute, and the king stood to receive the acclaim.

"My lords, ladies, knights of the realm. I shall

leave soon upon a God-given quest for the Holy Grail. Now I seek a champion to protect our country and the honor of our fair Queen while I'm gone!"

"I claim that honor, Sire!" Gawain shouted from the first rank of knights.

"Gawain, I hope you don't win!" Arthur called back, smiling. "You know I need you with me!"

The crowd laughed, and Arthur resumed his seat. The knights wheeled their mounts and broke ranks, half trotting to one side of the field, half to the other, to wait and prepare for the first charge of the day. Though the swords would be blunted and the lance points would be bare wood, not tipped in bronze, the falls would be real, and the Royal College of Chirurgeons were standing by to minister to the fallen.

"You should have let me compete in the tourney, Sire!" Sir Boris blustered.

"You're too old, Sir Boris," Arthur said kindly. The old knight was nearly seventy, and though he still talked a good fight, most of Sir Boris's great battles these days were conducted at the feast table instead of the field.

"Of course he's too old," Sir Hector said, standing at Arthur's side, "but I'm not!"

Guinevere joined Arthur in the general meriment at Sir Hector's jest. But beneath her gaiety, her thoughts were grave.

Arthur would be leaving in less than a month's time, leaving her to rule Britain in his place with the help of his wizard, Merlin—if Merlin ever returned from his latest expedition—and whoever won the tourney today. Despite what Arthur had said, Guinevere hoped it would be her brother Gawain. She knew and loved Gawain. He would protect her and support her decisions unquestioningly.

Though Guinevere had eagerly accepted the New Religion when her father commanded it, her marriage had not been what she had been taught to expect. She was the daughter of a king and a sister to princes. She had thought she knew what it would be to be queen—that at last she would have a place and a life that belonged to her beyond doubt—but Arthur had confused all her expectations. He didn't even seem to want to be alone with her, let alone help her to get a child to rule after him. Now she was neither wife nor maiden, caught between the two until Arthur achieved the Grail and became a husband to her in truth as well as name.

But though he spoke of his own sin and unworthiness, it seemed to Guinevere that Arthur thought that his queen was the one who was unworthy. That somehow he had looked into her and seen what she had always suspected was there—some flaw, some inadequacy, the thing that had always made her feel like a stranger, even in her own home. Undeserving. Sinful.

I am the daughter of a king, and I have committed no sin! Guinevere thought, her head held high. Her eyes flashed with pride, able to believe for a moment that she was right. She knew the Scriptures. In them the people were commanded to be fruitful and multiply, yet Arthur denied her a child. His was the sin, not hers.

If he did not love her, let him set her aside for another—and the green hills of Britain would run red with the blood her father and brothers would shed for such an insult. Let Uther's bastard son see what it meant to mock the proud Iceni!

But the flash of temper faded, and the Queen shook her head sadly at her own foolishness. A woman's place was to submit to her husband, so the New Religion taught. And if Arthur didn't want her, then surely the fault was hers, and she could see no way to repair it.

How? How had she failed him? No matter how often she asked him, Arthur only spoke of the Grail.

He said everything would be different once he had brought it back to Britain, but he also said the quest could take many years. He did not know what he was asking of her. How could she rule Britain alone for years? The thought of being left all alone at Camelot with a stranger questioning her decisions frightened her. She no longer knew what was right, and she was learning not to expect happiness. Arthur had turned her whole world upside down and made her question every certainty. Arthur had changed everything.

Still smiling automatically, the young Queen's attention was caught by movement on the field. It was Merlin—he'd come back!

The wizard was walking beside a knight on a black horse, a knight who was wearing armor the like of which Guinevere had never seen. It gleamed like polished silver, and the helm covered the whole of his head, so that nothing of his face could be seen.

Merlin led the stranger knight before the king. The closed helmet that he wore completely covered his face. It was polished brighter than Guinevere's own mirror, and she could see the sky and the trees reflected in its surface.

"Your Majesty, I wish to vouch for Sir Lancelot of the Lake, who wants to enter the jousts," Merlin said.

Guinevere darted a look at Arthur. He looked surprised, and the others around them were whispering together, speculating on where Merlin had been and the identity of this newcomer.

"So be it, Merlin," Arthur said graciously.

The knight rode off to the side of the field, and Merlin made his way into the royal box. Guinevere hoped she didn't look as dismayed as she felt, but she had always feared Merlin's power.

As a child, her older brothers had enjoyed frightening her with tales of the wizard Merlin, how he had slain Vortigern with magic and set Prince Uther upon the throne. As Uther had descended deeper into madness, the whole country had suffered. Guinevere's Iceni kinsmen had clung to the Old Ways longer than most, but even their gods Lugh and Epona could not save them from the Dark Times, and the common people had feared the magic that Queen Mab could wield on behalf of her followers.

When Uther died and Arthur was acknowledged by her father as the true king, Guinevere's people had discovered a king they could willingly follow, one who replaced the capriciousness of the Old Ways and the demonolatry of Uther with a religion of peace, light, and love. When Guinevere had sworn to the New Religion, she had been certain that the days of darkness and fear were over . . . until she discovered that the King's closest adviser was a wizard of the Old Ways.

Gawain had said that Merlin had not prayed with the army that day at Mount Badon, and Guinevere knew that though he was an enemy of Mab, he still used the magic she had given him. How could the weapons of Darkness be used in the service of the Light?

For questions such as these, the young queen had no answer.

The chivalry of Britain thundered out upon the field, and the air was filled with the sounds of clashing swords and shouting men. Merlin looked out over the melee, spotting Lancelot without difficulty. The knight which the Lady of the Lake had sent Merlin to find was holding his own against all foes. His sword flashed in the sun and the coat of his black charger gleamed like silk.

"Your Majesty," Merlin said, bowing.

"Oh, don't be so formal with me, Merlin!" Arthur urged. He reached up his hand to clasp the wizard's, his eyes intent upon the tourney field. "You used to be willing to call me Arthur—and much worse, too. Where have you been? You were gone so long—the others all said you'd left for good, but I knew you would not leave without saying good-bye."

"And so I would not," Merlin answered. "But magic is a tricky business. The moment that you think you're the master of it, magic will master *you*. But I survived well enough—and brought you Lancelot."

"He fights like no knight I have ever seen," Arthur

said, his eyes never leaving the spectacle before him. "Where did he come from?"

"The Lady of the Lake sent him," Merlin answered, "and so he is known as Lancelot of the Lake."

There was a crash on the field as Lancelot unhorsed a knight—it was Agravain, one of the Queen's brothers, and she gasped and stiffened, seeing him fall. Lancelot rode out of the melee, raising his sword to salute the royal box, then rode back into battle once more.

Squires and pages ran onto the field to capture riderless horses and help their masters to safety. The assembly rose to its feet each time a favorite was in trouble, the ladies crying out to the knights who bore their favors into battle.

The fighting continued for hours, and slowly the number of combatants declined. As the field thinned, the melee combat gave way to the joust, as knights rode to the sides of the field to claim their long ashwood lances, then thundered toward each other in a brutal contest of strength and nerve. The crack of splintered lances sounded over all the other sounds of the field, and slowly the number of undefeated knights diminished.

Gawain, on his huge blood-bay destrier, was still in the fight, and so was Bedivere, though Gawain's three brothers and Bedivere's cousin had been unhorsed and defeated earlier. Those knights not under the care of the chirurgeons had gathered upon the sidelines of the tourney field to watch the contest, for as the day had worn on, it gradually became clear to all those watching that Sir Lancelot of the Lake was a knight without equal . . . unless that equal was Gawain.

At last only the two of them were left.

Gawain rode to the edge of the field, taking a fresh lance from his squire Simnel. He turned into the rays of the westering sun. At the far side of the field, Lancelot was also accepting a spear. The setting sun gilded his armor, turning its silver into gold and his black stallion into a horse of blood.

Merlin had left the king's side hours before to go into the tents where the chirurgeons cared for the wounded. After the first few minutes, he had no doubt that his champion would defeat all others to become the guardian of the crown, and his healing skills were needed among the players of this rough sport.

If only he had some art that would turn Arthur from this unwise quest as easily as he had summoned a champion to support it. Let the king stay here where he was needed—others could waste their time seeking after the Grail.

Merlin's thoughts were so much an echo of things he'd said to Nimue over the years that he stopped, wondering if he was actually right or if he'd simply fallen into an unexamined habit. Perhaps Arthur had spoken the truth. Perhaps the spiritual quest was truly as important a task as the mundane rule of Britain. Perhaps one was not complete without the other.

Merlin shook his head ruefully.

Perhaps I have judged Arthur too harshly. Part of me, I fear, will always see him as the child I took into my care when he was but a few hours old. But if I have judged him, I have also helped him to do what he thinks is right. I've brought him Lancelot.

He heard the crowd roar at something that happened upon the field. Bradamante passed him, heading toward the stands. She had shed her armor for a tunic and breeches, for the woman warrior was under a vow not to assume women's dress until Jerusalem had been freed.

"Come on, Wizard! Gawain's in the lists—he'll take that Lancelot down a few pegs!" She clapped Merlin on the shoulder as she strode past him.

Merlin smiled. It was Gawain who was in for a shock, not Lancelot. He headed for the royal box. The moment he had been waiting for all day had come.

"Look, Guinevere. You'll get what you wanted after all. Gawain will face the stranger," Arthur said, taking her hand. "Your hands are so cold."

"I'm tired," Guinevere answered shortly, pulling away. She sat forward in her chair, staring at the field, clenched fists hidden in the folds of her skirts. All around her, the spectators laughed and cheered, while on the field the fate of Britain's queen was being decided.

On one side was her brother Gawain, a giant of a man, laughing and fearless, his gold-washed bronze helmet glinting in the evening light. On the other side of the field stood the stranger, Merlin's protégé, faceless and menacing in his shining steel armor. In a moment they would charge, and one would fall. Guinevere prayed with all the passion in her heart that it would be Lancelot who fell, and Gawain who would prevail and lend her his strength, just as he had since she was a small child.

The onlookers began to cheer as both men spurred their horses forward. As the charge began, each held his lance high, but as they approached one another, they lowered their lances into position, each aiming for the other's heart.

She could not look. And she could not look away. With helpless anguish, Guinevere stared as the two armored titans pounded toward each other on an inevitable collision course.

There was a crash, and both lances splintered, the pieces flying across the field to lodge in the turf like a flight of arrows. Lancelot swayed in his saddle, and for a moment Guinevere thought he would fall, but it was Gawain who fell, cartwheeling over his horse's rump to fall, spread-eagled and dazed, to the ground. The black horse neighed as Lancelot reined it in.

No one cheered. There was a long moment of silence, broken by a few groans of disappointment, then some of the spectators clapped forlornly.

"He's unhorsed Gawain!" Arthur said in disbelief.

But you knew he would. Merlin brought him here to do just that, Guinevere thought. She sat very still as the stranger knight on the prancing stallion rode up to the royal box, holding the stump of his splintered lance in his right hand. How Merlin must be exulting to see all his plans fall so neatly into place!

"Lancelot of the Lake takes the honors! He is the best—and the noblest—of the knights!" Arthur cried gallantly, rising to his feet. Guinevere rose with him, but her legs would not hold her. She sank back into her chair, staring at the stranger as the rabbit stares at the fox. He reached up to raise the visor of his helmet.

And time stopped. Lancelot was no monster, but the most beautiful man she had ever seen . . . and more. There was a melancholy in him, a secret sorrow, that tugged at her heartstrings. She felt herself reaching out to him, as if her whole soul could drown in those storm-blue eyes.

Merlin really makes this too easy, Mab thought with glee. He made all his plans openly, in the light of day, and trusted them to endure by their own strength. All she needed to do to thwart him was to wait until he acted, then destroy his hopes. And all the while at Castle Tintagel, Mordred was growing big and strong, and there was nothing Merlin could do to prevent Mab's eventual victory.

Invisibly, she appeared beside the Queen's throne. Merlin was only a few feet away, yet he sensed nothing of her presence. She watched as Merlin's chosen protector rode up to the royal box. Her hold on Arthur might be broken with Mordred's begetting, but his Queen could still be led astray by fairy arts. When Lancelot lifted his visor, Mab was there to whisper in her ear: *"He's very handsome, isn't he?"*

And the Queen whispered: "Yes. . . ."

"What did you say, my lady?" Arthur asked.

"Nothing," Guinevere answered. She leaned forward, the better to see Sir Lancelot.

"Your Majesty," Lancelot said, gazing up at the king and queen, "I offer you my sword—and my life."

Bright pearls of sweat stood out on his forehead, as if his skin were studded with diamonds.

"It is an honor, brave knight," Arthur answered easily. He raised his voice to be heard by all. "As Champion, Lancelot shall—"

With a moan, Lancelot crashed unconscious to the ground, cutting off the king's next words.

It was Gawain who reached him first, cradling his fallen opponent in his arms. "He's wounded," Gawain cried. "My lance splintered and took him in the shoulder—a fearful blow."

Though the tourney lances were deliberately blunt, not tipped with the killing points they would have in war, accidents happened. A splintered lance could pierce the defenses of even the finest armor.

"Save him!" Guinevere cried. Arthur glanced toward her approvingly, but Guinevere did not see. Gawain's shout had fetched attendants from the edges of the field, and under Gawain's supervision they carried the unconscious Lancelot off to Gawain's own arming pavilion. Guinevere watched until they were out of sight.

The tourney was over, and as the sun set the spectators rose from their seats to return to their lodgings.

"What about the feast, Your Majesty?" Sir Boris asked.

"The feast?" Arthur said blankly.

"The feast, Sire, with which you intended to honor the Queen's Champion," Merlin explained. He had heard people talking about it while he had been helping among the healers. "It will be a bit strange to have a feast for a man who isn't there."

"Nevertheless," Arthur said with a sigh, "I can't just change my mind. All those people would be so disappointed, and the cooks have been laboring for three days. We'll just have to hope that Lancelot recovers in time to join us."

When the others returned to their chambers to prepare for dinner, Guinevere slipped away and went to the tourney field. She did not think she could rest until she'd seen how Lancelot was. She wrapped her thick wool cloak around herself, hoping no one would recognize their queen. The knights would only think it was their right to bundle her back off to Camelot as if she were some unruly child. She was Queen, Guinevere realized, but she did not rule. No one listened to her.

"Jenny! What are you doing here?" a voice demanded from behind her.

She turned around, heart hammering in her throat, but it was only Gawain. He, at least, wouldn't send her packing.

"I came to see Lancelot. Do you know how he is?" she asked.

"No," said her brother, "but I know *where* he is. I was just going to see if the others are all right: you know Agravain, nothing can dent his hard head, and Gaheris was lucky as always, but Gareth's horse fell on him, poor lad, and he's broken an ankle. I sent Simnel to him, as he wouldn't have the doctors, and now I'm going to see how Lancelot fares. It was a grievous wound that he took, and I'm sorry for him."

"He can't die!" Guinevere gasped. Gawain looked at her oddly.

"I mean," she stumbled on, "that it would be very poor hospitality—to kill him—when he's only just come to us."

"You're right of course," Gawain said, walking along beside her. "Here we are."

He pushed open the door-slit of his arming pavilion so that his sister could precede him.

The interior of the pavilion was dark, and reeked of the smoke of herbs burned to clear away the foul humors. Gawain's armor and shield were shoved into a corner to make room for the three distinguished physicians who were debating the proper treatment for their patient.

"How is he?" Guinevere asked.

"Fair to middling," the Chief Physician said, "considering we haven't taken the lance out yet."

"And why not?" Gawain demanded, following her into the tent.

"There is a dispute—a scholarly dispute—as to whether we should take it out con or contra-wise, which means—to the mere layman—turning and pulling it to the left or to the right. . . ."

The other two physicians eagerly joined in the debate, but Guinevere ignored them. She moved on into the inner room, where Lancelot lay, still in all his armor, on the narrow pallet on which they had carried him from the field.

His face was pale and stark with pain, but he managed to smile when he saw her.

"Is there anything I can do for you, Sir Lancelot?" she asked in a low voice.

"Hold my hand, Lady," he whispered, reaching out to her. His fingers were cold and strong, and she could feel the tremors that the pain sent through his body.

"—as the planets Venus and Uranus will be the dominant influences—" came from the outer room.

"You're physicians! Instead of arguing about it— *do* it!" Gawain demanded loudly.

The three doctors regarded him with identical affronted expressions.

"Do it?" the first asked. "We must talk about it first."

"Indeed," said the second, "these are weighty matters, fit only for experts."

"Trust us!" the Chief Physician said. "If we treat a knight for a broken arm, that's what he'll die of."

But Gawain—simple, honest, straightforward Gawain—had lost what small store of patience he possessed.

"That's enough! Enough! Lancelot—"

He followed Guinevere to the inner room and looked down at the man lying upon the bed. "Are you ready, Sir Knight?"

"Do it, Gawain," Lancelot answered steadily.

Gawain bent over the bed and grasped the splintered end of the lance in his strong hands. The point of the lance had entered beneath Lancelot's arm, the weakest spot upon a knight's armor, and the silvery scale mail around the wound was dark with pooled

blood. Without warning, Gawain yanked the spear
point free.

Lancelot's hand tightened upon hers in a crushing
grip, but Guinevere would not cry out. Lancelot endured the agony in silence, his mouth open in a sound-
less scream as the point slowly worked free of the
wound. Suddenly his muscles went slack and his head
lolled to the side. He had fainted.

"*Now* make yourselves useful!" Gawain bellowed
at the men standing behind him. "Bandage the man up
before he bleeds to death, and a scurvy pox on your
planets!" He flung away the bloodsoaked lance.

As the doctors scurried to obey, Guinevere gently laid Lancelot's hand across his chest. The way he
had stared into her eyes through the pain, as though
he had stared into her soul! He had needed her. No
man had ever needed her before . . . not even her
husband.

The doctors were hurrying to obey Gawain, and
Guinevere stepped back to allow the doctors to do
their work. Some of the blood had gotten on her skirt,
making mahogany shadows on her gay red gown.

"Come on, Jenny. Arthur will wonder why you
aren't at the feast," Gawain said, leading her gently
out of the pavilion. The evening air was cool after the
heat of the tent and she shivered. "I'll stay here and
tend to him," Gawain added.

She stared up at her brother's face in the soft twilight. From the moment she'd first learned to walk,
Gawain had been there to protect her. But now some-

thing had happened—something for which she had no words—and Gawain could not protect her now.

"Your Majesty?"

She turned, to see Arthur's wizard behind her. Flustered, her hands darted about—to her crown, to her hair, to the folds of her skirt—trying to smooth away her disquiet. "Yes?" she answered, her voice higher and sharper than she intended.

If Merlin noticed her discourtesy, he gave no sign. "The king asked me to see if there was anything I could do for Lancelot."

"Gawain pulled the lance from his shoulder," Guinevere answered.

"The doctors are bandaging him now. I do not think there is any more harm they can do him, and in any event, I will stay to keep watch over him," Gawain said to Merlin. "Take the Queen back to Camelot. This is no place for her."

"I shall be honored," Merlin said, and offered Guinevere his arm. Reluctant, but unable to do anything else, she took it.

The Great Hall of the castle was still unfinished, but the torches that ringed its walls this April night dispelled the dark and damp, and the golden stone the king had chosen for his city shone warmly in the firelight.

The High Table was covered with a cloth of white linen and set with cups and plates and pitchers and trays of jewel-studded silver and enameled gold. Though Arthur had not yet reigned a year, the peace he had brought had already caused the land to flourish, and the Eastertide banquet held this night was evidence of how far Britain had come in just a few short months. Every savory treat that the cooks could provide had been set forth to delight the company assembled to celebrate the choosing of Arthur's champion, from whole roast swan and peacock in their plumage, to venison in spiced frumenty, to large cased pies of beef and pork. There were conserves of quince and roses, wines flavored with saffron and the Grains of Paradise that turned the vintage a deep ruby, glazed fruits in honey, and for dessert, a subtlety of a unicorn with a gilded horn made entirely of spun sugar and marzipan.

Arthur, seated at the High Table in a painted and gilded chair with his device—an image of the Blessed Virgin enthroned upon a crescent moon—carved upon its back, presided over it all. Around the King sat his closest friends and advisers—Lord Lot, Sir Boris, Sir Hector, and others—but one who might have been expected to be present was not.

Merlin, the enchanter.

Merlin's place at Arthur's court was an ambiguous one. He had ended the reign of one king and brought about the reigns of two others. And in the time it had taken him to do so, the customs of the nobility had shifted, subtly but unmistakably, away from the Old Ways and toward the New Religion. Vortigern's court had worshiped power, and Uther's had made uneasy alliances wherever it could, but Arthur of Britain was a Christian king ruling a land that would someday be wholly a Christian one, from which the dark magics of the Old Ways would be banished.

And as such, his court had no official place for a wizard. Many of Arthur's nobles, whether Christian since Roman times or newly-converted, distrusted anything that smacked of the Old Ways. And with good reason. The Old Ways had made Britain a battle-ground since King Constant's time, and those who felt they had escaped them were wary of anything that would once again entangle them in magic's shadowy net.

Arthur thought their attitude unjust, but in some ways, the idealism that Merlin had so carefully fostered in his royal charge was a liability in dealing with day-to-day matters. The years had made Merlin more of a realist. He would not intrude where his presence would spoil the trust that must grow up between Arthur and the nobles he ruled. Thus, this night Merlin sat not at the high table, but near the door, where the lesser nobility took its meal. The food was as good as that served at the high table, and one could come and go unobtrusively.

And, if one had the power of the Old Ways, one could hear the conversations at the High Table as easily as if one were sitting there.

Merlin knew that eavesdropping wasn't very good manners, but with Arthur's chosen champion lying injured, and the Queen looking so pale and wan, Merlin felt it was his duty as the King's adviser to know what was going on, so that he could ward off further trouble, assuming such a thing were possible. There were times when Merlin thought the old Saxon gods had been right after all: if a fate had been laid out for a man at the beginning of his life, there was no sense in trying to outwit it, for his fate would find him in the end.

But as Merlin watched Guinevere do no more than pick at her food, while beside her Arthur ate and drank as though nothing were amiss, Merlin knew he could not be content to watch from afar. He needed to *know*.

A small gesture, almost unnoticed by those who sat around him, and the words of the King and Queen came to him as clearly as if he stood behind them.

"How is Lancelot?" Arthur asked.

"He's past the worst," Guinevere said slowly, not looking at the king.

"Good," Arthur said. "That's good. He can hardly be your champion if he's lying in bed, now, can he?" The king smiled, hoping to coax his queen into a cheerier mood.

"Must you go on this quest?" Guinevere burst out, her voice low. Her hands clasped each other so tightly the knuckles shone white through the flesh.

"Yes I must," Arthur said firmly. "My lady, you know that seeking the Grail is the right thing for me to do. I can delay a few weeks, until Lancelot is more recovered, but that is all."

"And if I beg you not to go?" Guinevere persisted.

Arthur turned to her. "What are you afraid of, Guinevere?"

Whatever disturbed her, the Queen was not prepared to share it with Arthur, Merlin saw. She shook her head, and the long strands of pearls braided through her hair glimmered in the torchlight as they swung against her cheeks. "Nothing," she said. "I'll miss you," she added hollowly.

"I'll miss you, too," Arthur said patiently, "but I've given my word. To God."

"I need you more," Guinevere said, and the heart-felt cry seemed for a moment to echo Merlin's to Nimue. *I need you,* he had told her, over and over, and Nimue's answer had always been the same: *God needs me more.*

If the Queen was as lonely as he was in the midst of all these people, Merlin pitied her.

"But you'll have Merlin," Arthur said. "And Lancelot."

From the foot of the table, Merlin saw a flash of panic cross the Queen's face, and wondered at it. Surely she could not be afraid of Lancelot? The man was the soul of chivalry!

He saw Guinevere bow her head, and nod meekly, and suddenly Merlin did not wish to listen any longer.

But later, when the guests had departed and Arthur and Guinevere were alone together, the queen could not keep from pleading with Arthur once more. If only he could understand her feelings, surely they would move him to pity her and do as she asked.

They were alone together in Guinevere's rooms. She sat at the dressing table taking down her hair, while Arthur watched her from a chair by the door. These were not the royal apartments, which were not yet finished, but a set of simpler rooms on the ground floor of the castle. Arthur liked to sit with her for a few minutes here in the evening, but he always retired to his own rooms afterward, to pray to be worthy of finding the Grail. Leaving her alone, like a pair of unwanted shoes.

"You cannot go," Guinevere said. Blessed Virgin, make him hear the words she searched for in vain——let him know her heart!

Her hands shook as she lifted her pearl crown from her head and set it on the table. She stood and clasped them together, trying to still their trembling. Arthur was fearless—it was Gawain who had first told her that, and when she had met her husband she discovered it was the simple truth. And how could a man who did not know fear understand a woman's fears? She turned and walked to the window, standing before it and looking out so she would not have to see his face.

"We have gone over all this before, my lady," Arthur said, with what sounded like a stifled sigh of exasperation. She heard his chair creak as he shifted position. "I know it is hard, but you knew I meant to accept this quest before we were wed. I will leave you many competent, experienced men to help you rule the kingdom while I am gone—your own father, Sir Boris. The land is at peace. You have nothing to fear."

Nothing but the knowledge that she had always felt like a ghost traveling through other people's lives, flawed where they were perfect, only an encumbrance to them on life's journey. She had hoped marriage would change that, but it had not. She had thought she was resigned to her loneliness. She had accepted it as the natural order of things, until she had met Lancelot.

From the moment she had looked into his eyes, she had begun to question everything—from the way she was treated by Arthur's knights, to whether she really deserved the fate that was hers as Arthur's virgin queen. Lancelot would change her by his very presence in Camelot, and Guinevere feared that.

"Arthur—" she began. But how to put this formless dread into words that could sway a man as brave and fearless as her husband? She did not even know what she feared, only that she feared it very much.

Guinevere turned away from the window. "You're right," she said dutifully, forcing herself to smile and look at him. "I have nothing to fear. After all, I will have your wizard to protect me, as well as Lancelot."

She saw Arthur's face relax as he took her words at face value. "You'll do fine," he said, getting to his feet and coming over to her. "And I'll be back . . . as soon as possible," he finished lamely. He took her by the shoulders and gazed down at her tenderly. "Well, good night, then." He kissed her chastely upon the forehead, just as he had every night since they were wed.

"Good night," Guinevere echoed, watching as he walked from the room.

When he was gone and she was alone, she turned back to the window, wishing she were in a tower a thousand miles high. One leap, and all choices would be over, and the dread in her heart would be stilled. At last the slow tears came, when there was no one to see them.

Where will you go to seek the Grail, husband? How can you begin to know where it lies? Will you recognize it when you see it? Or will all of this building and planning be for nothing, only a beautiful dream that vanishes in the morning because you are not here to make it real?

The next ten days passed as quickly as moments, leaves torn from the Tree of Years by an autumn wind. Arthur made his final choices: Gawain and forty of the Round Table's bravest knights would go with him on his quest. They would begin by going to Avalon Abbey to offer prayers in the Grail Chapel, and there seek an omen that would lead them onward in their search.

Lancelot recovered swiftly from his wound, aided by Merlin's salves and cordials and the sincere wish of the attending physicians not to face Gawain's temper again. Much of the wizard's healing magic stemmed from the same source that Avalon's did; the herbcraft of the country people, taught to him by his Aunt Ambrosia, but just to be sure that no dark forces were involved, the Bishop of Camelot offered up a special Mass for Lancelot's welfare, and even Arthur took time from his preparations for departure to visit Lancelot almost every day. Whatever the cause, Lancelot of the Lake healed quickly and well, and was able to tour Camelot with Arthur a few days before the king's departure.

The golden city was expanding in all directions at once. Its buildings were shrouded by scaffolding, and its defensive walls were barely six feet high as yet. The great gates that would be hung when the walls were finished lay protected beneath a tarpaulin until they were needed. Outside the castle walls a small city of workmen's huts had sprung up; many would vanish when construction was complete, but the rest would remain to form the nucleus of the village that would be a part of Camelot, and of Arthur's dream.

He had told Lancelot much about his hopes for the future in the time they had spent together, and the two men had laid the groundwork of a strong friendship.

"When I go," Arthur said, "I want you to see that Camelot is finished just as I planned."

"Of course I will," Lancelot said warmly. "It is a mighty dream, my friend, and, God willing, a dream that will endure forever."

As they walked through the streets that would someday be a bustling city, Arthur pointed out particular details—here a gargoyle imported from France, there, windows that would someday be bright with stained glass crafted by skilled Flemish artisans. He spoke of the law-courts and hospitals the city would someday contain, of the peace and charity it would spread over all the land like the radiance of the Grail itself.

"Better that Camelot should become real than remain a dream," Arthur said. "I entrust that to you, Lancelot. You must make my city real."

"I will," Lancelot said. "Both the city and the dream."

It seemed to Lancelot that he could almost see the city through Arthur's eyes—its shining towers rising into the sky, its streets filled with happy, peaceful people. How like his own Joyous Gard it would be when it was finished. Already he could see ways in which he could make Camelot greater than Arthur's vision. He would lay the perfected Camelot as a gift at the feet of his friend when Arthur returned with the Grail.

"Ah, here's Merlin," Arthur said, his arm draped companionably around Lancelot's shoulder. "I was just showing Lancelot the city."

Arthur spoke as though Camelot were finished, and Lancelot saw Merlin smile.

"And what do you think of Camelot, Sir Knight?" Merlin asked.

"I think it will be a very great city," Lancelot said. "A city worthy of its king . . . and queen."

Late into the evening, a lone candle burned in a hut at the edge of the workmen's village. Even after all these years, Merlin still disliked being confined within stone walls, so Arthur had built for him a small hut at the edge of the builders' city. Inside, Merlin had all that he needed: a table, a chair, some books. The cool breezes of spring wafted through the walls; the woven withes would have to be chinked with mud before the hut would be warm enough for winter. But the thatched roof was tight, and the hut would be a pleasant place through the spring and summer.

A candle flickered in a clay candlestick upon the table. Arthur had promised to take a letter to Nimue when he went to Avalon, but Merlin was finding it hard to find the words. What could he say to her? That he loved her but dared not be with her? That their happiness could not be allowed to matter more than Arthur's kingdom? That he feared that any weakness he showed could be turned into a weapon by Queen Mab?

All of these things. None of these things. Merlin sighed. *Oh, Auntie A, I do miss you so. I am sure that if all of this had been left to you, you would not have made as much of a muddle of it as I have!*

He didn't even know that Nimue would be willing to read the letter. Each time he thought of what she must have felt that morning when she awoke and found herself alone, something twisted deep inside him. Did Mab's blood flowing in his veins count for so much that he could never bring anything but pain to those he loved?

But half of me is mortal. I had a mortal mother. I have a mortal heart. Surely those matter at least as much as magic?

The night did not answer. Sighing, Merlin bent to his task once more. Tonight was Beltaine Eve, one of the holiest days of the Old Calendar. It seemed somehow fitting that one who had rejected the old world and had no place in the new should spend this holy night in such homely tasks as these. The only place he had ever belonged was in Nimue's arms, and the place he wanted most to be was the one farthest out of his reach.

If nothing else, Merlin felt that he owed Nimue an explanation, but no matter how hard he tried, the right words would not come. The hours stretched on into the darkness just before dawn as his eyelids grew heavy and Merlin subsided, slowly and unwillingly, into Idath's lesser kingdom: sleep.

Merlin stood upon a mist-shrouded plain, hearing the clash of battle and the screams of the wounded as they echoed through the mist. Even in his dreams, he knew that this was no false phantasm, but a true vision of what would someday be. In the sky a blood-red comet bathed the landscape in a fearful scarlet light, burning like a red eye through the mist.

He saw men running wildly through the fog, their beards and their swords crusted with blood, and the knowledge came to him that Arthur's quest had been all in vain. That Mab had been right—she had charmed him and robbed him while still in the cradle of any chance to achieve the Grail. His quest had been for nothing, all for nothing, and this was its end.

Again he saw the warrior with the bat-winged helm. His sword was covered in blood—Caliban, the black sword, Excalibur's dark twin—and his black and silver armor bore the symbol of the eclipse.

Merlin had been sent this vision before, but this time the wizard knew the identity of the Knight of the Eclipse. This was Mordred of Tintagel, Arthur's ill-starred bastard, Mab's cat's-paw. Her final weapon upon this day of judgment.

YOU WILL NOT WIN. In the face of terrible defeat and the death of all he loved, Merlin was still defiant. He would not despair. He would not surrender. Even if this was how all his dreams must end, as long as he lived Merlin would fight. Mab would not claim the victory, nor would Mordred.

Even as Merlin watched, Arthur staggered out of the mists to confront his rebel son. They were like sunlight and shadow, glory and its dark echo. They fought like titans, but in the end, Arthur raised his sword and could not deal the death stroke, and Merlin's world ended in the dimming of the day.

YOU WILL NOT WIN. Again the vow came, as if

*from outside himself, yet a part of him, giving Merlin
the strength for what must be done in the time to come.*

*And the world dissolved in shouting and blood
and the promise of darkness. . . .*

Merlin awoke with a strangled cry. The candle had
long since burned out, and spilled wax had puddled
across his unfinished letter to Nimue. The grey light of
dawn was in the eastern sky. In a few hours Arthur
would embark upon his journey.

And all for nothing.

Merlin got to his feet, groaning with stiffness. He
rubbed his eyes, trying to force the jumbled images of
the prophecy into some proper pattern, but all he could
see was ruin and chaos, blood and war.

And there was nothing he could do to stop it. The
realization grew inside Merlin like a cancer. If he told
Arthur that his quest for the Holy Grail was doomed to
failure, Arthur would not listen. The king could not
bear to believe himself unworthy of the Grail. It was
something he could never accept.

*And so he will go, and he will fail. But my old
master Blaise would tell me that the attempt is as glorious as the achievement. Have I the right to take that
away from Arthur?*

Merlin knew the answer to that. His part in
Arthur's life had ended when he led the young king to
Excalibur. Now Arthur must forge his own destiny.

And Merlin must do what he could.

The first rays of sun shone through the window of
the little hut, onto the litter of spilled wax and spoiled
drafts. Merlin scooped up the papers and dumped

them into his brazier. A flick of his fingers set the papers alight.

There was no point in writing to Nimue. He had no words to give her. Everything that could be said between them had already been said. He must trust that she knew his heart.

Dawn. The land outside the gates of the city was filled with well-wishers eager to see the King depart upon his quest.

Arthur wore a suit of golden armor that was a gift from Lord Lot. A round helm, chased with figures of men and beasts in the Iceni style, protected his head, and he wore a shirt of golden plate-mail that caused him to shine like the sun itself on this Beltaine morning. The young King was a splendid figure in scarlet and gold, as proud and regal as the Old Gods themselves. Boukephalos had been curried until he shone, and many of Arthur's subjects, gazing upon the king among his knights upon this May morning, called not upon the gods and saints of the New Religion, but upon Llew Long-hand, Baldur the Beautiful, Hyborean Apollo, and other golden gods and heroes of ages past. In this moment, Arthur was more than a king to his people: he was a force of nature, a myth.

And like all gods of myth and heroes of story, his dark twin stood nearby. Merlin waited with the others to bid Arthur farewell, his thoughts somber. Beside him stood Lancelot and Guinevere.

The queen was very pale, but stood steadfast and composed, wrapped in the invisible cloak of royalty. Beside her stood Lancelot in full plate armor.

"Sir Lancelot," Arthur said, turning in his saddle. "Guard the honor of our sovereign lady, the Queen."

"I will, Sire," Lancelot said. He looked wistful as he watched Arthur prepare to depart, as though he wished more than anything to be going with him.

"Go in God's good grace, my love," Guinevere said. She reached up to Arthur, and he leaned down out of the saddle, kissing her with all the passion their marriage had lacked, as if he thought he would never see her again. Tears glittered in her eyes when she stepped back.

"Good-bye, Merlin," Arthur said.

"Good-bye, Arthur," the wizard said gently. "Come back to us."

"I leave the country in your hands."

Arthur reached out and took his standard from a waiting squire. The crowds fell back as he raised it up. Boukephalos began to step forward, and the blue silk billowed, exposing the silver image of the Lady. Arthur spurred his horse to a trot, and then to a gallop, and the knights who were accompanying him followed, the thunder of their hooves making harsh music on this golden May morning. In moments they were gone, a cloud of dust upon the road, gilded by the rising sun.

The others turned away, back to their daily lives, but neither Guinevere nor Lancelot did. The two of them ascended to the wall and watched after Arthur until even the last sign of his dust cloud was gone.

Merlin watched them as they stood, silhouetted against the morning sky, the flower of chivalry and the queen of Britain.

Arthur is gone. Merlin sighed, feeling suddenly old. *He goes to chase dreams—shadows.* The vision that had come to him last night weighted his bones with foreknowledge, but like Cassandra at the walls of Troy, it would do no one any good for him to tell what he knew. Arthur would not have listened, and how could any of them escape their futures?

Sadly, he watched Guinevere and Lancelot as they stood together upon the battlements, and waited for the future to begin.

THE
MERLIN
MYSTERY

Jonathan Gunson & Marten Coombe

The Secret Lies Inside . . .

The Puzzle – hidden in the enchanting illustrations and story of Merlin and the water-sprite Nimue is the most intricate puzzle ever created.

The Prize – is Merlin's Wand, an alchemist's staff crafted from gold, silver, bronze, crystal and lapis lazuli, and also an accumulating prize fund. *For every book wherever sold will produce an extra grain of gold*. THE MERLIN MYSTERY will be published simultaneously all over the world and for every copy of the book sold 20p will be put into a prize fund which will grow and grow until the puzzle is solved.

All you need to solve THE MERLIN MYSTERY is in the book, and the solution is as likely to be found by a bright and determined child as by an expert puzzler.

WHO ON EARTH WILL WIN?

ISBN 0 00 224675 9